I0598315

Dark Brew

by

Diana Rubino

This is a work of fiction. Names, characters, places, and incidents are either the product of the author's imagination or are used fictitiously, and any resemblance to actual persons living or dead, business establishments, events, or locales, is entirely coincidental.

Dark Brew

COPYRIGHT © 2016 by Diana Rubino

All rights reserved. No part of this book may be used or reproduced in any manner whatsoever without written permission of the author or The Wild Rose Press, Inc. except in the case of brief quotations embodied in critical articles or reviews.
Contact Information: info@thewildrosepress.com

Cover Art by *Debbie Taylor*

The Wild Rose Press, Inc.
PO Box 708
Adams Basin, NY 14410-0708
Visit us at www.thewildrosepress.com

Publishing History
First Fantasy Rose Edition, 2016
Print ISBN 978-1-5092-0843-2
Digital ISBN 978-1-5092-0844-9

Published in the United States of America

Kylah shut Ted's den door. She couldn't bear to look at the spot where he gasped his last breath. His presence, an imposing force, lingered. So did his scent, a blend of pine aftershave, manly sweat, and marijuana. His essence echoed his personality all over the house: the heap of dirty shirts, shorts, and socks piled up in the laundry room, the spattered stove, his fingerprints on the microwave. But she couldn't bring herself to clean any of it up. Painful as these remnants were, they offered a strange comfort. He still lived here.

Each reminder ripped into her heart like a knife. Especially now with the funeral looming ahead, the eulogies, the mournful organ hymns, the tolling bells...

These ceremonies should bring closure, but they'd only prolong the agony of her grief. She wanted to remember him alive for a while longer. Oh, if only she could delay these morbid customs until the hurt subsided.

"I'll find that murdering bastard, Teddy," she promised him over and over, wandering from room to empty room, traces of him lurking in every corner. "I'll do everything in my power to make sure justice is served. Another past life regression isn't enough anymore. I know what I have to do now. And I promise, it will never, ever happen again—in any future life." She inhaled and breathed him in. "Go take a shower, Teddy." She chuckled through her tears as the doorbell rang. Cringing, she broke out in cold sweat at the sight of the black sedan at the curb. "Not again."

No sense in hiding. She let Detectives Munn and Egan in.

Praise for Diana Rubino's New York Saga

FROM HERE TO FOURTEENTH STREET (Book One)
"Immigrant Vita Caputo escapes New York's Italian ghetto and secures a job in a Wall Street bank, along with a room in a Greenwich Village boarding house, thanks to Irish police officer Tom McGlory. When Tom's cousin is murdered and Vita's father and brother are arrested for the crime, the two team up to investigate and soon discover that they are falling in love. Vita and Tom face economic problems, prejudice, and cultural differences. Ms. Rubino's research is obvious."

~Kathe Robin, Romantic Times Reviews
~*~

BOOTLEG BROADWAY (Book Two)
"Diana Rubino has blended the history of the Depression and Prohibition, romance and the realities of getting mixed up with the mob into one compelling read. This may not be your typical romance, but it is one magnificent story."

~Deborah Brent, Romantic Times Reviews
~*~

THE END OF CAMELOT (Book Three)
"If one can overlook the well-worn conspiracy theory surrounding Kennedy's death and focus on the mystery of the heroine's husband's murder, this becomes an intriguing and fascinating story. The romance, though minor, develops nicely."

~Susan Mobley, Romantic Times Reviews

Dedication

To the memory of Kathie Close

Acknowledgements

This book was nearly twelve years in the making. Through its many rewrites, revisions, and incarnations, many folks helped me and believed in me. I couldn't have written this book without:

Irish cousins Mary, Andy, Clare, and Annmarie Cotter for their Gaelic translations.

My cousin Captain Paul Rubino of Jersey City, NJ, and Master Patrol Officer Dan Dolan of the Hudson, NH, Police Department for their time and their expert advice on police procedural.

Eddie and Christine Curran for explaining how to start a motorcycle.

Kathie Close for the herbs.

Siobhan McNally for the numerous plotting ideas and facts about Ireland, Druids, and dolmens in Carlow, in the Boyne Valley, Howth and Dowth, and *Brugh na Boinne.*

Josh Bartlett of the Barnstable Village Ghost Tour for the amazing stories and EVPs.

My editor Claudia Fallon for her invaluable advice and expertise, and for believing in me.

My publisher The Wild Rose Press, Inc.

Fellow Ricardian Pamela Butler for letting me use her name in the story as the author of the article on Alice. Pamela is the author of the actual *Ricardian Register* article that captured my imagination to the point of writing *Dark Brew*. It wouldn't exist without Pamela.

Visit Pamela at:

https://www.facebook.com/pam.butler.9212?fref=ts

Chapter One

Narrowback's Pub, South Boston, Massachusetts, summer before last

"We have a request. This is for Kylah and Ted McKinley."

The band struck up "Black Velvet Band."

"Her eyes, they shone like diamonds..." The lead vocalist sang and swayed to the lively old Irish tune.

"Come on, Teddy, it's our song!" Kylah grasped her husband's hand and pulled him out of his chair.

He drained his beer and plunked the mug down. "Okay, but after this, I'm outta here. You wore me out with the Gay Gordons."

They sidestepped around other couples heading for the dance floor. "But we can't leave before they play 'Killing Me Softly'," she insisted. "I wanted to slow dance with you."

"Tell you what." They glided past a dancer twirling his partner. "We'll go home, put our 'World's Greatest Love Songs' CD on, dim the lights and we can slow dance in privacy."

A thrill warmed Kylah to her toes. "Oh, you can be so romantic after a few beers!" She nipped his ear. "Then after this dance, I'm outta here with you."

When their song ended, he walked her toward the exit. "Be right back. Gotta make a pit stop."

As she waited for him, tapping her foot to "The Wild Rover," a lug in a wife beater tank top loped up to her.

"Hey, hottie. Wanna dance?"

He grabbed her wrist with his sweaty hand. His beer-soured breath made her gag. "I'm with my husband." She jerked her hand away and sighed in relief as Ted headed back to her.

"C'mon, one dance. He'll survive." The creep grabbed her arm.

Ted drew back and landed a left hook that sent him spinning.

Kylah's jaw dropped. A few curious heads turned their way. Ted steered her to the door.

"Why'd you hit him?" Expecting another barroom brawl, she shuddered. A stab of fear pierced her gut. "Why do you always have to start fights?" she shrieked over the music, the singing, the mishmash of voices.

"Nobody messes with my wife." He swung the door open.

"One of these days you'll pick on the wrong guy." Once again her warning fell on deaf ears.

The rain pelted the awning in a steady drumbeat. A spatter of raindrops slapped Kylah's cheeks as she stepped outside under the awning. "It's pouring. I don't want to get on your bike in this. Let's take a taxi."

"Come on, Ky, I know the roads." He fished out his keys.

"Teddy, please." A familiar premonition haunted her. Trembling, she cringed and chewed her bottom lip. "It's too dangerous. I'm calling a taxi. Leave the bike here." She fished in her bag for her phone.

He jangled his keys. "Go call one for yourself. I'm

capable of driving a bike in the rain. Just because you're a wuss." He strode to the curb and straddled his motorcycle.

"Teddy, please!" She dashed out from under the awning and tugged on his arm as he started the engine. He revved it up and shifted into gear with his boot. It purred above the spatter of rain.

He strapped his helmet on. "Now if you're coming, hop on. I'm wasting gas here." He twisted the throttle on the right handlebar.

She trembled as her teeth clenched in anger. "No, I'm taking a taxi, damn it!"

As Ted zoomed out into the street, a car swerved and headed straight for him. The headlights blinded her. A scream ripped from deep inside her. The car rammed Ted with a sickening thump. He struck the ground, his bike a mangled mess of steel. Tires screeched as the car sped off into the night.

Ted rolled over, moaning.

Dazed with shock, Kylah stumbled back into the noisy bar. She grabbed a waitress, knocking a tray out of her arms. Dishes and glasses crashed to the floor. "Help! Call 9-1-1! My husband got run over!"

Patrons turned to stare. The waitress pulled out a cell phone and shouted into it, "There's been an accident!"

"Hurry up, please, he's out there on the ground, please!" Kylah screamed.

"An ambulance is coming," someone yelled in her ear.

Tears blinding her, she burst through the door and back into the rain to Ted. His chest rose and fell. He still breathed, thank God.

"An ambulance is coming, Teddy, you'll be fine, I promise." She took his hand, pressed her fingers to his wrist. "Your pulse is steady," she assured him. As rain drenched them, she bowed her head and whispered the Lord's Prayer in Gaelic…"Ár n-Athair atá ar neamh, Go naofar d'ainim, Go dtagfadh do ríocht…"

****

Wailing sirens cut through the spattering rain. A whirring red light flashed on Ted making him look awash in blood. Two paramedics carried a stretcher and lifted him onto it.

"I'm right here, I'm with you."

She followed them and scrambled into the ambulance. On the endless ride, the siren blaring, she knelt at his side. "You'll be fine, Teddy, I promise…"

****

It all went by in a blur. She ran after the paramedics as they raced down the hall with Ted on a gurney.

"You can't go in there, ma'am," a nurse warned her, guarding the ER doors.

"I'm not leaving you, Teddy…" she promised as they wheeled him through the doors out of her sight.

Lightheaded from the odor of antiseptic, she collapsed in a plastic chair, clasped her hands and prayed. How many hours passed? She had no concept of time. Harsh fluorescent lights cast a cold glare on the tile floor and white walls.

"Mrs. McKinley?"

She looked up at a doctor looming over her. How did they know her name? Had she given it to them? Had she filled out forms? Shown an insurance card? She had no memory of any details.

"Your husband is in stable condition in ICU. You can see him now. This way." He gestured down the hall.

Kylah stood and stumbled. He held her up. Leaning on his sturdy frame, she entered the ward, beige curtains separating beds all around her. Her heels clicked on the floor. She approached Ted lying on his back, hooked up to an IV. A monitor beeped a steady rhythm as green blips ran across the screen.

"Teddy..."

His eyes opened; he mouthed words she couldn't understand.

"Don't talk, save your strength. You'll be all right, they said. And honey...I'll find out who did this to you, to make sure it never happens again." She left her premonition unsaid.

One detail she did remember about that horrific night: the doctor's words. They echoed in her mind, in her sleep: "If he wasn't wearing his helmet, he'd be dead..."

****

Ted survived, paralyzed from the waist down. "It was an accident. Nobody tried to mow me down," he kept insisting.

But she knew better.

Chapter Two

Barnstable Village, Cape Cod, last spring

Kylah halted Ted's wheelchair and pointed skyward. "Look, a shooting star." It streaked through the twilight over their heads. "Make a wish." She shut her eyes.

I wish to learn the truth.

Ted grasped her fingers. "Babe, this is even better than that eclipse the other night." His voice lilted, lightening her heart.

"It sure is. You can't wish on an eclipse." As they shared a laugh, she leaned forward and kissed Ted's bearded cheek. She resumed wheeling him down the tree-lined road past the dwellings and churches of centuries past. "It's quieter than usual, isn't it?" She inhaled the sweet fragrance of a lilac bush. "Mmm, I can even taste this."

Their neighbor's boy pedaled past them on his bicycle, waving as he whizzed by. "Hey, Mr. and Mrs. McK!"

"Hey, Ty." They waved as he vanished around the bend.

"Why hasn't Tyler ever come around for you to make an astro chart for him?" Kylah asked. "That paranormal investigation I did at his house turned up a lot of evidence. They have spirits in there, but nothing malevolent, just some kids who lived there in the eighteen hundreds."

"Maybe living in a haunted house is enough," Ted said over his shoulder. "Hey, you should ask the local station if they'll produce a TV show about your ghost hunts, like all those shows we watch."

"You'd want a wife with her own show?" She tugged his gray ponytail. "A TV series is very time-consuming. I'd never have time to run the store or ghost hunt. My podcasts are enough media for me."

A car approached from behind and passed them.

"Well, you're the star of your own show, TV or no TV, babe." His undying belief gave her a much-needed boost. "In the last chart I made for you, the sun in your fellow sign of Aquarius promises you'll be a star if you make an effort to shine. Sometimes you can be too low profile for your own good. Sounds to me if you launch the ship, it'll get you there."

"You know me, I prefer round trips," she joked. "But strange you mention a launch. Last week I did a tarot reading for myself that predicted 'a fated trip.' I was thinking of doing ghost hunts across the Cape and Rhode Island this October, for the Halloween season. Would you like to go with me?"

"Would I!" He plucked a few leaves off a low-hanging branch. "This beats Baltimore, but most of the time, I feel like part of the furniture."

"A change of scenery's always healthy." She squeezed his arm. "What about your chart?"

"I haven't done one lately. Been too busy giving the drum lessons and doing the meditation. The higher powers keep me outta trouble." He chuckled as another car passed by.

"Speaking of higher powers," she said, "I made an appointment for another past life regression with Laurie, for Friday."

"You just had one last night. And you got home so late, we didn't get to talk about it. What happened?"

"I learned more about my past life as Alice Kyteler, but I need to know even more." She waited for an SUV to pass by. "When I first went back to the thirteen hundreds, I saw myself dressed in black—I knew it had to be mourning, because an unbearable grief came over me and I cried my heart out. But I didn't know whose death it was." That vivid memory engulfed her once more. "I'm still a little depressed over it."

"It had to be somebody close. I'm guessing it was one of your—uh, Alice's husbands, right?" he asked her.

"Yeah, it had to be." She steered Ted's chair around scattered rocks on the dirt path. "It was that same past life I regressed to all the other times—rural Ireland. When I looked around, I saw that same cottage with the thatched roof, the crooked door, the herb garden…it was all so vivid."

"And in color?" Ted asked.

"Oh, yeah, living color." She nodded even though he couldn't see her. "I stood there, looking down at this closed coffin. Then I remembered—Alice's last husband John LePoer was murdered. And guess who was accused? Alice."

"He's the dude you think is me reincarnated?" Ted asked, his tone tinged with doubt.

"That's him. Alice was accused of his murder and of witchcraft at the same time."

Ted turned his head to glance at her. "Murder *and* witchcraft?" He whistled. "They had it in for you, all right—I mean her."

"She was the richest woman in Kilkenny, maybe in all of Ireland, and that's what they hated about her. A woman in the fourteenth century with all that dough? They had to put her in her place." Kylah took a deep breath and savored the aroma of freshly mowed grass. "Then the next thing I knew, I was standing in a stuffy courtroom. I could see it and hear it and smell it—" She wrinkled her nose. "Unwashed bodies, a judge sweating through his robe, the crowd hissing...Alice, Alice..." she rasped.

"You mean regressions switch scenes like that, like a dream?" he asked. "You're in one place one minute, another place the next?"

"It's very much like dreaming. All your senses are working—and I even thought what Alice was thinking. I kept saying, 'I did not kill John!' I know Alice didn't kill him."

"So the husband had his enemies too." Ted glanced up at her.

"Seems that way." A breeze carried the chill of early evening. "Maybe it was a bad business deal, who knows? Years before that, Alice was arrested for killing her first husband, William, but they proved he'd eaten bad lampreys and she got off."

"So where'd you wind up after that?" He stretched his arms over his head and flexed his muscles.

"That was the worst part." She cringed at the memory. "After the courtroom scene faded, I found myself standing in some dungeon or cell or—this dark creepy place with stone walls. Rats scurried over the

9

dirt floor. And, oh, man, did it stink!" She gulped a breath of fresh air at the memory. "It choked me—the nauseating stench of rotting flesh." Covering her nose and mouth with her hand, she gagged. "Oh, it was disgusting."

"Why'd they throw you in there if you weren't found guilty yet? Hey, sorry, I mean Alice…I keep saying 'you' but just smack me next time I do that, okay?" He smiled up at her.

"Glad to." She gave his head a playful slap. "But I was Alice when this went on. Then this figure appeared before me, I couldn't tell if it was male or female, I couldn't distinguish any facial features, just someone draped in a dark kirtle—you know, those flowing robes they wore. It pointed a bony finger at me and condemned me to a life of suffering."

"What did the voice sound like?" Ted asked. "A man or a woman?"

"Neither, it was—not so much a voice as a gravelly cackle." She stopped the chair and chased the gooseflesh from her arms. "It made my skin crawl."

"Hmm." Ted drummed on the chair arms with his fingertips. "You sound like you got more homework to do."

"I sure do." She wheeled him past their favorite haunted landmark—the oldest wooden 'gaol' in the United States. "That was the end of the regression. Laurie brought me back."

"So you need to know who's that sinister cackling character tormenting you—I mean, Alice," he said.

"That and who murdered her last husband. Maybe it's the same person. After I came home from Laurie's last night, I couldn't sleep, so I finished this book from the eighteen-hundreds, *The Annals of Ireland*. It kind of scared me." She paused, searching for the right words to tell him.

"Well?" he probed. "What'd it say?"

"Her husband John left a note. The way it was worded made it look like Alice murdered him," she said. "So that's more evidence against her."

He held up his index finger. "Hey, maybe John did himself in and made it look like Alice—"

An approaching engine's roar drowned out his words. She looked over her shoulder. A pickup truck veered off the road and sped toward them.

High beams blinded her. She shielded her eyes with her hand. "What the hell!" By instinct she shoved Ted off the path, but too late—the truck sideswiped his chair, hurled him to the ground and knocked her over. She yelped as pain shot through her elbow. The truck zoomed away.

Stunned, she knelt beside him. "Are you all right?"

"Yeah...just a bump." Wincing, he brushed dirt from his hands. "Damn, I can't believe the way kids drive these days."

She righted his chair and helped him back into it. Shaking, she leaned on the handles for support. Her elbow throbbed. "What if it wasn't some kid? What if it was—" She tried to stop herself but the words fell out. "The same maniac who knocked you off your bike outside Narrowback's last summer?"

"Oh, come on with your what-iffing. That would be like getting hit by lightning twice."

He looked down and massaged his paralyzed legs, tearing her heart apart. The horror of that night came rushing back to her. She shuddered.

11

"Teddy, I have the strangest hunch this is no coincidence. I can't explain it, but—I sense it." Taking deep breaths, she turned his chair around. "Let's go home before they really do kill us." She tried to flex her swelling elbow.

"Come on. It was just some jerk texting or smoking too much weed. Don't go all woo-woo on me." He wiggled his fingers.

"Our lives haven't been the same since you got mowed down that night." Her voice trembled. "Somebody wants to kill the both of us now." She chased the goosebumps from her chilled arms—but it wasn't from the nippy air. Raw fear iced her blood. "I just want to get us home and safe."

"Safe? Hah!" He turned halfway around. "A savage killer stalks us in the dark," he droned, "a scraggly hand with bony fingers splayed in the shadows, reaching, reeeechiiing—" His cold hand clamped down on hers.

"Stop it!" She halted the chair, the sudden lurch jolting him. "I hate when you use that creepy voice."

He faced forward and snickered. "You're being paranoid. If some nut wanted to kill us, they'd've plowed right into us, not just sideswiped us." He reached up and grasped her fingers. "When we get home, we'll brew some chamomile to calm you down, light one of your lavender candles, do some meditating in front of the fire…"

But as she pushed his chair, her mind whirred. "You have no enemies." She gripped his chair handles so tightly, her fingers ached. "But that's the key, isn't it? No *living* enemies."

"Oh, now you think it's somebody from the other

side?" His voice carried a note of annoyance. "C'mon, lighten up." He shook his head.

"Teddy, this is no random accident." She picked up her pace, anxious to get home. "When you got mowed down outside the bar, it was right after Laurie did a past life regression on me. Now this—after last night's regression."

"Babe, the entire universe is random—the galaxies, the stars, the planets." He waved his hands. "Formed at random. The only reason we're here at all is by pure chance, not some grand master plan."

"That's a theory, Teddy. Nobody knows for sure. Not the most brilliant astronomer, physicist or theologian—no mortal knows."

"But you never give me a reason," he insisted. "Why would somebody want to kill me? From this life or some past life?"

"That's what I'm trying to find out with the regressions." A few paces from their street corner, she breathed easier. "If there's a parallel to Alice and John."

"Like I always say, they call this stuff paranormal for a reason. It isn't normal." Ted pointed his finger like a stern teacher.

Relief washed over her at the welcoming sight of their red brick colonial. She wheeled him up the ramp lined with spotlights and onto the porch.

"It's perfectly safe. Here." He jangled the keys above his head.

She grabbed them and jabbed the key into the lock. She opened the door and maneuvered his chair over the threshold. Her cozy living room greeted her with the aroma of cinnamon, her rocker, her fireplace, her knitting in a wicker basket, her clocks of every size tick-tocking, and her latest extravagance: the 3-D TV.

Home. Just the way she'd left it.

She slammed and bolted the door. "You don't hear anything, do you?" She held her breath.

"No, Ky." Ted wheeled himself into the entry hall and peered around. "Only your army of clocks. We're alone. The Cape Strangler must'a took the night off."

Her heart calmed and her limbs stopped wobbling. She sat on Ted's lap and they shared a tight embrace. He held her hands and massaged her bruised elbow.

"Mmm, that's nice. You have such a healing touch. It really eased the pain." She flexed her arm and stretched it.

He slid the elastic from her hair and unwound her braid, stroking her wavy locks. She sighed in contentment.

"Are you calm now?" He nuzzled her ear.

"Not quite, but I've never been so glad to be home. Teddy, we have to talk about this."

"You need some tea first." He wheeled himself into the kitchen.

****

Settled at the kitchen table, she circled her fingers around her teacup and studied Ted's face. His setbacks and hardships never showed in his lively brown eyes. So he put on a little weight since the night they met at a Poe reading. But his eyes and his smile still held that spark of youth.

"I still feel threatened by the evil emanating from that—that spirit on my regression," she said. "It might be in the body of a living person, here in this world. I keep thinking that's who knocked you off your bike outside the bar. Now it looks like they're after the both of us. We're lucky to be alive. For now."

He slurped his tea. "I just find it a stretch that it's paranormal and had something to do with Alice and John seven hundred years ago." He tilted his head and gave her his cocked-brow "show me the money" look.

"From what I know about Alice and John, it's not a stretch. Look at the similarities in what happened. Their tragic history is repeating itself—or trying to." She glanced through the grocery coupons he'd cut from the Sunday paper.

He circled the rim of his cup with his fingertip. "If you look at any two events, you can come up with similarities. No, I can't believe we lived in some past life, together or apart." Ted shook his head as he spoke. "We only go around once, babe."

"Someday you'll believe me," she promised. "But meanwhile, I need to find out why this person from our past hates us."

"Here's my theory." He plucked one of her homemade oat squares from the ceramic cookie jar. "It's a woman, 'cause guys don't cackle. She had the hots for John and he blew her off. Or maybe she had the hots for Alice. Any women hit on you in this life?" Grinning, he chomped on his oat square.

"That's not funny." She shot him a glare. "Your habit of twisting everything into a joke irks me at times. But you're a master at dealing with life's crap," she admitted. "Alice didn't murder John. But this spirit, person, whoever it was—has a vendetta against us and I'm going to find out what it is."

"John LePoer was a moneylender, wasn't he? Maybe they had a dispute over a debt. Some dames just can't let go of a grudge." A smirk spread his lips.

She tapped her nails on her cup. "Look. You got run off the road outside the bar right after I was regressed to that life. But having done last night's regression, I'm convinced of a connection. That person's hatred was so powerful I can feel it spilling out into this life. I need to find out who it was and what went on, so I can figure out how it relates to this life. And Teddy—" She leaned forward, her heart racing. "I know the best way to find out." Her muscles tensed, her elbow throbbing again.

He took a slurp of tea and swallowed. "Okay, lay it on me."

She captured his hands. "We'll get regressed together."

His gaze roved around the kitchen, at her antique herb cupboard, at the Welsh love spoons on the wall, everywhere but on her. "Aw, come on, Ky, I don't wanna go under."

"It's not 'going under.' This will give us a huge piece of the puzzle. You were John in that life. Your lives parallel each other as closely as mine and Alice's. She was a Druid, I'm a Druid. She lived in Kilkenny, I lived in Kilkenny. She opened a business and grew herbs, so have I." She drew a deep breath. "You and he were both disabled by a hit-and-run vehicle—back then it was a wagon, this time a car. He married Alice and you married me. Our lives aren't just parallel, they're identical."

He fiddled with his spoon. "What if I don't come out of it?"

"That's impossible. While under hypnosis, you're still in control. You can open your eyes anytime, get up and go to the bathroom, or end the entire session. Just do this with me." She squeezed his fingers. "Please?"

He released a whoosh. "Look, we don't have to make this decision now, do we? Can we at least sleep on it?"

He wheeled himself over to her and caressed her cheek. His calloused hand felt rough, yet comforting.

"All right. But do we have to sleep?" she murmured, tingling under his touch. "You only had lobsta for dinner. I had oysters."

****

She woke before sunrise. Remembering last night's brush with death, she wanted to burrow under the covers and hide. But reality wouldn't wait.

Flexing her bruised elbow wasn't all that painful. As she showered and braided her hair, she longed to meditate and share the newborn day with the earth. She set Ted's cereal and bowl on the kitchen table and jotted him a note.

Taking inventory tonight, will be late.

Going to the beach before work. Txt me later.

xoxo

He had a full day of astro readings and drum lessons to teach. She didn't expect him to text her for a while.

She admired Ted's attitude, refusing to act the victim, keeping busy. He battled depression, but with the help of a psychiatrist, he handled it. He harbored no resentment, no bitterness. He forgave. Good God, the guy would never walk again, and he flipped it off as "one of them curve balls life throws ya." He sure did know how to deal.

Whether he thought some pothead or some texting

kid ran him over, it was up to her to learn the truth. She'd have to be regressed on Friday without him.

Before leaving, she made a circlet around her head with her braid. She clipped it with her favorite barrette that she'd made with shell fragments from her local beach.

She slid into her Mustang convertible and put the top down. Turning onto Old King's Highway, she avoided the scene of last night's near miss. She didn't want to see the path of Ted's tumbling chair in the dirt.

Refreshed and energized from the cool breeze, Kylah stepped on the gas. Her spirit in harmony with Earth below and infinity above, she tingled.

She parked next to the weather-beaten fence at the edge of the sand dunes. Kicking off her shoes, she crunched through the cool grains. Breathing and tasting the salty air, she gazed at earth's curve where heaven met sea.

Sitting cross-legged on the sand, she pulled her cell phone out of her pocket and tapped "Mike" on the contacts list. She needed her best friend now more than she needed him when he handled her divorce fifteen years ago.

"Please be there, Mike," she pleaded through two, three, four rings.

"You have reached the private line of attorney Michael Richardson. I'm unavailable at this time. Please leave your name and number…"

At the beep, Kylah blurted, "Mike, please call me, I need to talk to you."

She slipped the phone into her pocket. With the salt spray misting her face, she turned toward the morning sky, streaked with wispy pink clouds. "What did Ted and I do in that other life that was so terrible, someone wants to kill us?" Yearning for midnight's sprinkling of stars, she implored the glassy moon floating above the horizon. "Alice was a good person. Who is this spirit and why does it hate us?"

She picked up a scallop shell and ran her thumbnail over its delicate ridges. What precision, what symmetry. It would be perfect for the feng shui water corner in her house. She named it Murchadh—Gaelic for protector of the sea—and dropped it into her pocket. "Please let me learn the full story," she spoke aloud to the universe. "Then I can find out why this karma's coming around now."

Her phone rang and she checked the caller I.D.

"Hey, that was fast." She liked to picture Mike in her mind's eye when she talked to him, hunched over his desk, stubble sprinkling his chin, specs perched on the end of his nose.

"Hey yourself. What's up?"

His tone calmed her. She breathed deep. "Somebody in a pickup tried to run us over last night as I wheeled Ted along the road. I believe it's the same person that knocked Ted off his bike outside Narrowback's and the time before that." The words rushed out in one breath. "It can't be a coincidence. I don't believe in coincidence."

"Are you both all right?" His voice rose with a note of alarm.

"Yeah, just bruises," she assured him.

"Did you get the plate number?"

A gust of wind drowned out his voice. She pressed her palm to her free ear. "No, it all happened too fast. But I think it's..." She dug her feet into the sand. "I know we don't see eye to eye on this. But I believe it's somebody from Ted's and my past. I mean our past life together, before this one."

"Oh, that."

She pictured him rolling his eyes.

"If we can get together now, I have some free time," he said.

A pang of longing for his comfort seized her. She squeezed her eyes shut. "I'd love to. Petra will have to open the store, but she'll understand. Can you come here? I'm at Gray's Beach, next to the lifeguard chair. I'm the only one sitting. Everybody else is either jogging or dog walking or scavenging—that's the seagulls."

"Sure, I don't have to be in court until one. Maybe I can cheer you up a little."

"I wouldn't even mind some of your lawyer's gallows humor." She smiled. "I'll be here, meditating."

"Give me fifteen minutes. I just brewed a pot of Smooth and Mellow coffee. I'll bring some," he said.

"Smooth *or* mellow is good enough for me. See you in a bit." She dropped her phone back into its bamboo case.

Digging her feet into the sand up to her ankles, she let her thoughts drift.

What would have happened if I'd chosen that other path? If I'd stayed in Ireland after college?

Sometimes it looked like her path chose *her.*

****

As she hummed "Danny Boy," the breeze brought Mike's voice to her ears. "Ready for a coffee break?"

Smiling, she looked up and shaded her eyes. "Am I ever!"

He unfolded the chairs and poured her a mug of thick steaming coffee.

The aroma brought warm memories of her grandma's kitchen. "Chairs? Well, someday you'll be as earthy as I am and sit on bare sand."

"I like to get as down 'n dirty as the next guy, but I can't show up in court with Gray's Beach clinging to my behind." He lifted his trouser legs and sat. "Maybe when I'm a judge I can get away with it."

"Mike, thanks so much for coming." Her muscles relaxed as relief washed over her. "Oh, God, I was scared…"

"It's okay, you're safe now." He pulled his chair closer.

"I keep seeing Ted before my eyes, unable to walk, now faced with this. He's braver than I'll ever be." She drew a deep breath. "They're not going to stop until they finish us off."

"They?" He cocked his head to one side. "They who?"

She began with, "I told you about my past life as Alice Kyteler, accused of witchcraft and killing her husband John LePoer."

"There's more?" Skepticism crept into his tone.

"Okay, hear me out." She stood up and settled in the chair next to him. "At my regression the other night, I became Alice again, in a confrontation with this spirit who hates me and Ted, and it's determined to kill us. I don't know if it's male or female. But it was scary as hell." She shivered, inhaling in the rich coffee aroma.

"And you believe this—this encounter happened? You weren't hallucinating?"

She shook her head. "No, Mike. I confirmed

everything in history books and archives. Somebody had it in for Alice and her last husband John, and history is repeating itself with me and Ted."

He stared out at the calm waves. "I know you're going through hell right now, but hear me out. There's a practical, mundane way to handle this."

"That must be the lawyer in you talking." She forced her shaky lips into a smile. "Somehow I knew you'd get all mundane on me."

"Assuming you're right and some nut is after you, whether they came from the Middle Ages or the Stone Age, they're here now. Until this lunatic is caught, the best thing to do is hire security guards to patrol your property." He blew on his coffee and took a sip.

She heaved a frustrated sigh. "What good will guards do? It's history re-emerging. It's my karma, what goes around comes around," she pointed at herself, "unless I do something to stop it. This happens all the time, but people don't realize it, or refuse to believe because they're afraid to."

"Then what's better than hiring guards?" he challenged.

The wind blew her hair into her face and she smoothed it away. "I have an appointment for another past life regression on Friday. But after last night's close call, I asked Ted to regress with me." She took a sip of coffee. Scalding and strong, it stung her tongue. "But he doesn't want to 'go under' as he says."

"Does Ted believe he was John Le—what's-his-name in that life?" Mike asked.

She shook her head. "He doesn't believe in reincarnation. But I'm convinced what happened to him last year and last night was no accident. Someone wants to kill him. And now me, too."

"I take it he's not worried." Mike stretched his legs.

"No, it was some kid smoking weed or texting, he says. But he's not afraid to die." She took another sip. "He's a fatalist who doesn't believe we should try to change our destinies, even if we're empowered to. But if I get regressed to the right moment in my past life as Alice, I can find out exactly what happened and deal with this karma, so it won't happen now. Or ever again. It would work much better with Ted there, but I can do it alone if I have to. I've done it before." Chilled, she raised the mug to her face and let the steam warm her. "When I was waiting for you, I tried to put the question out there. What did Ted and I do to deserve his murder in a past life? Whether we did something to deserve it then or not, our lives are in danger now, and I have to fix it. What scares me most is that no one knows what happened to Alice. She just vanished into the mists of time. That's not exactly comforting."

"No matter what happened to Alice in the Middle Ages, I'm not convinced somebody is trying to kill you now," Mike argued. "From what evidence I see, it looks like somebody's tried to get you to leave town— somebody who's against Druidism and your ghost hunting and all that mumbo j—" He halted. "That stuff you believe in. It's probably some born-again fundamentalist who thinks you're the spawn of the devil."

"One of those 'warnings' crippled Ted," she reminded him, her voice flat.

"Yes, that was terrible," he admitted. "But in my view, going on present-day evidence here, nobody's out to kill you. A determined killer would have got Ted—and you. Trust me. He just misjudged how close he could get and hit Ted."

She sat up straight. "I see where you're coming from as a lawyer, but see my side, as someone who's seen my past life, and what's happened to me and my husband in that life."

He took a sip of coffee. "I can't wrap my head around your going on faith in all this. Me, I need evidence. I can't make a living without it. I've never put much stock in blind faith out of the courtroom either."

She breathed the salty air. "During one of my regressions, when I was in that past life as Alice, I was grieving for someone in a closed coffin, a loved one. I believe it was John. He was murdered and I got arrested for it." She gulped her coffee, needing that jolt.

"Is there any proof this hateful person existed?" he probed. "You need to get facts. All you're going on here is intuition."

"No, it's not intuition, it's past and present lives converging." She gave an emphatic nod. "I know Alice didn't kill John. I was Alice and I'd never kill my husband, in this life or any other. I always babble about being single again, but I'd never harm Ted or leave him—or kill him." She suppressed another shiver.

"Okay, but hire some security. I'll have some local cops patrol the area. If somebody's out to harm you, they'll get caught." He leaned toward her. "I'm not talking like a lawyer now. Just do what I ask, please."

"I appreciate your concern, but..." She had to humor him on this. The supernatural couldn't be handled by the mundane. "I hope when I come back from my past life on Friday, I'll know who's after us and why."

He eyed her with a raised brow. "Since Ted doesn't believe it's some past life spirit after you two, wouldn't he want to have some security around the house?"

She remembered Ted's behavior last night. "Ted keeps saying what you say. If somebody wants to kill him, they will."

"He's right." Mike refilled her cup. "But his helmet saved him. Still, it can't hurt to have security."

She wiggled her toes in the sand. "Whatever is going on, I'm determined to find out on Friday, either with or without Ted." She leaned over and sifted a handful of sand through her fingers, watching the grains fall away. "I wish I had all day here."

"Yeah, I used to walk or jog on Scusset Beach with the dogs before work. But these days, all the walking I do is back and forth to the bench." He patted the small paunch above his belt. "Middle age and gravity creep up on all of us."

"It's not growing old that I'm afraid of. I'm afraid of *not* getting the chance to grow old." She sipped her coffee and savored it before swallowing.

"We can only control so much." He tipped his cup to his lips, head back.

"But one advantage to being aware of our past lives is knowing we can learn from past mistakes and don't have to repeat history," she said. "We can fulfill our karma."

He drained his cup. "Hell, getting through this life is hard enough, without thinking of ways we screwed up our past ones."

Glancing at her watch, she said, "I still have a few

minutes. Aside from some maniac wanting to kill us, my life is the same old same old. What's new with you?"

He propped his elbows on his knees and they chatted about lighter things, her new café range, his goal to break 80 in golf. The small talk eased her prickly stress. She breathed easier.

After a pause, he said, "I may as well tell you now. Jen wants a divorce."

"Oh, Mike." Pangs of shock and pity took her off guard. She gave his hand a clasp and made sure not to linger. "Why didn't you tell me before?"

"You had your own problem to get off your chest. I'm not jumping off a cliff over it, but I'm not doing handsprings either."

"Is there another man or…" She sipped, let the cooling coffee linger on her tongue, and swallowed.

He shook his head. "Nothing that dramatic. Just general boredom."

"Well, you did marry her about an hour after you met her."

"Yeah, I wasn't thinking ten minutes into the future. But when she first suggested a separation, I agreed, figuring we could see each other on dates, do a little rekindling." He rubbed his eyes. "But who was I kidding? So she said a clean break is the best all around, and I agreed with her. The kids'll be in college by September. We're good at bridge together but…" He gave a one-shoulder shrug. "That's about it anymore."

"I understand." She took the last mouthful of her cooled coffee. "I love Ted, but I've never been truly free, except for those few years I lived in Ireland. That was so long ago, it's a distant memory. I spent my adult life taking care of other people. Sometimes I fantasize about being single and free. Then I hate myself for thinking that way and walk around drowning in guilt."

"Don't." He poured himself another refill. "We all need our fantasies. It's healthy as long as we don't act on them."

She itched to ask about those fantasies of his, but wouldn't dare. For all she knew, he might want to do three strippers at once, and she didn't want to go there. Another glimpse at her watch told her, "It's that time. Tonight's inventory night. I'm working late." As a gossamer cloud shrouded the sun, he helped her to her feet, folded the chairs and they trudged through the sand.

"Call me if you need me," he said as they reached her car. "But if it's around six, text me and I'll get back to you later tonight. I'm taking Mom for a birthday dinner at L'Espalier."

"Wow. I've never been there, but heard enough about it. Your mom gave birth to a heart of gold." She gave him a warm smile.

"Yeah, well—" He fished his car key out of his pocket. "She deserves it. I want to give her what Dad couldn't. I take her to fancy restaurants because all she did was cook for us."

"If I know your mom, she'd be just as happy eating colcannon at the Irish Village," she kidded him. "I've seen her ask them to add extra cabbage to the mashed potatoes."

"You mean add potatoes to the cabbage!" They shared a laugh. "She insisted I take her there last weekend instead of the Capital Grille. But that's 'cause Finton Stanley was playing."

"So that's where you get your love of kicking up your heels." She smiled. "Hey, what's your mom's number?" She dug out her phone. He gave her the number and she texted, "Happy Birthday, Rose, many more!" She turned to him. "Thanks for being here."

He leaned over and gave her a one-arm hug. "Any time, kiddo."

She didn't mind his calling her kiddo. It made her feel young. After all, he was on the wrong side of forty, but he sure didn't look it. Good genes; it had to be.

****

Her store, on the ground floor of a restored 1754 tavern, was already open with half a dozen cars parked outside. As she walked through the door, the ancient Celtic strains of Clannad soothed her. Sandalwood incense sweetened the air. Although her mind drifted back to her fourteenth century life, she chatted with customers and showed a young couple to her "Adam and Eve" room where she kept the adult DVD's, flavored body oils, and assorted "toys." People came in just to ask for that room, making her wonder.

Maybe I should make this a sex shop and sell all the other stuff in the back.

During a lull, Petra gushed, "Kylah, three Druids from Ireland were waiting at the door when I got here to open. They bought a bunch of crystals and books—" She took a closer look. "Are you okay?"

"I'm fine, I know I look like hell warmed over." She gestured toward the receipts. "You're a sales wizard."

"It was nothing, really, this stuff sells itself. Let me make you some tea. Red, white, or green?"

"No, thanks, not right now." She paused and took a

breath. "I'm not going to blab this to just anybody, but I want to tell you. A truck tried to run us over last night. I know someone's trying to kill Ted again—and me, too, this time. I'm afraid it's the same person as the other times." Her voice shook. She swallowed, her mouth dry.

Petra came around the counter and gave Kylah a hug. "Oh, I'm so sorry. Should I ask my dad to talk to Ted? They've always been on the same page about most things, you know, both being ex-bikers and all."

"I don't think Ted needs motivational coaching." Kylah shook her head. "It hardly affected him."

"Did either of you get hurt?"

"He got dirty hands. I got a bruise." She held up her elbow. "But I'm having another regression Friday with Laurie. I hope to find out what happened to Alice once and for all. I asked Ted to regress with me, but he won't."

"He's afraid, huh?"

"Not afraid of regression. Just afraid to believe." Her cell rang and she swiped the screen. "Hey, Teddy."

"Hey, babe. You were so scared last night, I thought I'd tell you we're well protected now."

"What do you mean?" Sweat sprang out on her palms.

"I got the arsenal out. I'm keeping my forty-four on the table in the den so I can reach it. I also loaded the shotgun with deer slugs. It's in the living room."

"Oh no, please be careful with those." A jolt frayed her nerves.

"Ky, if there's one thing I can still do, it's hit a bull's ass with a handgun. Don't worry about me. I got the twenty-two out for you, too. I put it in the piano bench. I think you should start packing."

"I don't want to carry firearms." Her fingers clenched the phone. "We'll talk about it tonight. I made you a tuna casserole. It's in the blue dish. I put extra garlic in it for you."

"Ah, sweet. That'll scare a killer away. Sounds like it's to die for. No bad pun intended. But think about it. You have the *right* to protect yourself. Catch ya later."

"Catch ya back." She couldn't dwell on the merits of the Second Amendment right now.

The steady stream of customers helped her push last night's terror from her mind. The sterling silver jewelry went especially fast; she made a note to order more Claddagh rings and Celtic knot pendants. One customer bought the St. Brighid's cross pendant right from around her neck...she'd run out of them on display and the woman begged her to buy it. Another customer asked if she sold mushy peas. That got her thinking...maybe expand into Irish groceries.

****

Kylah enjoyed her bi-annual inventory ritual. She closed the store early, sent Petra home and locked herself in the back room, a long-ago kitchen. She sat in her own world, a fire in the hearth, her crystals, amulets and books all around her. Nobody knew where she was. Relaxing to Enya's entrancing melodies, she lit vanilla incense and sipped matcha tea. Time flew as she counted her supply of rings, bracelets, pendants, amulets, crystals, books, hooded capes...she was way low on 'adult' items from the back room...flavored condoms always moved fast.

Before she knew it, it was 9:30 and dark out. She called Ted, but his voice mail picked up. He was either asleep or in his den with the TV blasting.

By now he would've devoured the tuna casserole, but she craved the cinnamon buns they'd baked the other night. Thoughts of the warm buttery crust made her mouth water.

On the drive home, she wondered about her past life with Ted as John LePoer in the long-ago misty Ireland of green hills and white sheep, the smell of wet earth all around them. It all ended in his murder. For all she knew, Alice was murdered, too. On Friday, she planned to uncover the rest of that life, shrouded in centuries of mystery.

When she got home, the Red Sox game blasted from the den and a stale beer smell wafted out. "Oh, no, he's zonked again." She headed for the den, knowing she'd have to hoist his dead weight onto the bed...

At the doorway, she halted in shock so severe, she couldn't scream. Ted lay on his side on the floor, rigid and lifeless, his wheelchair knocked over. His eyes stared unblinking, his lips a sickly bluish gray. His hands clutched his middle, as if he'd suffered severe pain with his last breath. An empty teacup and her half-eaten casserole sat on the table.

She rushed to him and pressed her fingers to his wrist. No pulse.

"Oh, Teddy!" Sobbing, she collapsed on her dead husband.

Chapter Three

Kilkenny, Ireland, May 1324

Alice Kyteler snipped a leaf from the basil plant in her herb garden. As she inhaled its sweet essence, her copper wind chimes tinkled. A sign at her door asked visitors to chime her upon arrival, and they did—the ones who could read.

Peering at her cottage, she brushed soil from her hands. "A fine morn to you, sir."

"Mighty fine, Alice, but no need to address me so formal. 'Tis only I."

"Arn, may that be you?" Indeed, twas her dear friend Arnold Wolfe. "Come in, join me in a cup of chamomile. I'm about to brew a kettle—"

"Alice, this is no social call, I fear." Removing his felt hat, he wiped the sweat from his forehead and took a hesitant step forward. "I come to you not as a friend, but as Kilkenny's steward."

"What is it? You look positively gray, mind." Short of breath, dread clutching at her heart, she approached him. "Oh, no. Is it John again? I know his moneylending brings disquiet when his dunning zeal gets the best of him. Has he been bedeviling patrons again? Whom did he pommel this time?"

"He won't be returnin' to you, Alice." His voice cracked. "He's passed on."

She staggered backwards.

He seized her arms to steady her. "I'm sorry, Alice. Lean on me, look."

"B—by the rood, what happened?" she stammered.

"He was found at the top of the road up yonder, at the mile marker for Dublin, nigh on an hour ago. His mount is went. He had coin in his pouch, so it was no robbery."

She blessed herself with a trembling hand. "O, the poor soul, he wasn't long for this world, but I hoped he'd expire at home, warm and snug." She longed for release of her grief, to sob, to take deep breaths and wail out loud. But the tears wouldn't come. "Arn, I cannot say the news is a right shock. He'd been ailing for some time, but no doctor could diagnose his malady. Indeed my herbal remedies made his final days bearable. Where be he now?" She paced in circles, opening her hands to inhale the soothing basil fragrance. "I must make arrangements. He wished to spend eternity under the east oak in the churchyard, and he had sundry final requests."

Arnold cleared his throat and stumbled over his next words. "Michael Artson found him, came back here and called for you. Receiving no answer, he reported to us. We collected John's body and brought him to Dr. Butts. On examination, he gave cause of death as a mixture of herbs. Evidence points to the possibility of poisoning."

"Poisoning!" She blanched in disbelief. "No one would harm John. He was beloved in these parts. But who is this Michael Artson?"

"A land speculator and defense counselor. He owed John a sum of money and was coming by to repay him, says he. He's being questioned at the constabulary."

"Michael Artson?" She silently mouthed the name twice. "I know him not. He murdered my John?"

"He's not accused as yet, Alice. But meanwhile—" Arnold cleared his throat and grasped her hand. "I must take you to the chancellor. He needs question you."

She recoiled. "Surely he cannot believe I—"

"Of course I don't believe you could ever harm John." He shook his head. "But he wants a word with you. They fear John was murdered. And—and—" he stammered, shuffling his feet, "You and Artson are suspects." Arnold lowered his head and crushed his hat between his hands, staining it with sweat.

She nodded. "Then as I've naught to hide, I shall fetch my cloak and satchel."

Entering her inn, she glimpsed herself in the looking glass. No longer bright with passion for life, her eyes portended a fearsome outcome. They gazed back at her, dark and questioning, her cheeks pasty, her lips pale, forming questions she feared asking. "You're a widow for the fourth time," she whispered to the flustered image, as if informing someone else, too mired in shock for grief to flood her.

Arnold offered her his mount, but she preferred to walk to the chancellor's offices in town. She took comfort in her daily walks, her feet pounding the hard earth, stopping to inhale a flower's fragrance or breathe in the scent of laundered sheets fluttering on a line. But now, head down, she trudged along, imploring, "Oh John, how could you meet such a direful end?"

She strode alongside Arnold as he rode, heedless of his attempts at chitchat. No defender however expensive would convince the chancellor of her innocence. They hated her for being the richest proprietress in Kilkenny since hanging her shingle on the Kyteler Inn, nigh on twenty years ago. Now this was their grand opportunity to make her pay for her prosperity.

The chancellor's office was in a timber framed cottage set apart from the town's crowded dwellings and shops. She and Arnold climbed five rotting steps to the pockmarked door. Arnold leaned on it and it gave way with a groan. They entered and the door creaked shut. Darkness engulfed them.

He led her down a corridor to a stuffy room. Chancellor Edward de Burgh stood with his back to them, hands clasped, staring out the window.

Upon hearing their footfalls, he turned and with two strides, towered over her. He puffed out his chest and pushed her down into a hard chair. "Dame Alice, where were you in the last three hours?"

She rattled off her entire agenda for that day. "After cooking breakfast for my patrons at the Inn, I went to market and returned with my purchases. Next I went into the garden and toiled there. At exactly noon, because I glimpsed the sundial, John approached and announced he was going to inspect his tenants' dwellings, and would return afore nightfall."

"Can anyone vouch for your whereabouts after you arrived back home?"

"Nay." She shook her head. "I was on my own."

"We are in possession of evidence that points to the murder of your husband. His sons brought us this proof of *malefecia* they'd obtained from your own kitchen." de Burgh pointed to an opened sack on the floor.

"Dame Alice Kyteler LePoer, you are hereby under arrest for the murder of your husband John LePoer by casting a witch's spell with *malefecia*. And that you use the enchanted skull of a beheaded thief as your cauldron." He spewed forth the accusations like gobs of grease from a hissing spit.

She sprang up. "Witch's spell? I am no witch. I am a member of the Druid order, as you well know. I never have nor will I ever practice witchcraft in any form. How do you propose to prove this wild accusation?"

"At eleven of the clock this morn, your stepsons, driven by your husband's sickly appearance, examined the contents of your kitchen. They seized a sackful of horrible and detestable things and turned them in for evidence. At two of the clock, the victim's body was found. Dr. Butts pronounced the death of poisoning, from the very contents of your kitchen."

"'Tis not *malefecia*. I use my herbs for remedies, medicines, cures," she counted on her fingers, "which I've been giving John since the day we wed. I well prolonged his life, not ended it!" Alice turned to Arnold, pleading with her eyes.

His gaze softened with pity. "Alice, 'tis easy to mistake your herbs for a lethal brew."

"But I've never harmed a soul with my herbs." She clutched Arnold's meaty hands. "You know what happened, Arn. His sons—they're galled that I be beneficiary of John's estate. They covet the inheritance for themselves, 'tis what this is all about. Tell him!"

Arnold spread his hands and appealed to de Burgh. "That part be true, sir. The LePoer lads do begrudge Dame Alice her share of John's estate."

"I'm innocent, I tell you." Alice stepped up to de

Burgh and poked him in the chest. "I did not kill my husband. If you want the true murderers, look to those ingrate sons of his. At least be fair."

"Nevertheless, you are under arrest for his murder. Pending trial, at which the facts shall prevail, God willing, you shall bide here," de Burgh recited with practiced confidence.

She pinned him with her sharp gaze. "If you've any sense of fairness, my lord de Burgh, I implore you to subject his sons to the same scrutiny and indignity you're inflicting upon me."

"I shall see to that as I deem fit," came his answer.

"You have it in for me. You always have. Mayhap someone should question *you*, sir. Where were *you* this morn when my husband met his end on that deserted lane?"

De Burgh sputtered, his face turning splotchy, matching his crimson robe. "How dare you spout at me this way! You shall live only long enough to regret that indiscretion, Dame Alice, that you may count on!"

Arnold slid his arm round her shoulders. "I shall procure the best defense possible, Alice. As you're the most upstanding citizen of this town, if not in all of Ireland, I know the judge will let you post bail pending trial. Meanwhile, I'll commence preparing your defense and ask for you to be released on bail. If anyone wants to get his hands on your money, tis *him*." He tossed his head in de Burgh's direction.

A burly constable led her out into the sunshine. She trod the spongy earth beneath her garden slippers and watched the swaying trees obey the breeze. Will I ever again gaze upon the stars and tread upon the soil? she wondered through her grief.

The gaol, an ancient cottage, boasted a central fireplace, sturdy oak benches and rushes strewn on the dirt floor. At least she wasn't shackled or clapped behind iron bars. "Bide quietly and pray for your salvation." The constable walked out and bolted the door behind him.

The last thing she wanted to do was bide quietly, or bide at all. She'd happily pay her entire fortune in bail to get out of here.

She paced in circles, her heart light, for she appreciated the blurry slice of sky visible through the smudged window.

A rustling sound came from the far end of the cottage. Presently, a man appeared in the doorway, straightening his doublet. He tipped an imaginary hat in welcome. "And you be the widow. I am Michael Artson, the other accused." He bowed.

"Accused?" She gaped at him. "You were arrested as well?"

"Minutes afore you arrived. They allege I conspired with you, as they suspect I had motives of my own. You need convince them that you know me *not* on an intimate basis."

She held out her hand. He clasped it and held it to his lips.

On instinct, she squeezed his fingers, desperate for human contact. "I am in such shock, I pray I'm in the throes of a nightmare and shall awaken with John at my side, rattling the rafters with his snoring." Her voice quivered with a sob.

"I fear neither of us is dreaming, Dame LePoer. I be in this as thick as you."

"No one has ever called me Dame LePoer. I've

always been Alice Kyteler and I prefer to retain my identity." Something in his demeanor put her at ease. Her heart calmed. Her elemental senses blanketed her with comforting trust. "Alice is plenty sufficient, Michael." She forced a smile.

He returned her smile, adding a nod of reassurance. "As you wish, Alice. Since our fates are similar and all but set and sealed in stone, let us be somewhat familiar and cordial to each other."

"So tell me what happened," she urged. "How come they to accuse you as well? And let us stand by the light, I abhor the thought of being imprisoned. The reality of it all will strike me soon enough."

They walked over to a weak ray of sunlight from a dirty window in the charred cooking area.

"I'm accused of killing John, as I was in debt to him. I'd sunk far into debt with land speculation," he explained. "I was paying him back, albeit slowly. John was ever so patient with me, unlike some of his other debtors, from what I've learnt."

"John and I were in the moneylending business together and I run the Kyteler Inn," she said. "Tis ever so busy with travelers to and fro, and I run a tight ship. Every groat is accounted for. I keep an accurate log, stock a full larder, and scrub the house sparkling clean."

"I know of the Kyteler Inn. I've been a patron there a few times." Michael gave her a smile, a faraway look in his eyes.

"Have you?" She took his features in more carefully. Curly mahogany hair framed a smoothly shaved face and angular jaw. "I confess I don't recall you. But so many folk come and go all the time. I would've remembered your—" She gestured at him up and down. "—height."

His cheeks flushed and he turned away. "I stopped there last several years back, so I don't expect you to remember me. But I do remember you." He gave her a wink of approval.

"Was your visit for a brief tryst with a colleen?" she asked.

He shuffled his feet, craning his neck to peer out the window, clearly embarrassed by this bold line of questioning. "What have I to lose at this point? Aye, my lady, I would depart afore sunrise."

"'Tis what gives my inn the reputation as a house of ill repute." Alice assumed a mock-chiding tone. "'Tis, however, a most respectable establishment. I do serve the heartiest breakfasts in all of Kilkenny."

"Ah, that you do, my lady. My mouth waters as I can taste it now, the eggs, generous rashers of bacon, fat and juicy pork sausages, black and white pudding—pardon my rumbling tum." He rubbed his midsection. "But it helps to take me mind off this predicament we're mired in. It was spotless, unlike any other inn I'd ever lodged at, with their vermin-infested mattresses and unemptied chamberpots."

"'Tis why it's popular. But why did we never chat when you stopped in?" She looked him over again. He was easy on the eyes, but she couldn't remember seeing him before.

He shrugged. "I'm not one for chatting. I'm rather bashful."

"Should we survive this ordeal, and I've faith we will, I shall remedy you of that malady, Michael, my dear," Alice's voice trilled in glee, "and it will have naught to do with magic. I shall bring you out your shell so quickly, you'll not know it was cracked."

"Speaking of which, how d'you reckon they'll treat us in this—confinement? Accused murderers hardly rate along with mere highwaymen and thieves, do they?" he asked.

"I know not, my dear sir." She shook her head. "But the constable assured me the chancellor is most merciful with detainees and he shall grant me release on bail." She took a step closer. "I trust you're not a murderer."

He looked her straight in the eye, unblinking. "My lady, nay. Is that what you ask me? If I murdered John? I merely stumbled upon his lifeless body and reported it. I didn't even touch him. I trust all this will come out as truth when the trial commences."

"I pray so as well. The steward, Arnold Wolfe, is a dear friend of mine. He's patronized my inn for donkey's years. He's going to defend me. Who is preparing your defense, Michael?"

"I myself am a defense counselor, but I dare not defend myself in this. My barrister is one Murtagh Teague of Dublin. One of the most prominent with an impeccable record. I dispatched him a message immediately I was accused. I trust he'll arrive in two or three days' time to prepare my defense. I pray he'll arrange bail for me, too." He held out his hands in offering. "If I wasn't accused of this horrid crime, I'd gladly defend you."

"Thank you." She nodded. "I fear I'll need all the defense I can procure. One can't rely on magic all the time."

"Magic?" His eyes brightened in admiration. "Ah, you be the witch they referred to."

"Let us clarify one thing presently, Michael." She placed a fist on her hip. "I never have nor never will practice black arts. I am a member of the Druid order. We do only good for others and for ourselves. So please banish the notion of witchcraft presently. That is one of the trumped-up charges against me. I believe I know who murdered John. You and I are falsely accused. The sooner I clear my name with all my power to do so, the better."

Surprise widened his eyes. "Who do you believe did the deed, then?"

"By simple deduction, I've arrived upon his sons as the suspects. Three ne'er do well ruffians in the prime of their youth, they resent me as John's beneficiary, despite no love lost between them and their father. They raided my kitchen and brought the 'evidence' as de Burgh called it, with the equally absurd idiom *malefecia*. My herbs are harmless unless ingested in monolithic doses or combinations. My husband would never ingest a lethal amount at will. He was forced or he wasn't aware the herb combination was lethal. And—" She crossed her heart. "That, I can swear on the graves of all my departed loved ones, is what happened."

"His own sons murdered him?" He leant forward and she caught a whiff of the spearmint sprig he chewed on.

"Aye, they poisoned John, like as not, but I am a most convenient scapegoat. And you, poor soul, you be another victim, finding his body, having been indebted to him and having stopped at my inn. You've fallen victim to three unfortunate circumstances."

"God Jesu." He clasped his hands together. "I pray

you be proven right."

"I know I'm right. I know I didn't kill him, nor instigate it. And can I be reasonably sure neither did you?" She cast him a penetrating glance.

He answered with an assuring nod, "My lady, I would never murder a living soul nor assist in so foul a deed. 'Tis the Sixth Commandment, 'thou shalt not kill.' Commit a mortal sin? Never."

"Then your wife is a lucky lass."

"I've no wife, Alice." He shook his head, eyes downcast. "Never found the right lass."

Surprised by his revelation, she took a step closer. "Never say never. Whichever lass snags you will be a lucky one indeed."

He gazed at her, eyes a-twinkle. "Ah, then. If we escape this alive, my lady, I shall ask you to marry me."

They shared an uneasy, but welcomed laugh.

"I needed that brief interlude of levity." Alice sensed the sincerity in his expressive eyes and tone. But she picked up on what wasn't said. Innate instinct told her that Michael Artson was as innocent as she. It filled her with hope.

"D'you hail from these parts originally, Michael?" she asked.

He shook his head. "Born and bred in Callan but now live in Ballymack."

"Then you're not familiar with the denizens here. They thrive on making other folks' business their business, and what isn't true, they conjure up. I'm despised in these parts because of my prosperity and because I am a Druid. I'm subject to many a false and cruel rumor I care not to repeat." She closed her eyes and sighed. "But I refuse to let them nettle me. I go about my business, and the folk who care about me stand behind me."

"I never encountered a Druid before." He regarded her with wide eyes. "I know next to naught about that tradition, except that they built those stone circles, one being—what is it called—the one on the Salisbury plain?"

"Stonehenge," she said. "'Tis unknown whether Celts or Druids built it. Celts dwelt in Britain two hundred centuries before Christ, so Druids may not have built it, but they do use it. We have dolmens in Carlow. 'Tis so large, two-hundred men may stand up with room to spare. But I specially love the ones in the Boyne Valley, north and west of Dublin. So we have plenty of them."

"I've never been partial to any religion, though I'm from a Catholic family," he told her. "I wish to learn about all of your activities, Alice. You're an intriguing lady and I'm eager to know you better."

"'Tis not something you can learn in a week, Michael. A full Druid must study for nineteen years. A lifetime commitment." She smiled, adding, "Like marriage."

"I be a man of my word, Alice. I shall never disappoint you," he vowed. "And I trust justice will prevail and we'll not pay for this horrid crime."

A recollection came to her and she felt comfortable enough to share it with Michael. "One eve not long ago, John lay ill with the sweat. I sponged him down and tried to ease his suffering. He told me, 'Wife, afore I am cold in my grave, someone will love you and care for you just as you care for others.' I thought he spoke out of delirium, but now—"

Michael nodded and took her hands in his.

Had John prophesized this very moment? As she looked into Michael's eyes, she harbored the same as he: apprehension, fear and comfort in the company of a compassionate stranger destined to know the other.

"He was right, Alice," came Michael's answer. "I never break my promises," he vowed. "I'd wed you tonight should a priest wander by."

She uttered a sad laugh. "Ah, that would testify to our innocence. The two conspirators marrying. Nay, even when this ordeal is behind us, I deem it prudent to wait a respectable amount of time. After all, we're both accused of his murder. Marrying so soon will only stir up suspicion anew."

"May I make one overture first?" He approached her and drew her to him, holding her close. "May I kiss my betrothed?"

She touched her lips to his and rested her head on his chest. "When I woke this morn, I had a premonition that a life-altering event would occur today. Something tragic. And I was right. At times these premonitions are a curse. But you came along and now I feel alive again."

"Thank you, Alice." His cheeks flushed.

"I've never lived a day such as this." Her gaze fixed on the sputtering flame in the distance. "In one day, I've been widowed, accused of murder, jailed and betrothed. Just yestermorn toiling in my garden, I'd itched for a spark of excitement. I must cease wishing for things. Because every time I do, I get what I wish for."

He captured her gaze. "You must be precise when wishing. There's more than one kind of excitement."

Chapter Four

Numb with shock, Kylah waited for the police, drapes clutched in her fist. Grief drenched her as driving rain pounded her windows. A cruiser pulled into her driveway. Imposing footsteps beat the same tattoo on the walk as her hammering heart.

Shivering with cold sweat, she fumbled with the lock and opened the door.

"Mrs. McKinley? I'm Officer Hughes and this is Officer Everett." With no outward signs of sympathy the taller one introduced them.

They stepped in, shaking water off their hats, splattering her floor.

"Where is the deceased, ma'am?" Hughes asked.

Her trembling hand waved toward the den. An ambulance pulled up behind the cruiser and two paramedics rushed in with a stretcher.

"Last room on your left," she directed.

They too disappeared down the hall.

She crept to the den doorway, trying to make out their words. She glanced in and saw Ted's bare feet. Shuddering, she turned away. The cops came out and radioed for a medical examiner.

Flipping open a pad, Hughes said, "We need to take some information for the report, ma'am."

She pleaded with her eyes. "I came home and found him like that—"

"I just need his age, medical condition, a few details."

As she answered his questions about Ted, the paramedics approached. One pulled a stethoscope from around his neck. "He's deceased."

So final. So abrupt.

Part of her mind still couldn't accept this. "I just—I came home and found him on the floor with no pulse. What happens now? Where will you take him?" she babbled. "This has never happened to me before." An absurd statement, but she couldn't think straight and made no apologies for it.

Everett said, "When the M.E. arrives, he'll make a pronouncement, do a preliminary exam to determine approximate time and cause of death. If he determines it's a natural death, the body will be removed to the morgue. Any hint at foul play and the body will be subject to further examination and autopsy."

"Foul play?" She staggered backward. "No, he must've died of a heart attack. Or he drank himself to death. He always drank Scotch, sometimes with a beer chaser. There was no foul play, for God's sake!"

"That's for the M.E. to determine, ma'am. But if it's apparent that there was, we'll call the commanding officer from the Criminal Investigation Unit. He'll have the detective lieutenant send some detectives out to photograph and collect any evidence." He paused. "Do you have anyone who can be with you right now? Family member? Friend?"

Do I want Mike here?

"No, I'd rather be alone."

As tears blurred her vision, she wandered into the living room and collapsed on the sofa. The cops ambled into the entry hall, talking in hushed tones.

She covered her eyes with her hand, forcing steady breaths. Now she had to face the most painful task of her life. She called his brothers, his niece, his closest buddies. "I'm calling to tell you Ted passed away," she repeated what seemed like a thousand times.

She called Mike and repeated the same message to his voice mail. "But don't come over yet," she added. "I want to be alone a while."

Drained, she rested her head on the sofa arm. Approaching footsteps startled her. She pushed herself upright to face a stocky man with horn rims. "I'm the medical examiner, Mrs. McKinley. Where's the body?"

She couldn't accept Ted as "the body." The atrocious reality made it more unreal.

Clutching the sofa for support, she pointed to the den. "My husband is in there." He charged down the hall and the cops followed. Steadying herself with one hand, she looked out the rain-streaked window at the official vehicles barricading her house. A few neighbors' lights blazed. The gossip must be simmering...

When will reporters come banging on the door?

The medical examiner stomped back out and pushed his glasses onto his head. "We have to take the body in for further examination, Mrs. McKinley. I can't determine the cause of death at this time."

"I still believe he had a heart attack." Wasted breath, she knew.

Dazed, she watched him pull out a cell phone and call the morgue. In a blur of white coats and blue uniforms, with gruff voices and the earthy aroma of outdoors, they carried her sheet-enshrouded husband on a stretcher to the waiting ambulance.

Officers Hughes and Everett came out of the den, Hughes carrying Ted's spiral notebook.

She blinked in surprise. "What are you doing, searching the place?" slipped out of her mouth. "Don't you need a warrant?"

"We weren't searching, Mrs. McKinley." He held it out to her. "We found this on the table next to your husband's body, this page facing out."

She leaned forward to see a blur of words in red ink. "I don't have my glasses. But Ted liked to write in red. He has a ton of notebooks on his Poe shelf. He was a huge Poe fan," she blathered, needing to talk. "He wrote poems and short stories, all replicating Poe's macabre tone. Some of them were even creepier than Poe's. He—" She would have rattled on if he hadn't stopped her.

"Ma'am, this is no poem. Evidently it's the last thing he ever wrote, in the final moments of his life." He stepped closer. "You want to fetch your glasses or have me read it to you?"

"You read it."

He cleared his throat. "You did what you had to do. And I forgive you. I'm going to a better place and can go with a clean conscience. I had nothing to live for here anyway. Whoever I was in any past lives, I hope to return to Earth as a writer as gifted and with a sense of humor and the macabre as the man who, with pen and paper, created worlds beyond anything we mortals can imagine on Earth or beyond, who I idolize more than any other: Eddie Poe. Gotta go. Ted." Hughes stepped back and shut the notebook as Everett held out a plastic bag to slip it in. "Could be a clue to what happened to him. We need to take this for evidence, ma'am."

"Of course I want you to find out what happened to him!" came out louder and more forceful than she'd intended. One strange thing hit her as Ted's last words echoed in her mind: past lives? Return to Earth? Ted never believed in any of that. What could have changed his mind in less than one day?

She stood in her doorway and watched them take Ted away, rain pelting down on him. Unable to bear the sight of the departing motorcade, she closed the door and faced her suddenly empty house. Her vision blurred on the oil painting from a Provincetown gallery, Ted's wedding gift to her. The blend of tranquil pastels, the azure sky blending into blue ocean and pink sand, reminded her of their honeymoon. She couldn't bear to look at it now.

The rain let up, the silence tomblike for a few beats.

The doorbell rang. The chimes echoed like distant church bells tolling for the dead.

No, she couldn't face any more of their probing questions.

She made some valerian tea to knock herself out. Turning out the lights, she sat in the gloom. Thoughts of Ted, full of life and energy, raced through her mind. As she sipped her tea, her breathing synchronized with the steady backdrop of rain and her ticking clocks. She drifted off to a faraway world.

Chapter Five

After drinking valerian tea, Kylah always dreamed in vivid color...

Daylight struggled through the wavy windowpanes into her drafty kitchen. She stood on hard flagstones, chopping lavender and sage at her butcher's block. The cold seeped through her thin slippers. She turned to the iron cauldron hung over the fire in the charred hearth, bubbling with her latest brew. She inhaled the tangy aroma, tasting it on her tongue. Blending her herbs, she hummed a lively tune as her hands kept busy, her fingers stiff with cold. She peered out the window at her courtyard. Moth-like snowflakes swirled and stuck to the glass. Her beloved spouse entered the kitchen and stomped his snowy boots onto a reed mat.

"Good morrow to you, my sweetness," she greeted him, breathing in leather as he captured her in his arms. She warmed his lips with hers and wound her hands through his hair. A spark of desire surged. "Care to retire to our chamber?" She pressed her body to his. A low moan rumbled in her throat as he hardened against her.

"Any time you're ready, my lady, I stand at your command."

His breath tickled her earlobes. She responded with a shiver of delight. "I want you now. Take me right here. Before the hearth."

She led him to the fire's warmth, removed his surcoat and waistcoat. She untied the drawstring of his britches, eager to explore his body, tease him into a frenzy, play her fingers over his muscled thighs, feel him throbbing inside her. He planted kisses on her neck.

She purred with pleasure as he lowered her to the fur rug. Their mouths mingled in fiery passion. She ached for him. He lifted her skirts and nestled between her parted thighs. She drew her knees up and wrapped her legs round his back. Her hips rose, ready to welcome him...

Loud ringing jolted Kylah. Her heart surged. She opened her eyes, no longer in her beloved's arms before a hearth in a medieval kitchen, but on her sofa. Her cell phone lit up as it rang.

Her body still tingled. She tried to recapture that long-ago world, her virile lover longing to ravish her. What was that all about? She'd never dreamed anything like it. Even his scent lingered. Some corner of her mind remembered him with fondness and she missed him.

She emerged from her foggy reverie. Forcing herself to reality, she swiped the phone screen. "H'lo?"

"Kylah, it's Mike."

"What time's it?" she mumbled.

"Nine," he answered.

"A.m. or p.m.?"

"It's p.m," he answered. "I got your message. I've been trying to call you for ages. I'm so sorry, Kylah." His voice broke. "Are you all right?"

"I must've not heard the phone. I drank some valerian after they left." She rubbed her eyes.

"Why didn't you want me there before? I'd have come right over."

She sat up. "I just wanted to be alone. But I appreciate it."

"I'm on my way over," he said. "I wanted to call first." His engine rumbled in the background. "I should be there in about ten minutes. Nine minutes. I just made this light."

He was there in eight minutes with a thermos and a paper bag, barely enough time to make herself presentable.

He wrapped her in his arms. They embraced for a long time.

"I'm so sorry, honey. Anything I can do, anything…" came his muffled words.

"Thanks." She broke the embrace and wiped her tears.

"Thought I'd bring you a special treat." He held up the bag. "Mocha Java and a batch of mushroom turnovers. You need a break from kale and mineral water."

"Thanks for all this. I'll get some mugs." As she went over to the mug tree, she halted in her tracks. "Huh?" She bent down. "Look at this. The door to my herb cupboard is wide open."

"You didn't leave it open?"

"I always close this door and turn the key in the latch so it won't fall open." She peered inside. The pungent aromas of herbs seeped out. "Something's wrong."

Mike placed his hand on her shoulder. "What?"

"Somebody was in here. Some of my jars are opened and others are missing." Her mind sped ahead.

"Was Ted in here? Oh, my God, if he—no, I can't even think that!"

"What? Kylah, what is it?"

"Ted got in here and took those herbs." A jolt kicked her in the gut. "He committed suicide."

Chapter Six

Dominic Bugbee stood before his floor-to-ceiling mirror and admired his dashing figure in his 'gently worn' designer suit. Business wasn't what it used to be, so he cut corners, buying his apparel in thrift stores. He extended his arm, displaying his knockoff designer watch. After he slipped a handful of his autographed books and CDs into his briefcase, he headed out to his rented limo. He'd be doing his own driving if business didn't pick up by year end.

Dashing his youthful dreams to escape poverty, he found his true calling as a life coach, motivational speaker and self-help author. But he no longer commanded the standing-room only masses he'd once captivated in theaters. His audience was growing up and deserting him. He needed some serious PR, but he had to let the publicist go.

Tonight he would address an audience of two hundred. Whenever his girlfriend called them fans, he gave her a playful swat on the rump. "They're my adherents, Judy, my believers, and I'm their life coach. Fans are for actors. I don't act. I'm the real deal."

He wished Judy were meeting him later, but she had night school, so his daughter Petra was joining him. She cut a dashing figure on the stage, and when his wife, Viv, also appeared, they created the illusion of the model American family. Only close friends knew the truth. Viv was his ex-wife. But tonight, only Petra accompanied him to a high school auditorium in Hartford, Connecticut. The two-hour ride would be another chance to bring his child to her senses.

"You're doomed if you fall into the clutches of that cult, Pet." He wagged a finger at his daughter as the chauffeur pulled away from the curb.

She turned away from him, staring out into the night and at the traffic whizzing by. "Dad, for the gazillionth time, Druidism is not a cult. It's a philosophy. Druids are philosophers, their main concern is with the meaning of life on Earth. I love being close to nature and the sacred Druid trees. I enjoy working in Kylah's store, and she's making me a part owner soon. You want a secure future for me, don't you?"

"That woman hoodwinked us all," he snarled. "When she first married Ted, she looked so sincere, a good South Boston girl. If only I could've warned Ted off. The poor soul. At the mercy of her evil hand, Ted is doomed too, now." He pressed his lips together.

"Oh, you were always so nice to her, now you're throwing her under the bus." Petra threw her arms up and they plopped back at her sides.

"Will you start casting spells next?" He clutched at her shoulder to make her face him.

She slid out of his grasp. "Kylah doesn't cast spells. But spells aren't like curses—they're the universe working under the laws of nature."

"She's a witch, Pet. A hell-bent witch."

"If she's a witch, I'm a witch," she retorted. "Yes, Druidism and Wicca can overlap, but it's not the same thing. Look, maybe I shouldn't go with you to your seminars anymore. You obviously disapprove of my lifestyle, and I'm beginning to feel sorry for these 'adherents'"—she held up finger quotes, "you herd into your clutches."

"I motivate them to attain success, set goals and get on the right track. You've seen my mail. It's from folks who've become successful because of my seminars and books." Besides the mail from bill collectors.

She gave a dramatic eye roll and *tsk*'d. "It's like a cult, Dad."

"No more of a cult than followers of the Grateful Dead or that hip-hip stuff you kids go for. We'll talk later," he warned her.

She reached forward to open the bar. "Good, cause I need a belt. And it's hip-*hop*." She plucked a bottle of malt whiskey. "Glad you can still afford the hard stuff. I'll know your...er, 'adherents' abandoned you when the next limo doesn't have a stocked bar."

"Enough of that, young lady."

She snickered as she poured herself a shot.

****

Kylah and Mike stood before her herb cupboard and stared into its depths. It looked almost sinister in its disarray.

"Why would he kill himself, Kylah?" He paced up and down, hands behind his back. "You sure you didn't leave these bottles opened and take some others out and leave them somewhere?"

"Never. I keep it like a quartermaster with military precision. I know it so well, I have each bottle and its position in there memorized. I consider it a private space and he respected that, just like his den was his private space. He never interfered with my herbal remedies. He had absolutely no reason to come anywhere near here. Not unless he wanted to do himself harm. I told him many times that certain combinations were lethal, even in small doses." Looking past the disturbance, she took comfort in the untouched rows of bottles and jars lined up alphabetically, others labeled with their special mixtures. But that comfort was short lived when she realized one special bottle was open and lying on its side. "Oh, my God, Mike." She took out the dark blue bottle and held it up. "Half my moonsbane is gone."

"What's moonsbane?" he asked her.

"It's a spore from a wild fungus that only releases its spores in moonlight. It hasn't been seen since the fourteenth century. A fellow Druid gave it to me in Ireland, and I'm the only Druid I know of in the United States who has any. It's the only bottle I didn't have labeled, and it's blue, to keep out any light. Light contaminates it." She pointed. "And look. Ted's metal claws for reaching things are leaning against the cabinet. He was in here." Shivering underneath her cardigan, she stepped closer to Mike.

"Then call the police and give them that information," he ordered. "That'll shed a whole new light on everything if it was a suicide."

She nodded and stumbled over to the phone. "I didn't think I'd be talking to them again so soon." Another thought entered her mind. "I should look for his daily journal. He wrote in it every day, his thoughts, his to-do lists, shopping lists, everything."

She entered Ted's den, avoiding the spot where she'd found him, his Colts blanket spilled on the floor, a cushion plopped over it. She pictured them kicking it aside when they hauled him away.

Mike followed, looking around, but not touching anything. "Did he write on the computer?"

"No, he wrote in longhand in notebooks, like that one the cops found on the table here. But he had a daily journal with a brown leather cover." She peeked into corners and under the couch and chairs. She shivered at the sight of his handgun on the bookshelf. "I can't find it. It must be in this pile of magazines here. He was kind of disorganized." She found his red pen on the table and closed her fingers around it.

Finding nothing in the den, she searched the rest of the house for any note he might've left in an obscure place: his medicine cabinet, his bureau drawers, even the computer hard drive.

"Did he have an e-mail account?" Mike looked over her shoulder at the monitor.

"No, he never went on the Internet. He just used the computer for games and his checking account on Quicken." She scanned every document in Word, just in case. "No, nothing here hints of wanting to end his life. There isn't even a reference to his accidents or his stepson's death. Nobody searching this house would ever believe a suicidal handicapped man lived and died here." Grinding her teeth in frustration, she clicked the mouse on the 'shut down' button.

"They'll come back and do a search for anything connected to a suicide," Mike assured her.

She stood and their eyes met. "I can't face another cop, Mike. I just want him buried and—" She gasped. "Oh, no. Suicide victims aren't allowed burial in consecrated ground. He bought this plot in Baltimore where Poe is buried—"

"It used to be that way, but I don't think so

anymore." He placed his hands on her shoulders. "Don't worry about burial yet. Just call the police and tell them you have reason to believe he took his own life."

Forcing herself to call the police, she fought a negative emotion—anger—that tightened her chest and boiled her blood. "Oh, why did he keep it all bottled up inside, without the slightest hint he was so desperate?" She moaned, despair tormenting her.

The operator transferred her to a lieutenant of the Patrol Division. He took all her information down to the last detail, including which herbs were missing.

She put the phone down and turned to Mike. "The last thing the lieutenant said—it just hit me."

"What?" He followed her out of the den, closing the door.

"He told me they'll be in touch. What for?"

"It means they'll get back to you after the autopsy. They have to tell you when the undertaker can collect him."

As they sat on the living room sofa, she fixed her gaze on Ted's old wine stain on the carpet. "I don't think I should've made that call. The lieutenant sounded kind of suspicious."

"Of course you should've called." He crossed one leg over the other and grabbed his ankle. "They need to know."

"The more I think about it, I'd rather they didn't know Ted committed suicide." She looked over at him.

"Why not, if that's what really happened?"

"You already know this—" She paused. "The last two or three years, we had a rocky marriage. His first wife's family never liked me, even though he divorced

Jill before he met me. I was never the 'other woman.' I—" She took a breath, ready to share something very personal. "I didn't even sleep with Ted until our wedding night."

He shrugged, looking away. "You don't have to tell me any of this."

"I want to. We loved each other, but were sometimes at odds with each other's habits, we had completely opposing political beliefs—you know how we argued about politics. Once, after his stepson died, we had an argument, Ted drank too much and hit me." She touched her hand to her cheek. "Once. Not hard, but he promised never to do it again, and he never did. Then once, he called me a—the 'c' word and I smacked him. Not hard, but—" She splayed her fingers as Mike nodded his understanding. "If word gets around that he took his own life, of course the blame is going to land right here." She hugged her arms to herself. "On my shoulders."

He moved closer until their knees touched. "Don't blame yourself for this, if he really did commit suicide. He must have been going through a deep depression. He was seeing a psychiatrist, right?"

She inched closer to him. Their thighs touched. She needed that physical contact. "Yes, after little Jeremy died. But his sessions weren't on a regular basis. He just went once in a while."

"Ted wasn't the type to give any hints of his suffering." Mike shook his head. "He didn't wear his heart on his sleeve."

"I can't help it." She wiped sweat from her hairline. "I'm trying to see the whole thing through his eyes, and to him, I believe suicide was the only way out. No, he didn't display any outward signs of depression or suicidal tendencies. He had a positive attitude about what happened to him. But I knew deep down it bothered him that he couldn't bike and hike across the country, go skydiving..." She closed her eyes, remembering all his lofty dreams. "When he got knocked off his bike the first time—" She stopped for breath, letting out a shaky sigh. "He became interested in astrology and yoga and it made him more spiritual. It gave him purpose. Then he found out Jeremy was terminally ill, and to top it all off, he found out Jeremy wasn't even his son. My God, Jill had another man's baby and Ted never even suspected. He felt so betrayed." She forced her gaze from the rug. "Now it all makes sense. I should've figured on suicide before. But a heart attack is the first thing anybody thinks of with a sedentary middle-aged man. He was just lying there on his side, clutching his middle..." Tears filled her eyes.

His fingers squeezed hers. "Let's just get the facts, Kylah, wait for the autopsy report. There's no sense beating yourself up over something that might not even be true. You're still in shock and aren't thinking straight. Just try to relax and go to sleep."

Once again her lids weighed on her like sandbags. "You're right, I can't keep my eyes open. I feel the entire world on my shoulders and just want to escape for a while."

"Then do what your body wants." He stood and pulled his keys out of his pocket.

She nodded. "Oblivion is the best place for me right now. I'll brew some more valerian tea. Mike, can I ask you a big favor?"

Their eyes met.

"Will you stay here until I fall asleep? I don't want to be alone."

He dropped his keys back in his pocket. "If that's what you want, sure. I'll be right here."

She microwaved the mushroom turnovers he'd brought. In a fit of self-indulgence, she devoured three. "My appetite's finally coming back."

"Good. You do look a little gaunt." His eyes roved over her and he quickly averted them.

"I'm going to sleep in the living room from now on. We once shared the bedroom I use now, but—" She fidgeted with her watch. "We hadn't shared a bed since the last—accident. He moved into the spare bedroom. It was just easier for both of us that way."

Mike tried to look unfazed, but failed to keep the surprise out of his eyes. "Oh, well, I didn't know—but you didn't have to tell me that."

"I wanted to tell you."

Her tea brewed, she poured a cupful and brought it back into the living room, curled up on the sofa and pulled the afghan over her shoulders. "Thanks so much for staying."

"No problem. I'll just be over here, reading." He went to her bookcase and selected a biography of Aaron Burr. "If Hamilton had kept his trap shut, that duel never would've happened," he commented as he settled in a chair.

Her grandfather clock in the corner gonged ten times.

"I should sleep about seven hours on this cup," she told him before finishing the last gulp.

"Okay, I'll let myself out in a little while."

Another clock chimed, then another, across the

room. Mike looked around, brows knitted as yet another chime rang from the antique mantel clock. Then two more clocks on the end tables chimed. "Hey, what's with all these clocks?"

"I set each clock less than a minute apart because I love to hear the chimes. It's like a mini symphony. Having them all go off at once would be too much of a cacophony."

He nodded, his expression still dubious. "Ah, I see."

"I can also see you're not too impressed with my chime-fest." Her body went limp and sank into the soft cushions. She slipped into an exhausted sleep.

****

The phone woke her and she answered groggily in the dark.

"Just me calling to see if you're all right."

"Fine, I was sleeping," she said.

"Sorry, go back to sleep then. I'll check with you later."

Savoring the comfort of Mike's voice, she drifted off.

Where would I be without him?

She cringed, fearing the answer.

When the phone rang again, weak light filtered through the drapes. She guessed it was early morning.

"Hey Ky, it's Petra. You okay?"

"I'm fine." She closed her eyes again.

"I'll take over the store, I just wanted you to know everything's cool there, I added some extra hours to Cassandra's schedule…"

Her words hardly registered. Craving more sleep, Kylah mumbled thanks as the phone slid from her hand.

****

The symphony of chimes woke her. She drifted off to sleep once more, but another chime rang out. This one was her doorbell. She opened her eyes. Sunlight streamed through the living room window. Then the horror rushed back.

Ted is dead. His corpse is on a morgue slab. I'm a widow.

She belted her robe and peeked out to see a black sedan parked in her driveway. Heart hammering, quaking with fear, still exhausted and in shock, she pulled open the door.

A tall man and a stout woman stood on her porch in khaki pants and shirts. The woman looked younger than Kylah, but the hard edge to her features bespoke years of witnessing crime scenes. He appeared more kindly, as if resigned to accepting the bad, knowing it always got worse. Veins crisscrossed his cheeks. They held up badges.

"Mrs. McKinley?" asked the man.

She nodded silently.

"I'm Detective Lieutenant Frank Munn and this is Detective Gail Egan from the Barnstable Police Criminal Investigation Unit. May we come in?"

"Of course." She stepped aside.

Munn let Egan enter first. They didn't remove their sunglasses as they crowded her entry hall.

"Mrs. McKinley, we have the results of the autopsy from the medical examiner," Munn said. "Your husband died from a massive overdose of four herbs, which he ingested raw. Foxglove, mandrake, hemlock and another herb, unidentified as of yet. It's being analyzed now. The stomach contained large quantities, which are lethal in the doses he took. It will state that on the death certificate."

That combination sounded vaguely familiar. She'd heard of it many years ago, and couldn't remember why, but sensed that it was dangerous. She looked from one detective to the other, their expressions flat, unreadable. Their sunglass tints began fading.

"How would he know about a combination like that?" she blurted, thinking out loud. She didn't expect them to answer her, and they didn't.

"We need to ask you a few questions, ma'am."

"Yes, of course." But she was the one who needed answers.

They followed her into the living room. She stammered an apology for the mess and they got down to business.

Their questioning seemed reasonable. Where were you yesterday and last evening? Had he threatened you? Had you threatened him? Did he often take herbal tea or herbal remedies? What was his state of mind when you saw him last? Had you fought recently? Nothing she couldn't answer.

The initial shock had worn off, but she was still shaken up. They maintained eye contact through their now-clear glasses and alternated with practiced precision. Some questions such as, "What time did Ted usually get up in the morning?" seemed irrelevant, but she didn't dare question them. They replied to each of her answers with a curt nod, as if assuring her she could get on with her life. But nothing would ever be the same.

Munn confirmed those fears when he asked, "Can anyone vouch for you as to where you were between 4 and 7 p.m. on the day of your husband's death?"

"Me? I closed the store at five o'clock. I was by myself until nine-thirty, in the back taking inventory. Then I came home," she rattled off her alibi.

"No one saw you between the time you closed the store and seven o'clock?" he prodded.

"No, I'm afraid not." They had her there. She could not verify her whereabouts during that time. "I got home about quarter to ten and found him on the floor. That was it," was all she could offer.

"Did you always buy the groceries?" he asked.

"Yes, I always do."

"And the herbs?" came out in a more accusing tone.

"I grow them in the garden. But they were—I called last night and told the lieutenant it looks like Ted committed suicide by taking a lethal combination. After his stepson died, he was depressed a lot of the time. He saw a psychiatrist for a while." She didn't know why she added that; it didn't seem to faze them.

They thanked her and ushered themselves out, but didn't go back to their car. They walked across her next door neighbor's lawn and knocked on their door.

She turned and faced the empty living room. She longed for the security she felt the other night when she bolted the door behind herself and Ted, breathing in cinnamon, safe from a killer.

Enshrouded in eerie silence, she shivered. It wasn't the same without Ted's television or stereo blaring— without Ted. The words 'Criminal Investigation Unit' echoed in her head, leaving her stunned. Forget the suicide theory. They hadn't even considered that. They sounded reasonably convinced Ted had been murdered.

They didn't say so. But they didn't have to.

"I'm a suspect," she muttered over and over.

But she still had duties to carry out: the next round of phone calls, to his priest and the funeral home.

First she had to look something up. She went into her library and unlocked her bottom desk drawer. She took out a fragile manuscript from nineteenth century Ireland. She had this since becoming a Bard, one of a select number of Druids who studied for the full nineteen years.

She carefully turned each brittle page until she found what she wanted. Nausea overcame her. She sank to the floor. The pages slipped out of her hands.

"No." She shook her head, unable to believe what she'd just read. It all came back to her now, that ancient spell known only to the Bards.

The spell was thousands of years old, an exact combination of foxglove, mandrake, hemlock—and moonsbane. The spell explained that Druids used this combination for one reason.

To poison a deadly enemy.

Chapter Seven

Kylah tapped "Mike" on her phone's contact list.

His voice mail answered, but she didn't want to leave her sordid details floating in space. "Mike, come over as soon as you can, please. I need a lawyer."

He arrived in the growing shadows of twilight. "What happened?"

"Two detectives from the C.I.U. interrogated me," rushed out of her before he stepped inside. "It looks like they're ruling it a homicide. But they're not saying anything yet. That's their car parked out there." She pointed. "They went to the Regans next door, and now they're across the street."

"I thought next door was selling their house and aren't living there anymore." He glanced in that direction. "The realtor's sign is on the front lawn."

"They might be, I don't know. Most of the neighbors didn't want much to do with us."

They went inside and he sat on the sofa, but she stood and stared out the window. "Oh, no, they're finished across the street and coming back. What could they want now?" She took a few deep breaths. It hardly calmed her slamming heart.

When she let them in, they did their badge-flashing routine with Mike. "We saw your car outside, sir. We need to question all Mrs. McKinley's contacts," Munn said. "Are you a friend, relative, what?"

"We're very close friends," he replied with no hesitation.

That wasn't enough. They hammered him with questions about his relationship with Kylah.

He kept his courtroom composure. "Kylah and I are not having, nor have we ever had an affair, detectives."

"And tell us your whereabouts on the day Mr. McKinley died, hour by hour, sir." Munn maintained his cop stance, stone-faced, feet spread.

"I was in court from one o'clock until five, then went back to my office in Hyannis. I got home at ten, or just after," he gave his airtight alibi, with a judge as a witness.

Scribbling notes in their spiral pads, the detectives made it obvious they'd check that alibi out.

The detectives finally left them alone, and she collapsed on the sofa. "I just found out something horrible. That combination of herbs they found in Ted's stomach at the autopsy—that's an ancient poison mixture, only known to certain Druids—Bards. I'm one of them. When I was in Ireland, another Bard gave me a rare manuscript that lists these mixtures. Bards use them as spells. I've kept it locked in my bottom drawer. Ted never would have found it. When ancient Druids wanted to kill an enemy, they combined four herbs." She took a ragged breath. "Three of them are the herbs they found in his stomach. The fourth one, which they couldn't identify, must be moonsbane. It's so rare, I'm one of a few Druids—" she took another breath and released a sob, "who has any. None has grown since Alice Kyteler's lifetime." She clutched his hands. "Mike, this was no suicide. Someone who knows that exact combination of herbs came in here, gave it to him and killed him." She couldn't stop shaking.

He sat next to her and ran his hands up and down her arms. "Did you check for forced entry, any sign that somebody else was in here?"

"No forced entry. I did check. Whoever was in here didn't leave a trace. Just my missing herbs in the cupboard—*those* herbs."

"The cops can dust for prints and check for hair fibers or footprints or any sign of an intruder," he said.

"Mike, he—or *she*—didn't intrude. Ted let this person in."

"So someone he knew, one of these Druid Bards, killed him with this secret combination? Do you know any of these Bards?" he asked.

"The only ones I know are in Ireland. They've never even been to this country. But I haven't seen them in years. They wouldn't know Ted from Adam." She cradled her head in her hands as her temples throbbed. "That's why I'm telling you it has to be someone from our remote past. Ted didn't put up any resistance. There was no blood, no stab wounds, no bullet wounds. Just poison. And now they think I did it. I couldn't have killed him. Or anyone. I'm not a murderer. And I loved him." She swept away tears.

He pulled a few tissues from the box on the table and handed them to her. She wiped her eyes. "Somebody came in here, somebody from our past life who hates us this much—"

"Hey, honey," he cut in, "let's just get you a drink or something to calm you down."

"But I'm a suspect! Good God, how do they think I could have murdered my own husband?" She crumpled the tissues and shredded them, unable to keep her hands still. "I told you about that spirit who came to me during the regression. Well, in human form, it tried to run us over and crippled Ted. Now whoever it is finally killed him, with that Druid combination of herbs. It's not known to the general public or the medical profession, you can't Google it. And the cops have no reason to accuse anyone but me. Now do you believe me?" She looked into his eyes.

"You're saying the human incarnation of a spirit tried to run you over and crippled Ted?" The dubious tone of a skeptic accompanied his stare.

"Yes, a live person with the spirit of someone who knew us in a past life," she explained, but explaining to nonbelievers was always a waste of breath.

Oh, if only Mike could understand!

"Don't get ahead of yourself." He helped her to her feet, walked her into the kitchen and snapped on the light. "There's no evidence pointing to you. Besides, they haven't yet officially ruled it a homicide. They need evidence before that can happen."

"Turn it down." She shaded her eyes. "I can't stand bright light. It reminds me of an operating room and Ted in the morgue. Use the dimmer switch."

He dimmed the recessed spotlights and bustled around her kitchen, opening cabinets.

"What are you looking for?" She pulled out a chair and sank into it, still shaking.

"I don't know. Anything. Coffee, vodka, whatever you have." He moved jars and cans around. "Aha, peanut butter. To bring out my inner child."

"There's vodka and gin in the cabinet over the microwave there." She pointed. "Take whatever you want."

He got the vodka, then rummaged around her fridge and took out cranberry juice. "Now what can I get you? I'll make you a PB and J if you have any grape jelly."

"Nothing, just nothing." She waved the offer away. "I can't believe this is happening. I'm the prime suspect." Unable to sit, she stood and paced the floor. "Just because I was his wife, I do paranormal investigations, have a New Age store and an herb garden? I suppose being a Druid doesn't help, either." She stopped at the stove, splattered with bacon grease from Ted's last breakfast. The thought of food sickened her.

He splashed vodka into a glass of ice and topped it off with the juice. "Like it or not, when someone dies and foul play is suspected, the spouse is the first suspect. But what they're doing is standard procedure. They're not ruling anything or anybody out. When someone dies under suspicious circumstances—in this case, a lethal amount of herbs—everyone in their immediate circle is questioned. They question the spouse first, that's the most obvious. After any alleged suicide or homicide, everyone in the local area is questioned. They're not singling you out. It's nothing personal." His eyes met hers. "Don't worry. I'm here for you."

"Thank you. I don't know what I'd do without you." She groped around for his hand until she was able to grasp it. "But I can't tell them some person from our past life seven hundred years ago killed him. They won't put me in jail, they'll haul me off to a psych ward."

"We have to look at every possibility here." He took a sip. Ice cubes tinkled. "Now, if I'm going to be defending you, I have to show reasonable doubt. The actual burden of proof is on them. You don't have to tell them who you think did it, if it's somebody from seven hundred years ago, or his own mother. Just let me work up the defense. And God willing, they will find whoever did kill Ted, and I can tell you with certainty that it's somebody from this century."

Her spirits lifted a bit as a shred of hope lightened her heart. "You're very grounded, Mike. I suppose I need that right now."

"Yeah." He took a swig of his drink. "Now I know that grounded and earthy are two different things."

****

"He what?" Dominic Bugbee's whiskey bottle slipped from his hands and thudded onto the shag carpet.

Petra picked up the bottle, toying with the top as if deciding whether she needed a belt, too. "Ted passed away, Dad. Kylah came home Tuesday night and found him dead on the floor. I thought it better to tell you in person."

"Well, what happened?" Dominic rubbed his eyes, shaking his head in disbelief. "Ted was healthy, wasn't he? Aside from his disability."

"He wasn't exactly healthy, Dad. You know he had a recurring drug habit and binge-drank. Kylah thinks he had a heart attack. When she found no pulse, she called the cops, they got the medical examiner in and took his body away. I don't know what's happened since then. The night before he died, a truck hit them and knocked them over. She thinks it's the same person who hit Ted last summer outside the bar." She glanced through his liquor supply.

"God rest his soul." Dominic stretched his arm and studied his timepiece. "Well, it's been what, forty-eight hours? Call her and see what else she found out. By now they must've done an autopsy."

"I'd rather wait to hear from her," Petra said. "She's probably frantic and doesn't need me bugging her. I called her yesterday to see if she was okay."

"Was she?"

"She was sleeping." Petra pulled a shot glass off the shelf. "I told her I'd run the store and increase Cassandra's hours."

"Run the store?" He scrunched his lips as if he'd bitten into a lemon. "Don't you work long enough hours?"

"Since I'd like to be a part owner someday, I'm happy to work long hours. You should know about that better than anybody, Mr. Success Coach." She twisted the top off the bottle, turned to his horseshoe bar and poured herself a shot. She knocked it back and let out a satisfied breath. "Ooh, yeah. Good stuff."

He fingered his cubic zirconia-studded tie clip. "I hate to say this, but I have the strangest hunch it wasn't a heart attack."

"Well, I didn't come over here to speculate, Dad. I'm not getting into a bunch of conspiracy theories either. Now I have to get back to work. But first—" She poured herself another shot. "One for the road." She knocked it back, rinsed the glass because her father no longer had a maid, and wrapped her arms around his ample middle. "I'll let you know anything as soon as I hear it."

"All right, poppet. Drive carefully."

As his daughter saw herself out—he no longer had a butler either—Dominic took the few paces out to his terrace. After a long pull of his whiskey, he leaned against the railing and stared down into his overgrown, weedy garden. Poor Ted McKinley suffered one mishap after another from the beginning of that doomed union. Two years into their marriage, his stepson Jeremy died of leukemia. Then Ted was run off the road by a hit-and-run driver. It happened again last summer, leaving him disabled.

Dominic invited Ted to his seminars and gave him front row tickets. But Ted didn't want to partake. He'd sat in the wings, looking bored, unwilling to share the audience's passion and enthusiasm.

But Dominic knew the cause of Ted's downfall. It was that woman he'd married, who worshipped oak trees and mistletoe, donning robes and chanting around a circle of rocks. She sold strange concoctions of herbs in her store to unsuspecting dupes, claiming these potions cured every malady from constipation to cancer.

Ted must've fallen victim to her spells somehow. Because Ted wasn't the first one. Ted's poor ex-wife Jill committed suicide, and then little Jeremy perished.

A shot of panic stabbed at his heart. How could he save his beloved Petra from being the next victim?

Ted didn't die of a heart attack, he'd bet on it. And he doubted the Barnstable Police C.I.U had the wherewithal to uncover the truth. They weren't of Boston's caliber. No, those small town coppers needed some horse sense, from a source who knew more than they could ever dig up—a personal friend of the deceased, blessed with the power of the media.

****

"Children, sit down." At seventeen, her twin grandson and granddaughter were hardly children. But to Enid Streetman, they'd never be adults as long as they lived with her, unemployed and unable to fund a checking account, let alone balance one. But she kept it that way. She'd die of loneliness without them.

"I have terrible news. Your stepdad passed away last night. Kylah called and told me." As she spoke, she looked straight at Charlotte, then at Charles.

Charlotte gasped. "What happened?" she shrieked, while Charles, who internalized every emotion, good or bad, stared at the floor.

"She came home and found him not breathing." Enid repeated what she'd heard.

"Do they know what he died from?" Charlotte began to tremble. She tugged on her earrings, twirled her hair, pulled on her friendship bracelets.

"I haven't heard back from her. But my guess would be a drug overdose. We know he had a recurring drug problem. I'm so sorry, children. It's very sad. He loved you like his own flesh and blood." Before Enid added, "I know you loved Ted back," she bit her tongue. They didn't love Ted back. He'd been a cash register to them and little else.

Charlotte flicked her hair over her shoulder and sobbed, smearing tears and green mascara. "Now I have no father figure, nobody to take me to concerts and clothes shopping and for ice cream—" She gulped. "All those things are gone because of that witch!" She wiped her nose and tears with the back of her hand. "We'll see if it was a drug overdose, Gran."

Enid blanched. "Charlotte! How could a granddaughter of mine have such a suspicious mind? It's all those crime shows you watch. Nobody trusts anybody anymore."

"Never mind TV shows, Gran." She fixed her teary eyes on Enid. "I hope the police are grilling Kylah, and good."

Enid returned her granddaughter's stare. "I had no idea you felt this strongly. Why do you think Kylah would—" She pursed her lips, leaving the rest unsaid.

"Because Ted was handicapped, Gran. He was a burden to her. He cramped her lifestyle, her free spirit, kept her from doing all those things she likes to do. He was an albatross around her neck, just like Jeremy was. I'll bet she did a jig when he died, too!" Charlotte shouted loud enough to hurt Enid's ears. "I never trusted her. If Ted hadn't met her and chased her all over the place and caught her, Mom never would've committed suicide. I'll always hold her responsible for Mom's suicide, and I'll never forgive her for it."

"Your mom divorced him *before* he started chasing Kylah," Enid reminded Charlotte. "Oh, why bother?" She twisted her ring around her finger.

Charles sat in silence, arms clasped across his chest, chewing his lip. He stood and hiked up his jeans. "I wanna go play my guitar," he said as the doorbell rang.

Enid went to open the door and jumped at the sight of the man and woman wearing dark sunglasses, holding up badges. Their bodies filled the doorway.

"Mrs. Streetman? I'm Detective Lieutenant Munn and this is Detective Egan from the Barnstable Police Criminal Investigation Unit. We need to ask you some questions. Are Charles and Charlotte at home?"

"Why, yes." She stepped back and let them in. "Children!" she called over her shoulder.

Charles grabbed Charlotte's arm with both hands. With unblinking and unflinching resolve, Charlotte approached the detectives. Charles skittered along next to her like a conjoined twin.

"I'll tell you who you should be questioning, detectives." Charlotte spread her pink glossed lips in her broadest sneer. "Ted's wife. I mean, his grieving widow," she said with a sarcastic roll of her eyes. Outspoken as always, Charlotte gave them an earful.

"Charlotte!" A hot flash hit Enid as she turned to the detectives. "She's very distraught, detectives. I just broke the sad news to them. So I wouldn't take anything she says seriously." She got out her hankie and mopped sweat from her neck.

"Oh, you'd better take it seriously!" Charlotte shrieked, shaking her brother off her arm and fixing her fists to her hips. "My stepfather claimed he met that woman *after* he divorced my mom. But I think they hooked up *before* that. Mom committed suicide. Then he made Kylah beneficiary to his estate, leaving us with nothing. Maybe you didn't know that minor detail. Do some more detective work and you'll find out she's one of those Druids, who casts spells and dispenses potions. You'd better make sure it was a drug overdose he died from and not some evil spell."

The detectives glanced at each other.

Enid caught a signal flash between them. "Charlotte, that's hearsay." Enid turned to the detectives with clasped hands. Her rings glittered. "Officers, my daughter Jill did commit suicide, but I can't say for certain it was because she was jealous of Kylah. Jill and Ted were already long divorced. It's all circumstantial."

Charlotte broke in, "Don't change your tune for them, Gran. She made Mom kill herself and she murdered Ted, I know it. And you know it. Now *they* better know it." She stabbed her finger at the detectives.

"I think so too, Gran," Charles spoke through tears. Wiping his eyes, he turned and slunk from the room.

"Thank you for your cooperation. We'll be in touch." The detectives saw themselves out.

Charlotte watched as their car pulled away.

Enid took the rosary beads she'd pulled off her Saint Patrick statue and rolled them around her fingers. "God willing, the right person will be apprehended in good time."

"They will, Gran." Charlotte hugged her grandmother. "I mean *she* will."

Chapter Eight

Kylah shut Ted's den door. She couldn't bear to look at the spot where he gasped his last breath. His presence, an imposing force, lingered. So did his scent, a blend of pine aftershave, manly sweat, and marijuana. His essence echoed his personality all over the house: the heap of dirty shirts, shorts and socks piled up in the laundry room, the spattered stove, his fingerprints on the microwave. But she couldn't bring herself to clean any of it up. Painful as these remnants were, they offered a strange comfort. He still lived here.

Each reminder ripped into her heart like a knife. Especially now with the funeral looming ahead, the eulogies, the mournful organ hymns, the tolling bells...

These ceremonies should bring closure, but they'd only prolong the agony of her grief. She wanted to remember him alive for a while longer. Oh, if only she could delay these morbid customs until the hurt subsided.

"I'll find that murdering bastard, Teddy," she promised him over and over, wandering from room to empty room, traces of him lurking in every corner. "I'll do everything in my power to make sure justice is served. Another past life regression isn't enough anymore. I know what I have to do now. And I promise, it will never, ever happen again—in any future life." She inhaled and breathed him in. "Go take a shower,

Teddy." She chuckled through her tears as the doorbell rang. Cringing, she broke out in cold sweat at the sight of the black sedan at the curb. "Not again."

No sense in hiding. She let Detectives Munn and Egan in.

"Mrs. McKinley, we need your permission to do a search and take some of your husband's possessions from the house," Munn said.

"What for?" She met his steely stare. "I looked everywhere and found nothing."

"Mrs. McKinley, the cupboard door was open, four jars of herbs are missing, and the autopsy showed he died of herb poisoning. *Those* herbs," Munn added for emphasis, as if it had slipped her feeble mind. "Foxglove, mandrake, hemlock—and an as-yet unidentified one," he read from a report. "The M.E. determined it was a lethal dose."

Sherlock Holmes got nothin' on him.

"Where's this cupboard, ma'am?" Detective Egan spoke up.

"Right there." She pointed, its door gaping exactly the way she'd found it that night. Munn went over to it and peered inside.

"Ma'am, it would be better if you left the house for a half hour or so. Please leave a number where you can be reached," Egan ordered.

Munn glanced down the hall. "Where is your bedroom?"

What could they want in the bedroom? "It's at the top of the stairs on the right. But we didn't sleep together," she offered, as if that would faze them.

It didn't.

After giving him her cell number, she got into her

car and drove to the beach.

An hour later, she let herself back in and looked around. They'd taken the computer, her thumb drive, her remaining herb jars, Ted's handgun, and left her alone with one horrible fact she spoke out loud: "This is now a homicide case and I am the prime suspect."

Chapter Nine

Dominic headed to Cape Cod to make sure his daughter wasn't overworked running that woman's store. Then he planned to pay a visit to the suspect herself. But as he crossed the Sagamore Bridge spanning the Cape Cod Canal, he decided to go straight to Kylah and get the required niceties out of the way.

Once on Route 6, he hit the 'media' button on his steering wheel. At the command, he ordered, "Call Brooke Hill." She always broke for lunch at one o'clock sharp.

Babbling Brooke to her rivals, she hosted and produced *The Cutting Edge: The Only Newsmagazine Show That Matters.* Like all stars, Brooke was not readily accessible, but always dropped everything for Dominic. They met at one of his seminars early in her career and became fast friends.

Back when Dominic had A-list celebrities clamoring to speak at his seminars about hitting the big time, he'd invited Brooke to tag along—rather, cover the events for her local cable station. His influence catapulted *The Cutting Edge* to the Top Ten of tabloid TV shows, and now A-list celebrities waited in line to appear on *her* show. With each Emmy win, Brooke thanked "my mentor, Dom," clutching her award to her cleavage.

"Brooke, it's Dom. I got a story that could keep

your show at the top till hiatus time. You don't even have to go out and scrounge for dirt. I'll spill it right at your feet."

"Sweet, Dom."

Her voice brimmed with eagerness as always. A real hustler was his Brooke.

"Something the entertainment industry is long overdue for. A possible spousal homicide. But here's the kicker. The husband was in a wheelchair after suffering a—wink, wink—'accident,' which we won't go into right now. Suffice it to say, he's dead now, and suspicion is pointing to the wife, but the authorities need a nudge to help them along. I know these folks personally, the husband was a good friend of mine, and I'd stake my career that she did him in. And you know how public opinion can sway a jury in cases like these. So, Brookie, wanna help see justice done? And boost your ratings into the stratosphere at the same time?"

"Sounds fascinating, Dom. Where are you now? Can we get together so I can take some notes?"

"I'm on Cape Cod heading for the suspect's house. I'll throw her off guard while I'm there to pay my respects." He overtook a slowpoke in an SUV. "I'll see which way the wind blows. Then you and me can have a powwow and get the ball rolling."

"Be better if she was a local celebrity."

"In a way, she is," he said. "She has a store that sells all that woo-woo stuff and she leads a ghost hunting team. She's one of those Druid witches. She casts spells, all that magic mumbo-jumbo. With Halloween coming down the pike, that'll be a good hook. Get all the punters glued to the tube. Anyways, I got my suspicions that she did her husband in with some brew of hers. He was on pot, but I can't see him o.d.'ing on something that mundane. You smelling a story here yet? Hmm?"

"Smelling a story? I'm seeing a movie!" Brooke's voice came through his car speakers in stereo. "This could be the blockbuster of the year, if we can scoop it. Do you know if the local media got wind of it yet?"

"Doubt it." He changed lanes. "My daughter works for her, and she said no reporters from the Cape Cod papers or any media has come in. Just the local dicks, course, and the M.E. who autopsied the victim, but I haven't heard any results yet. It's a matter of time before they officially rule it a homicide. How 'bout I meet you at your office, say at six tomorrow night."

"Great, Dom. I'll look forward to it. I'll tell the security guard I'm expecting you. He'll buzz you in."

"Later, chickie."

He disconnected his phone and mentally rehearsed his standard condolences as he exited Route 6. A tinge of remorse dampened his spirits. So, Ted was kinda off the wall and edgy, with that war-vet-type angst, but a kind soul deep down. Too bad he met such a pitiful end. But revenge is mine, saith the media.

Pulling into Kylah's driveway, he saw the living room curtain stir. All the drapes were drawn. He hoped the reporters and paparazzi weren't harassing her already. He needed this feather in his cap. Attendance at his last seminar was woeful and he needed a boost in the worst way, else it was Chapter 11 for him. He had to play this hand right.

But it wasn't all designed to jump-start his life coaching. He genuinely liked Ted, and tried to save the boy from destruction more than once. Now he had to save his little Petra from that cult.

He poked the bell a few times. When she didn't answer, he cupped his hands and hollered, "Come on out, Kylah, it's only me, Dom," while trying to peek through the crack in the living room drapes.

The door opened. A hint of recognition lit up her eyes, but she looked like she'd crawled out from under a rock. Her red hair lay flat and dull, her face sallow and blotchy with no makeup. A sweater covered in lint pills hung on her like a gunny sack. If she didn't give a hoot what she looked like, he almost couldn't blame her.

"Dom, I'm sorry, but I've kept the drapes drawn since..." She drew a sigh. "I just don't want any company, you know, the neighbors are so nosy—"

"I understand, doll." He strode up to her and opened his arms wide. "Here, give Dom a big hug." He patted her on the back. "Now, now. You're doing just fine. You're in my thoughts and prayers ever since Petra told me the news. They're holding a service in his memory tomorrow night at Our Lady Star of the Sea, but I understand if you're not up to it."

"Thanks, Dom, but I've got so much to do here." She waved her hands around. "The funeral preparations, his family coming in from Baltimore—"

"Where's he laid out?"

"At Sullivan's in South Yarmouth. But he wanted a closed casket. And his plot at Westminster Graveyard in Baltimore is all taken care of. He bought that a long time ago, because Edgar Allan Poe is buried there and Ted wanted to be near him."

Dominic guffawed. "That's our Ted, macabre to the finish. He always did seem moony over death, but never feared it." He needed to steer the topic his way. "He never converted to your Druid thing, did he now?" He tried to loosen her up.

"Druidism is a tradition," she informed him, her voice flat as her hair. "There's nothing to convert to."

"We had some intense discussions about passing on, and Ted never feared it. In fact, he once said he looked forward to it." Dominic observed her body language. She stood facing the drawn drapes, staring through the narrow opening, hugging herself. "It must've come as such a blow to you. Everything was going so well for you kids, wasn't it?"

"As well as..." She hesitated, as if carefully choosing her words. "As well as could be expected for any married couple."

"Have the police given you any more clues, information, on what happened?" Dominic prodded.

"Not yet." She shook her head. "I only hope he went peacefully." Her voice wavered and she began to cry. He rushed over and enclosed her in his arms once again.

"They rule it a heart attack or suicide or accidental or what?" he asked after a respectable thirty seconds or so. By "or what" he meant homicide, which he left hanging in the air.

"No." She wiped her eyes with her sleeve and slumped into a sagging lounge chair. "He swallowed a lethal mixture of my herbs from my cupboard." She waved in the general direction of the kitchen. "They're questioning everybody they can find who knew him. I don't suppose they got to you yet."

"No, but I'll go down there and tell them anything they want to know from me. I did think the world of

Ted, even though I couldn't get him to take my seminars or books seriously." He looked around the cluttered room, his gaze snagging on a teapot with two cups and saucers on the table. Tea for two?

This was no suicide, and he'd bet the cops knew that, too. If they were worth their salt, they'd be building a case against her right now. Prime suspect. The disgruntled—and possibly sexually frustrated wife.

Just wait 'til Brooke hears all this!

His delight bordered on lust. He licked his lips, top and bottom, wondering how much of a cut she'd give him for this scoop. A villa in Grand Cayman would make a nice love nest to whisk Judy off to…

"If there's anything at all I can help you with, just let me know," he offered, his voice brimming with practiced sincerity. "And of course, Petra is at your side always."

"I know. I have some good friends I can depend on." She forced a smile. But the furrows between her brows deepened.

"I'll be at the wake. Meanwhile, call me if you need to talk."

"Sure. Thanks," she croaked, her voice barely above a whisper.

He bent down to kiss her cheek and enclosed her small hand in his large paws. "I'll be thinking of you."

He let himself out, bursting to tell Brooke the bereaved widow looked guilty as sin. Herbs! It was original, he had to give her that. But he had to get out of earshot first. He squeezed into the car and pushed the 'media' button before he even shifted into gear. She wouldn't mind interrupting her kale smoothie for this!

****

Later that evening, Kylah ventured out of the house to pick up the last few days' mail and newspapers. Even under cover of darkness, she stayed alert for nosy neighbors. Her luck held so far. Not one of them called or peeked in. But the hedges and picket fences didn't always stop the neighbors' constant snooping.

"Mrs. McKinley!" someone called from behind her.

She spun around, ready to ward off an opening salvo of phony condolences. But it was Tyler, the teen who'd said hi to them on his bicycle that last night of Ted's life.

"I just wanted to tell you how sorry I am about Mr. McK. I liked him a lot." Visibly nervous, he tugged at his baggy low-rise pants as he kicked her mailbox pole, looking everywhere but at her.

"Thanks, Ty. I appreciate your coming over to tell me that."

"I wanted you to know, um—" He pulled his baseball cap off. "I took the drum lessons from him, 'cause at first, I was like, just doing it 'cause I wanted to ask Charlotte out. I felt like I used him. But I got to really enjoy the lessons."

"Charlotte?" Then the name registered. "Ted's stepdaughter?"

"Yeah, I'm trying to, like, get her to go to the prom." He gave her a nervous laugh.

"How do you know her?" She leaned on the mailbox.

"We're in the same English Lit class. We both love Dickens, and she was my study partner last semester. We're like soulmates." He twitched, unable to stand still.

"Ty, exactly what do you mean by soulmates?" She had enough complications without talking about past lives with him, too.

"You know, like, we have the same interests and all." He shrugged.

She wasn't aware Charlotte had any interests. "Well, I hope she says yes."

"Me too. I did ask her out once. She was all, 'No way,' but later she got more friendly. Mr. McK said he'd put in a good word for me, and I think he did. But I didn't get the guts to ask her to the prom yet. I just wanted to tell you I'll miss him a lot." He kicked at the ground.

"Thank you, Ty." She forced a smile. "And I hope you and Charlotte do hook up. You'd be good for her."

"Yeah, I think so. And my mom wants you to come back for another ghost hunt. When you're ready. Well, see ya." With that, he loped on down the street.

Charlotte and him? She couldn't see it, but she knew all about raging teen hormones. That's how she got married the first time.

Inside, she dumped her mail on the coffee table and opened the *Cape Cod Times*, skimming each section. She didn't even know what was going on in the world. But a small article snagged her gaze.

Barnstable Village Man Found Dead In Home

Police are investigating after a man was found dead in Barnstable Village Wednesday night. Officers responded to a call of a deceased person around 10 p.m. and found the body of local resident Theodore 'Ted' McKinley, 40, on the floor of his residence. Investigators have yet to release the results of the autopsy but a source inside the department confirms the death is deemed 'suspicious'. The source also said the police believe the public is not at risk. Police are expected to release more details on Monday.

Of course anyone who read the paper knew about this by now. She knew the reporters would start harassing her now. Maybe it was time to get that security...

Chapter Ten

"Brooke, go make more room on your mantel. This is the stuff Emmys are made of!" Dominic gave Brooke one of his bear hugs at the doorway to her plush office, the walls covered with blown-up photos of her with every A-list star alive, and a few dead ones, too. "This'll be, what, five for you now?"

"Six, but who's counting?" Brooke tossed a curtain of streaked blonde hair over her shoulder with a throaty laugh and offered him a seat on her leather sofa. "What's your poison this time?" She headed for her bar cabinet.

"Whatever hooch you got, babe. Straight up. It's not officially ruled a homicide yet, but the wife was kinda cagey. I formulated my own theory, from what I know of this woman. Now get this. He died from swallowing a lethal mixture of herbs from her cupboard. That came from the horse's mouth—the wife, that is. Puttin' two and two together was never easier."

"Herbs, huh?" Brooke poured their drinks and sat across from him in her lounge chair. "So who is she anyway?"

"Kylah McKinley. She has a big herb garden and a store selling all that woo-woo stuff and does ghost hunting all over Cape Cod. She's a Druid." He paused for effect. "I knew Ted first. Met him through the

Baltimore biker club in my salad days and we got chummy. Anyway, he met her through some group of Poe disciples, them both being poets. He was newly divorced." Dominic sipped his drink. "He followed Kylah to Cape Cod and wooed her. She gave in and married him. Not long after, his ex-wife Jill took her own life." He wet his whistle again and leaned forward, ice cubes clinking. "Now comes the spooky part. Two years into the marriage, he had an 'accident'. He was run off the road, but that's another story. It happened again last summer and it crippled him." He took another pause for two beats. "Then, the other night, it happens again, a truck tries to run him over. And Ted turns up dead the next day. But she kept trying to steer me into thinking he just by chance swallowed a killer dose of herbs." He cocked his brow. "Swallowed it, not smoked it."

"Any suspects in custody?" Brooke asked, taking notes.

"Not yet, but it's a matter of time before they name her as the prime suspect. She's the spouse, and the one who found his body. And my daughter tells me nobody can corroborate Kylah's whereabouts when it happened. She's got no alibi to speak of. So it's just a matter of time before they charge her and bring her in. The clock's a-tickin'."

Brooke scribbled more notes, sipped her Scotch and sneaked a peek at her lipstick in the mirror. "There won't be a story until she's charged and booked, if she ever is. It's no big deal if she's just a suspect. There are probably several right now. We can run a few teaser segments mid-week to get the ball rolling and get the names before the public, but it won't be a full-blown item until she's booked. 'Once they're booked, the viewers get hooked,' is what I always say."

One more swallow emptied his glass. "I intend to give the sleuths a hand. Meanwhile, let's shoot the breeze over dinner, say, at Elaine's. Can you command your regular table?" He knew she had an expense account there.

"If it's all the same to you, I haven't had a hot dog in ages." She smoothed the sleeves of her tailored blazer. "My treat."

"Sure, why not? It's humbling to go slumming once in a while." He was glad she offered to treat. New York hot dogs weren't cheap.

She linked her arm in his and they trotted off to the nearest street vendor.

****

At eight the next morning in the Barnstable Police Station's lobby, Dominic strode up to Detective Lieutenant Munn, hand extended. "Pleasure meeting you, detective."

"Mr. Bugbee." They shook hands. "Thanks for coming in. What can I do for you?"

"Well, detective…" Dominic clapped Munn on the arm, "I thought I'd help you boys along with your latest homicide case."

"Which is?" He gave Dominic a narrow-eyed look.

Dominic returned that with, "How many homicides happened on Cape Cod in the last week?" His inflection rose, as if demanding an answer.

"Just tell me what you have to tell me, sir." Munn gave him a beady-eyed stare.

Dominic straightened his tie pin. "Detective, I happen to've known Theodore—er, *Ted* McKinley a mite better than you boys, and what I know may provide some assistance to gather enough evidence to nab the perp."

"And what can you tell me about Mr. McKinley?" Munn slid a notepad and a pen out of his pocket.

"For one thing, he never ingested herbs. Might've smoked it, and may've been a little heavy on the sauce at times, but that herb dosage was forced down his throat. He didn't take it by his own hand. Kylah gave my daughter a job in her store, The Ancient Oak, in East Sandwich. It was a tavern in Revolutionary times. She sells all that woo-woo stuff and she tells everybody the joint is haunted. I don't approve of the store or the job, but my daughter seems to like it."

"Your daughter? Petra, is it?"

"Yes." A shot of fear blindsided him. "You've met her?"

"We questioned her the other day."

"Good Lord, that infernal woman didn't get my girl involved in this heinous crime, did she?" He clenched his fists.

"No, sir. And it's an investigation, not a crime until we determine that one was committed. We just needed to ask her some routine questions. We have to question everyone we know who's connected with the McKinleys. If we realized you knew her, we would've questioned you, too." Munn relaxed his stance. "But it looks like that won't be necessary now, since you're telling me everything I need to know. Aren't you?" Once more, he narrowed his eyes at Dominic.

Dominic didn't flinch. "Ask away." He opened his arms to demonstrate true accessibility.

"First finish telling me everything you wanted to

tell me, sir."

"There's a money motive here you should look into," Dominic said. "Kylah got herself made beneficiary of Ted's estate before the ink dried on the marriage license. This is no hearsay, Ted told me all this. At the time, he had a fat bank account with proceeds from a house he sold in Baltimore. She raided that account to buy that old tavern she uses as her store."

Munn jotted all this down. "Thank you, Mr. Bugbee. All this is good to know."

"You may deduce the crime was drug-related, and he was killed by some pusher he owed money to. But with herbs? Unlikely. Now, for the big kahuna." Dominic rubbed his hands together.

Munn's pen sat poised on the pad, his gaze fastened on Dominic.

Dominic leaned forward. "He got run off the road three times. The first time he got a concussion. The second time he got crippled. The third time only she gets a bruised elbow, and he dies the next day. You see a pattern here, don't you, Detective?"

"There are a lot of lousy drivers out there," Munn said.

Dominic shook his head. "No way. These were all hit and runs. But they couldn't be random. Three's a pattern. Throws a few more ingredients into the mix." He tapped the side of his head.

"When was the last time you saw Mr. McKinley, sir?" Munn asked.

He patted his lips with his fingers. "Hmm, oh, not for a while. A year ago at Christmastime, we went out with my daughter, and I didn't have any more contact with him after that. It was the last time I saw him alive." He made the gesture of wiping away a tear with his monogrammed handkerchief. "Alive and well, that is."

"Would you sign a witness statement form that says you're willing to testify under oath at trial, sir?"

Dominic blustered and fumbled with his tie tack. "Trial? Whose?"

"So far we haven't enough evidence to arrest anyone. But if someone is brought to trial, would you be willing to testify?" The detective rapped his pen on the pad.

"Why, of course I would. But I hope by now you will have enough evidence." He stood erect, thrust out his hand and gave Munn the classic 'minister's handshake,' placing his left hand on the detective's upper arm.

He flashed a smile at everyone who looked his way as he exited the precinct. Too bad there wasn't a reward for information leading to the capture of Ted's killer. A private jet would boost his image—for business purposes, of course.

****

"Now you hang back, don't let her see you," Dominic warned Brooke as he opened the passenger door of his convertible for her. He caressed the door handle, knowing his days with his pet vehicle were numbered. He was three months behind with the lease payments.

"Leave it to a pro." Brooke slipped out and smoothed her black suit. "I'll be part of the woodwork."

"You sure don't look like woodwork, but you're not your usual stylish self," he commented as he walked her across the parking lot to the funeral parlor's entrance.

"Well, it is a wake, and I can't afford to get recognized." She slipped on a pair of large black shades and patted the tight bun at the back of her head. "But I must admit, after ten years of wearing stiletto heels, these flats sure are comfy."

They entered and an usher led them to the chapel where Ted's casket lay, his name in white plastic letters on a board like a featured movie. "Nobody's here yet, but there's the widow," Dominic whispered out the side of his mouth. "Now scoot and come back in about twenty minutes. It'll be crowded by then."

"Are you sure?" Brooke asked. "This guy knew enough people to make a crowd?"

"She does." His brows wiggled up and down.

"All right, I'll go get a latte."

She turned and exited while Dominic hovered in the doorway, letting Kylah have a few moments with her husband. He stood observing her. Jeepers, her crocodile tears were almost as good as his own.

****

Kylah knelt before the closed casket and bowed her head. Viewing hours didn't start until seven o'clock, but there would be no viewing. He wanted a closed casket, and that's what she gave him. "Oh, Teddy, if only I hadn't worked late that night…" The cloying scent of flowers engulfed her as she took a few gasping sobs. "Whatever happened, I'll find out, I promise." She ran her hand over the polished oak. "The truth is somewhere in time, and I'll find it." The thought lightened her heart and eased her grief.

Soft footsteps made her turn around and stand. She

pulled a tissue out of her purse and dabbed at her eyes. "Dom, so good of you to come."

He stepped up to her and held out his arms. They hugged. "You want to be alone with him a little longer, doll?"

"No, I'm glad you're here." She stuffed the crumpled tissue into her pocket.

"Did you get to view his body before they shut the coffin lid?"

"No," she answered. "But he wanted to be buried in his Bagir Eco Gir suit, made from recycled beverage containers. With his Colts blanket covering him. Odd, I know, but we all have our quirks."

"He's dancin' up a storm with those dead— whatever you said." He released his embrace, stepped up to the casket, and knelt.

Soon the chapel begin to fill as Ted's relatives and friends drifted in. She was surprised when Ted's ex-mother-in-law, Enid Streetman, showed up with his two stepkids. Charles and Charlotte held back as Enid gave Kylah a crushing hug, squeezed her hands, and walked her over to the side aisle. Her fusty perfume clashed with the flowers.

"Kylah, I don't know if I'm supposed to tell you, but two detectives came over the other day and questioned us. Why us, I don't know. It was unnerving, but if there was foul play, I hope the truth comes out."

Kylah had been fully expecting this from Enid, the in-your-face type, never knowing when to shut up. "I know, Enid. They're questioning all the people who knew Ted or me, neighbors, friends, everybody."

"They think it was murder?" Enid's eyes widened, concealing the blobs of blue shadow on her creased lids.

"Not yet," Kylah said. "They have to question more people and do a lot more investigating first."

"Was your marriage on the rocks, dear?" Enid could've been asking a clerk if they had her size girdle, she was so casual about it.

It was easier to answer that personal question than to tell her to mind her own business. "Not at all. He did get depressed, although he hid it well most of the time."

"His whole life was one sad episode. Just like my poor Jill." Enid shook her head. "But he made the most of what he had."

Kylah could tell Enid was trying to force tears that wouldn't come. She always knew Enid didn't like her. His stepkids made no secret of their hostility. They were downright rude to her, even tonight. They hadn't even said hello. While Charles hung back in the doorway, Charlotte crept up to the casket, knelt for a few seconds and skulked away, giving Kylah a sideways sneer.

"He was a brave soul." Kylah glanced at the casket. "He had his moments, especially after Jeremy died."

Enid nodded and turned her mouth downward, a horrendous imitation of sincerity. Orange lipstick feathered on her pursed lips. Without looking Kylah in the eye, she dismissed herself with another hand squeeze. Her rings dug into Kylah's hand. "I'll leave you be now. If there's anything you need…"

"Thanks."

As the matron vanished into the milling crowd, the useless sentiment hung in the air like the choking fragrance of the flowers closing in on her.

When Mike appeared at the entrance, she caught

his attention with a subtle wave. He nodded, but stopped at the casket first, knelt, blessed himself, and took the front row chair next to her.

"How you holding up?"

"Barely. But I have support here. Besides you, of course." She ached for his warm embrace. "Ted's brothers are here, his drum students, and some biker buddies of his."

"I don't see any bikers." He glanced around.

"They don't wear leather and chains to wakes, Mike. Besides, they're all businessmen, doctors and lawyers. Don't you know any lawyer bikers?"

He glanced over his shoulder and shrugged. "Probably. But they don't ride bikes to court or wakes. This looks like a Lions Club meeting."

"Most of his friends were older. Ted had older brothers and hung out with his brothers' friends. He preferred people older than he was. He had friends in their seventies."

"Do you know if they were all questioned?" he asked.

"I didn't ask. But why would guys in their sixties and seventies want to do him harm? They've all been to the house to shoot pool, to watch ball games. No, I can't imagine any of them wanting to harm him. I told you what I believe happened." Her voice dropped. "But when anyone asks, I stick to the suicide theory. He ingested a lethal dose of herbs. That's it."

At that moment something drew her to the casket. "Excuse me." She got up and knelt before it again. She sensed Ted's urging her to find his killer. She heard his voice in her mind, clearly as if he were whispering in her ear. "I know what you want me to do, Teddy." She let a little smile break through her tears. "It's what I planned to do all along."

She managed to get through that first night of the wake. After she shook every sweaty hand in the place and the chapel emptied out, she approached the casket one last time and knelt.

"Good night, Teddy, I'll talk to you later." She turned around for one last glance before she walked out.

****

"It was nice meeting you, Mr. Bugbee." Enid turned to leave the funeral parlor.

"The pleasure was all mine, I assure you, Mrs. Streetman." Dominic offered his hand and wrapped it around this intriguing woman's fingers. "I do hope we'll meet again, under more cheerful circumstances." Before she had a chance to reply, he plowed right on with, "Care to stop somewhere for coffee? I'm at loose ends for the rest of the evening."

"Why, yes, I'd like that." Enid's face brightened. She looked surprised that he'd found her attractive enough to prolong this encounter. "But I've got my grandchildren with me." She waved a diamond-ringed hand. "Oh, they can see their own way home, if you can drop me off later."

"I'd be delighted, ma'am." Thank heaven Brooke had cabbed back to the airport, once she'd sized up the media fodder potential here. "My car is right this way. Just a toy."

He omitted to mention that in nine days, it would become some other middle aged has-been's toy.

****

As Kylah walked to her car, Dominic's convertible pulled out of the parking lot, Enid in the passenger's seat. A sardonic smirk spread Kylah's lips. *They deserve each other.*

A horn beeped. She turned and saw Mike get out of his car. "Just thought I'd wait for you and see if you wanted any company."

Joy fluttered through her, filling the emptiness. "I'd love that, Mike. Just follow me."

When they got to her house, he brought it up before she did. "Was that Dominic Bugbee I saw driving Enid out of there?"

"Sure was." She flipped on the kitchen switch. The lights flickered on. She dimmed them.

"I wonder what those two are up to." He spooned grounds into the coffeemaker's filter.

"I could care less." She got out the sugar bowl and creamer. "It never occurred to me before, but they're made for each other."

"None of my business, Kylah, but what did she say to you at the wake? Somehow I doubt she showed up just to pay her respects."

"She was more civil to me than she was when Ted was alive." They sat at the kitchen table waiting for the coffee. The comforting aroma brought cravings for crumb cake, but her stomach just wasn't ready. "She threw in a few digs, but I didn't bite."

"Maybe she had a change of heart and realizes there's no reason to be mean to you anymore. It took Ted's death for her to see the light. That does happen. It's always too late, but sometimes hard feelings get buried too."

She leaned forward and straightened the centerpiece she'd made out of clam shells. "No, I know her, and it was all an act. After Jill committed suicide,

Enid called Ted at all hours to tell him he was doomed to eternal damnation for divorcing Jill. She just couldn't accept that Jill asked *him* for the divorce."

He glanced over to check on the coffee. "When did the damning calls end?"

"After we got married she seemed to mellow out, when she saw how good he still treated Jill's kids, Charles and Charlotte. You saw them there, the twins with the lip piercings and blue hair and smartphones, ignoring me. When Jeremy was diagnosed and we took him in, it seemed to smooth Enid's ruffled feathers. I think it was because she was glad to have Jeremy out of her sight. She wasn't willing to care for a terminally ill kid. She started treating us like human beings around that time, but the hostility always bubbled near the surface. She never warmed up to me."

"You never know," he mused. "This tragedy might change her mind."

"It's big of you to give her the benefit of the doubt, Mike. Spoken like a true defense lawyer. But it no longer matters." She got two mugs from the mug tree. "We have no connection to each other now that Ted is gone. But who knows what goes on in people's heads? Maybe she did come to terms with it. Of course I sympathized with her for losing her daughter. That's tragic for anyone. But she'll never see that Jill wasn't the picture of purity. "

"What do you mean?" He looked up. "She cheated on Ted or something?"

She shook her head. "There's no 'or something.' Jill led a double life. She had a lover while married to Ted, and only after Jeremy got sick did Ted find out Jeremy wasn't his own son. Ted still raised Jeremy, just like he did with Charles and Charlotte. He loved those kids like his own. He was very understanding about Jeremy not being his, even though it put a strain on their marriage."

Mike folded his hands on the table top. She noticed the absence of his wedding ring. "Yeah, you told me that before. Jeremy wasn't even his kid."

"So he had good reason to divorce Jill." She got spoons from the drawer. "But he stayed with her until— well, until she asked for the divorce, so I'm not the reason he left her. She couldn't put up with his drinking and his pot smoking."

"And Enid doesn't know any of that?" Mike asked. "Jill's affair, Jeremy's real father?"

She shook her head. "None of it. Ted never told her, and as far as I know, Jill never told her either."

"So now she's carousing with Bugbee. I'd give five bucks to see where it ends up." The coffee ready, he brought the carafe to the table.

She inhaled the rich aroma as he poured. "The life coach is coaching right this minute."

They shared a strained smile.

"Hey, you know what?" He peeked into her breadbox. "A hunk of crumb cake would go down just right with this."

Chapter Eleven

After coffee and some idle chitchat about Ted's friends, Kylah's exhaustion got the better of her. "Mike, I can't keep my eyes open."

He pulled his keys out of his pocket. "I'll get out of here and check in with you tomorrow."

They shared a warm embrace. He topped it off with a promising but respectful kiss, as if he knew she couldn't handle anything more intense. What a gentleman.

She put a Caroline Myss meditation CD on and crashed on the sofa, but her muscles couldn't relax and her mind whirred like a top. So she wheeled the vacuum out and trekked through each room, aware of Ted's presence, welcoming the strange comfort it gave her.

Valerian or chamomile tea? Valerian always knocked her out. She went for it.

****

Seated at a cozy table in the coffee shop, Dominic wondered what drew him to Enid, much older than what usually turned his head. It had to be her worldly appearance and demeanor: her high-falutin' attire, diamond rings, pearls draping her neck, the regal way she carried herself. He stretched his arm out to let his gleaming timepiece peek through. A bit of braggadocio always lured them in.

"I came up the hard way, Enid. Grew up working poor in East Boston, but I had a ticket out: my ambition and drive," was his overture after ordering two cups of coffee and slabs of key lime pie. "How about you?" To show some table manners, he placed his paper napkin on his lap.

"We were lower middle class, from Worcester." She dropped her gaze. "But I was always ashamed of it. I made up stories about my background. When my daughter Jill brought Ted home, I was thrilled for her—a nice boy from a respectable family. But their marriage was never made in heaven, and couldn't endure, especially when Ted wouldn't give up booze and drugs." She glanced at her manicured nails. "Then little Jeremy was diagnosed with leukemia. I prayed with Jill constantly, but believe Jeremy would've won his battle if Ted had handled it better. I always felt the boy sensed he was a burden to Ted, and just slipped out of the way."

"Oh, no, Enid. I knew Ted, and he did the best he could. He loved Jeremy with all his heart." He folded his hands on the table top.

"I'm sure you're right, I'm just too close to it emotionally to be objective." She pressed a hankie to her eyes, smudging blue makeup all over it, folded it and stuffed it into her oversized purse. "After Ted and Jill divorced, she took her own life. I still miss her, even after seven years. And poor little Jeremy."

"Of course you do," Dominic empathized. "I lost my oldest son Scott. Boating accident on Long Island Sound. But as you know, the Lord giveth and the Lord taketh away."

"Yes, and much as I miss them, it's a comfort

knowing they're in heaven." She took a breath and looked into his eyes. "What do you really think happened to Ted, Mr. Bugbee?" Her tone took on a conspiratorial quality as her eyes darted back and forth. "I'll keep whatever you say strictly confidential."

"Please call me Dom, Enid." He tilted his head in his classic King-Kong-gazing-at-Fay-Wray style. "I pray it was natural causes and not a murder." Hoping to wheedle some lowdown from her, he didn't want to commit further than that—not yet.

"What does Kylah think?" she asked. "I can't get a straight answer from her."

"She wants us to believe he took that lethal dose of herbs himself. But I'm afraid her story won't hold water much longer." He halted, not ready to spill more.

"Why not?" Her eyes widened.

"As an old friend of Ted's, I knew about their marriage. It was a bit on the rocks." He left the rest of that dangling.

"She told me everything was hunky dory." Enid ignored her pie and leaned forward. "My goodness, you sound awful suspicious."

"Well, knowing the cops need as much help as they can get, I went to them. They asked a few questions and I told them what I could." He shook his head and felt his jowls jiggling. He picked up his knife, gave his reflection a quick glance, and smoothed his comb-over. He wasn't ready to blab that he'd given the detective dirt they could never dig up. "I told them a few things Ted told me." He shoved a forkful of pie into his mouth.

"Ted confided in you? That's unusual for him. He was such a private person." She cut into her pie but didn't eat any.

Dominic tried to hide his frown. He needed some scuttlebutt that he could feed Brooke. Too bad Ted had been so closemouthed. "He made Kylah beneficiary of his estate," he blabbed, hoping she'd blab something in return. "His sole heiress. Or heir, however they say it these days."

She nodded. "I knew about that. The kids had a fit over it. But he did leave them each something from his insurance policy."

"I can't fathom what force brought him and Kylah together," Dominic mused. "They were so mismatched. He was fiercely independent and she wanted to nurture him—or should I say smother him. I know he resented that. Especially after the accident."

"There were three accidents," she clarified.

"I know," he softened his tone. "Terrible things to have happen. Who would do such a thing? And why? I find it hard to believe those incidents were unrelated. Ted must've had some deadly enemies." He baited her further, hoping he could pull something out of her.

"Whoever it is, I hope they get their comeuppance. Or karma as some people say." She thoughtfully stirred milk into her coffee. "But that's not for us to decide."

"Nope, we're neither judge nor jury," he agreed, keeping his voice soft and soothing.

So she knew nothing about who might've caused Ted's 'accidents." Oh, well. It was worth a try. "It was a doomed marriage from the start," he ventured. "I even tried to talk him out of it. But he was hell-bent on marrying her. He wooed her for ages."

"Don't I know it. It's why my Jill is in her grave." A bitter scowl crossed Enid's face as she stabbed at her pie. "I never came into contact with Kylah all that much, just family gatherings over the years. Mostly what I know of her is through the children. They'd come home from visits there and tell me certain things about her…" Her voice trailed off.

"Oh?" he tossed out, tore into a packet and spilled sugar into his coffee. "If they're like my Petra, they must idolize her."

"Hardly." Her orange lips spread into a sneer.

Now he was getting somewhere. "What do you mean, Enid? Isn't Kylah a charming, fascinating, resourceful woman?"

"Not with my grandkids, she isn't. They always came home telling me about her—uh—friends. One in particular." She emphasized that word so strongly, she provoked his pushing further.

"What kind of friends? More of those Druids?" He screwed up his face, cringing.

"That smarmy lawyer she runs around with. Mike something. He was there tonight talking to her. Didn't you see them huddled together? Deplorable. And in full view of Ted's casket." She scowled into her coffee cup. "When Charles and Charlotte used to visit Ted—" she paused and took a sip, "Kylah and her *friend* would go out together, ostensibly to give Ted time with the kids. But teenagers being teenagers, they pick up on certain things, and got an inkling she's more than friends with this dashing attorney. Ted would bring the children back to his house, and Kylah and her *friend* would still be out gallivanting."

"Did the kids ever say how Ted felt about this?" he inquired.

She shook her head. "No, Ted kept his cards close

to his vest, as you said. And Mike did pro bono work for them, so Ted couldn't kick him out of their lives. Charles and Charlotte told me how cozy those two were, snuggled on the porch swing, strolling through her garden arm in arm, singing mushy songs at the piano together. Far too cozy, if you ask me."

So the lawyer dude was Kylah's squeeze on the side. Dominic pondered the implications of that for a moment as he savored his pie. What better motive…besides the money, of course.

"Enid, I'll be frank here. You're a very attractive woman, and I'm single and lonely. I find your companionship delightful, and I'd like to get to know you better. Do you find that objectionable?"

She swallowed a hunk of pie and gave him a come-hither raise of her plucked brows. "Of course not, Dom. I'm alone, as you know, a widow. What did you have in mind for the immediate future?"

"How about coming back to my place for a nightcap?" Now it was his turn to squeeze her hand.

Just then the waitress passed by.

Enid almost knocked over the table grabbing her. "Miss, may we have the check, please? Now."

Chapter Twelve

The next morning, Kylah cursed her ringing doorbell. It wasn't Mike's ring, or any of her friends coming over to comfort her. A glance out the window told her it was the police again. She trudged to the door to open it. Detective Lieutenant Munn stood there. Alone. "Sorry to disturb you again, Mrs. McKinley, but I need to ask a few more questions."

She nodded. "Come in."

Munn entered and flipped open his notebook. "Mrs. McKinley, police were called to this house by your neighbors in the past on complaints about loud music and parties, and once for domestic violence—"

"No!" she broke in. "It wasn't violence, just fisticuffs between Ted's friends. They drank a bit too much, had words, and one of them took a swing at another guy. Ted broke it up. The cops came because a nosy neighbor called them. There was no violence. Nobody pressed charges. I want to clear that up right now."

He let her finish and came out with, "Did your husband ever hit you?"

That sucker punched her. "W—well—" she stammered, stalling. What would happen if she lied? "Well, he—"

Better tell the truth.

"He hit me once, but he didn't hurt me. I didn't

113

even think of pressing charges." She glanced out the window, knowing the neighbors hovered behind their curtains dishing dirt about the 'witch lady' and her dead biker husband.

"That's your vehicle out front? The white Mustang?" He pointed his pen at the front window where her car sat in the driveway.

"Yes, it is."

"Did you drive that vehicle to your store on the day he died?" he asked.

"Yes, I always do."

He gave a curt nod. "You had it with you all that day?"

"Of course."

Another nod. "Where do you park it at your store?"

"In the building behind the store—it's the former carriage house."

The next nod came with a *hmm*. "And it was parked there until you drove it home?"

"Yes, sir."

What's all this about the car?

She itched to ask, but didn't want to push him.

"Two of your neighbors said they saw that car parked here in your driveway between four and seven o'clock on the day of your husband's death," he stated.

"That's impossible!" Stunned, she hugged her arms across her middle, fighting nausea. "You can't rely on them. They don't know what they're talking about. My car couldn't have been here."

"White Mustang convertible. That's what I have down here." He tapped the notebook with his pen.

"But I didn't get home until a quarter to ten. How many times do I have to tell you that?"

His stare bored into her. "Did someone borrow your car that day?"

"No, I have the only set of keys, which were in my purse the whole time, and no one ever borrows my car."

"Do you know anyone else—friends, relatives, neighbors—with the same make and model car as yours?" he prodded.

She let out an exasperated breath. "No. I've never seen another one like it anywhere on the Cape. But you can't rely on neighbors. People always get dates and times mixed up. They think they see what's not there."

"Mrs. McKinley, we have a photo a realtor took that day with a digital camera, of your next door neighbor's house, which is for sale. The photo shows the time and date it was taken. Part of your car in your driveway is visible in the corner of the photo." His tone took on an accusatory note.

She'd heard about cops forcing, browbeating and badgering innocent suspects until they confessed under duress. But they usually did the 'good cop/bad cop' routine. So where was the 'good cop'? "I tell you, officer, I wasn't here and neither was my car." She struggled to keep her voice down. "I was in my store until nine-thirty. I didn't touch my car all day." Her mind raced: what next? A false accusation? Getting handcuffed and hauled off to jail? Never again to see trees, flowers, the sky, the sea, her garden, her store, her Mike...

"The date of that photo is wrong, the camera was set wrong," she insisted.

He didn't nod or comment or *tsk* or *hmm* this time. That further terrified her. She hugged her arms tighter to her chest to stop shaking.

"That's all for now. Thanks for your time, ma'am." He broke eye contact and let himself out.

She dragged herself to the sofa and sank into the cushion, her worst fear now reality. "They're building a case against me," she said, over and over. She had to get out of the house.

Where's a more comforting place than the beach?

****

As Kylah entered her store, Petra dashed out from behind the counter. "Hey, so great to see you!" They shared a hug.

"I had to come back here, the only continuity in my life now, it seems." Kylah gazed at the colorful stones, beads and crystals on display, closed her eyes and inhaled the exotic scents of mingled incense. Oh, how comforting, how familiar.

"Yeah, it's the best thing for you." Petra nodded. "The place was packed yesterday and the day before, we had to stay open an hour after closing. This is the first lull we've had in ages."

"Glad to hear that," she murmured. "But to be honest, I'm past caring about how much money the store makes. A tragedy eclipses everything that once seemed important. Puts it all in perspective." She pulled off her street shoes and slid into her crimson satin slippers, wiggling her toes. "I'm wondering when I'll get through an entire day—and night—without the sight of Ted's lifeless body in my mind."

Petra gave her a sympathetic nod. "You will. It'll take time. But the best thing you could do is come back to work. We missed you." Petra moved aside to let Kylah stand behind the counter.

"Yeah, this is a big step." She swept her fingers

across the hanging necklaces on a revolving display. "I physically pushed myself out of bed this morning and choked down a smoothie without even tasting it."

"You'll come alive again. I know how strong you are." Petra gave her hand a squeeze. "Just stay busy."

As she greeted customers and accepted condolences, she eased back into her routine. She slipped some new moonstone rings on her fingers, enjoying the light glinting off the gems. Tourists swarmed in, milled, browsed and purchased. She chatted with them, gave out incense sticks, and made notes to order more merchandise.

"Karma will take care of what is meant to be," she recited the wise old saying. Her muscles relaxed as she looked forward to meditating in a warm bath.

"Mrs. McKinley?" A gruff voice cut through the serene strains of Enya. She turned to face two uniformed policemen.

The crowd parted, stared, whispered, and stuck around.

"You're under arrest for the murder of your husband, Theodore McKinley. You have the right to remain silent..."

The reading of her rights and the escort to the police car went by in a blur. Dazed with disbelief, she slid into the back seat.

Petra dashed out after her. "I'll call Mike!"

"It can't be, I didn't murder him," she insisted when she found her voice. Leaning forward, she placed her hand on the passenger's headrest, but snatched it away. They might think she was trying something and handcuff her.

Getting arrested for murder in her own store full of

customers mortified her enough.

****

Her arresting officers escorted her through the Barnstable County Correctional Facility entrance. A rookie cop with sympathetic eyes led her to a holding cell.

It wasn't cold and damp with rats scampering around her feet. But it wasn't the Four Seasons either. Grimy linoleum curled at the floor's edges. A cot stood against the wall next to a metal folding chair. The steel basin and toilet made her cringe. Her mind whirring, she sat on the cot. The frame squeaked and groaned as she sank into the sagging middle.

She peered out the small grime-streaked window facing a brick wall. Karma will take care of what is meant to be...

She jumped at the sound of clanging doors and approaching footsteps. The cell door opened. A bleary-eyed Mike stepped inside and held his arms out to her.

She leapt into his embrace. "I can't even cry, I'm just too stunned," was all she could say.

"You don't need to cry. I'll tell you what's going to happen."

As she sat on the cot and he pulled up the chair, he explained the procedures at the arraignment, the bail hearing, and about filing discovery. "The prosecution has to get more evidence. Then there will be a drawn-out process where both sides have to file dozens more motions and petitions. The judge will set the trial date. Don't show any emotion at the arraignment, don't break down or lose your temper, no matter what anyone says." Stripped of softness and emotion, his tone sounded like that of a lawyer advising a client.

"Of course I won't. But tell me honestly, now." She hunched forward. "Will the judge grant bail?"

He nodded. "You're a respected business woman, you're not a flight risk. I'll personally vouch for you to be held in my recognizance. He might take away your passport, but he'll let you out on half a mil or a million dollars."

She let that sink in.

"I don't know what I have in cash. I have to—" Her voice shook at the heartbreaking thought. "I have to sell my house. I don't even want to mortgage it. I can't go back to living there."

"Don't worry about that." He lifted her chin with his thumb. "I'll help you raise the funds if you need me to."

"Thanks, I appreciate that." Their eyes met.

"We can talk about it later."

"But I can't wait till later." She trembled, her heart pounding. "I have to pay for my trial." As another ugly reality hit her, she recoiled as if struck. "I'll have to sell the store, too."

"Stop worrying about all that." He took a deep breath. "I was going to wait, but I can't." He clasped her hands. "I loved you from the minute you first walked into my office, a young vulnerable beauty divorcing your first husband, owning up to your mistake. I thought I was way too old for you back then. But this is now. And because a husband always takes care of his wife…" He knelt on one knee before her, her hands still clasped in his. "Kylah, will you marry me?"

She gasped, adoring his eyes, the green of the forest they'd traveled together centuries ago, the same eyes that gazed at her in that faraway time. "Oh,

Mike..." She caught her breath, flooded with joy. "Of course I'll marry you."

He glanced around. "I know this place is the farthest thing from romantic, but I couldn't wait for soft violins and candlelight. I'll propose again at a more appropriate time."

"I love you, too, and it's been so hard to keep it bottled up inside." She drew him back into her arms and captured his lips. Their kiss held new meaning. She wanted to melt away and consume his patient passion for her. She reached up and touched his hair for the first time. "It's so soft," she whispered, kissing his neck. As if they both knew what would happen next, they pulled apart.

"We need to save it. It'll be worth the wait."

Her heart danced in anticipation. She saw their future in his eyes. "From now on, we share the same life. We did once before, but this means we're doing it again. And we will again, in the next life."

He traced his fingertip along her jawline. "We'll make it through this." He spoke as if reciting his marriage vows.

No marriage vows meant more to her than this promise. She caught her breath. "But how long will this take?"

"Since this isn't a big city like Boston, the duration won't be more than a few weeks until the trial begins. You will not spend your life behind bars." His voice resonated with the conviction of an attorney willing to stake his life on his client's innocence. "They'll never come up with enough evidence linking you to Ted's murder. This isn't even a hiccup in your life."

"Mike, if this does work out, I'll marry you the

same day I'm acquitted." The words rushed out of her.

His eyes sparkled. He displayed such a happy smile, her spirits leapt. "The same day?" His voice softened. "Without the gown and the flowers and the seven-tiered cake?"

"I had all that the first time around. And I don't want to wait."

He raised his right hand as if taking an oath. "I promise and swear on all that's holy, I'll get you acquitted, no matter who killed Ted, because I know you didn't. Now just bunk down here and get some sleep. I'll see you tomorrow."

She grabbed his arm as he moved to stand. "Mike, wait. Do something for me, please."

"What?" He sat back down.

"Will you bring me some of my herbs?" Fists clenched, her nails dug into her palms. She flexed her fingers, forcing the tension from her muscles.

"Tea, you mean?"

"No." She shook her head. "This isn't tea. I need some of my herbs. From my herb cupboard. The one that got broken into."

"What for?" His steely look unnerved her.

She took a deep breath. "I love you too much to lie to you, and at this juncture, lying would be the ultimate betrayal of your trust. I know you'll have a hard time understanding this, but I have to tell you."

He leaned forward and focused on her. "Well?"

"You know how we—I mean Druids in general, believe in the otherworld and the afterlife."

"Sure. If that's what you believe." He spread his fingers. "What's this got to do with herbs?"

"It's not just any herbs, Mike. There are certain

herbs that Druids have taken for thousands of years, special mixtures for specific results. And there's a mixture for something specific that I need."

"Uh-oh." His tone grew anxious.

She released a long sigh. "I hope I can explain this right. You know about my past life as Alice."

"More than most people, I presume."

"The bishop found her guilty of murdering her last husband. The night before her execution, she vanished from the face of the earth. Not another word was ever written about her. I don't know if she escaped, if she was executed, or what her fate was. I'm still trying to track her ending, but leads are few and far between." She twirled her braid around her finger. "But this is exactly what's happening to me now. I've been wrongly accused of killing Ted, just as she was with John. I need to find out how she dealt with her situation. That will tell me how to handle this, give me a clue as to what will happen, and I hope it'll point to who killed Ted. You see where I'm leading here?" She wiped sweat off her forehead.

"Taking herbs will help you find out?" he quizzed.

"I may not be able to leave the country, but I can leave the century. My spirit can, anyway," she declared, determined to carry out her quest. "Taking the right mixture of herbs will send me back to her time. They'll transport me back into her body, into her life. Other Druids have done this, have gone back to re-live past lives, to give them insight into their present lives, especially when something terrible like this has happened."

He folded his arms across his chest. "They don't just put you into a trance so your imagination can run riot?"

"To an observer, it'll look like I'm lying here, sleeping." She gestured at the cot. "My body will be unconscious. But my spirit will go back to 1324, and my past life as Alice."

He gave his head a quick shake and pinched the bridge of his nose. "This is too out there. I don't understand how this can possibly work."

"Because it always does," she replied calmly. "It's been done many times. It's not a past life regression under hypnosis. I'll physically return to 1324 to see, hear and feel exactly what happened to her, and prevent it from repeating now. If I can learn from my past life, history can't repeat itself. I have to do this before Ted's killer succeeds in destroying me."

"You've never traveled back this way before, have you?" His eyes expressed a mix of skepticism and fear.

"I never had reason to," she said. "But now it's a matter of life and death."

He slid his glasses from his pocket and polished them on his shirt. "I promised I'd get you acquitted. You don't need to live a previous life to find that out."

"Oh, yes, I do." She sat up straight. "It's not just about being acquitted now. It's about unresolved karma. Of course I trust you and believe you'll have me acquitted."

His expression changed from that of tight-lipped doubt to hope as his eyes brightened. He nodded, as if trying to believe her.

"The most important parallel," she went on, "is Alice was accused of killing her last husband and so was I. So I must go back and find out what happened to her. I need those herbs. And you're the only one who can get them to me."

He stood, paced the cell and sat back down again. The cot sagged and groaned. "I respect your beliefs even though I don't share them, but—pardon my bluntness, this idea is a disaster in the making. What you want to do can be harmful. My God, look what happened to Ted."

"I'm not taking the combination that killed him, Mike. I'm taking rosemary for protection, calendula to increase visions, angelica for luck and chamomile to relax."

"What if it brings you back to the wrong person's life in the wrong century instead of Alice in 1324?" he continued his line of questioning.

"The other part of the ritual is saying a specific chant and prayer in Gaelic, to voice my exact intention to when and where in time I need to go. This has worked for millennia, and will work now," she assured him. "It will bring my spirit back into Alice's body, if I focus my awareness on that life while I'm saying the prayer."

He shifted his body and cracked his knuckles, one at a time.

"I know it will work. It always does," she assured him, her tone forthright and sure.

"Going back to this past life is dangerous as hell." His posture stiffened and he leaned forward. "What if you get stuck in that godawful time?"

"I can't get stuck," she insisted. "I use the same herbs and prayer to return here."

His expression hardened. "Honey, past life regression by a medium or hypnotist or whatever—is one thing. That's entertainment. But your spirit traveling backwards in time under the influence of herbs and entering another body is beyond reckless. It's downright suicide. You know what conditions were like back then. Ireland was a wild untamed wasteland crawling with robbers and murderers and disease." He closed his eyes and rubbed the back of his neck. "Medicine was primitive to say the least." He shook his head. "I don't want you to do this."

"I'm sorry, but I need to." She took a ragged breath, holding back a flood of tears. "Someday I'll make you understand."

"Someday." His body tensed. "But right now, I know Ted would agree with me. Something will happen when you're back there, and you'll meet with a horrible end." The sunlight streaming through the window made two pinpoints of light in his eyes. "I admire your courage and determination, but come on. Don't you realize even one day in those times can kill you—of plague or something?" he challenged, in courtroom mode. His eyes pleaded.

"I didn't tell you this to ask your approval, Mike. I need your help. But I'm sensing that you don't have any confidence in me."

"It's not your competence I'm doubting." He rubbed his chin. "It's the diseases. And the murderers and highwaymen and other assorted thieves and maniacs back in those days you'll be up against. Can you tell me how you plan to stay safe from all that?"

"Alice survived all that. I'll be in the same body," she explained. "We know she lived through to her trial."

"That's the other thing. You're hell-bent on believing that you were Alice. I just—" He looked away, then back at her, "can't believe it without any concrete proof."

"I said I'll prove it to you someday, and someday soon." She added for emphasis, "Just wait and see."

They sat stalemated for a few beats.

Finally he heaved a weary breath. "I'm worried sick about you doing this. Don't you understand what I'm telling you, Kylah? I don't just love you. I'm in love with you."

How she'd hoped they share this moment in a different setting…sipping brandies and savoring bonbons before a fire in the hearth. Not in a holding cell.

"I fell in love with you too." That came straight from her heart. "I thought I loved you like a close friend, but it's so much more. While I was married to Ted I denied it. But I wasn't being true to myself. I had feelings for you at the same time I loved Ted. Oh, I was so torn. And I carried around all this guilt…" She hung her head and stared at her feet.

"It's entirely possible to love two people." He gave a knowing nod. "It happens all the time. That's why I never pushed you. I knew it would work out if it was meant to. But now it is. When you and Ted had problems, I hoped you'd split up, then hated myself for being so selfish. But I can't help it, that's the way I feel." His shoulders relaxed, as if he'd unleashed a heavy burden.

"So, my first request as your future wife…" Her heart raced. "Is for you to bring me the herbs I need. I swear I'll return before the arraignment."

He hesitated, then broke away and paced the cell again.

She followed him. "I believe you lived that life with me then, too. On a regression, I met a Michael Artson, and I knew in my heart he was you. Do you know that everyone we love in this life, we've loved in other lives?"

This time he smiled. "I knew you—and loved you—seven hundred years ago?"

"I've never been so sure of anything in my life. Any life. So, please?" She clutched his sleeves. "Will you go to my house, get the herbs and come back? I swear nothing bad will happen."

He sat back down. "If it means that much to you, then I have no right to try to stop you." He kissed her knuckles.

She let out a relieved sigh. "Oh, thank you!" She circled her fingers around his.

His brow furrowed as his grip on her hands tightened.

"Now text this to yourself," she instructed. He got out his phone. "I need one quarter teaspoon of rosemary, one quarter teaspoon of calendula, one third teaspoon angelica and one teaspoon of chamomile. Put them in separate sandwich bags. The bags are in the drawer under the microwave. Petra has a key to my house. She's working at the store. Got all that?"

His nodded. "Got it." Then, with a parting kiss, he left her.

She flopped on the rickety cot and bunched up the thin pillow. Closing her eyes, she forced herself to face the future—getting out of here, clearing her name, returning to her store, her herbs, her future husband.

He came back an hour later with the correct doses of herbs measured out in separate sandwich bags, just as she'd instructed him. "And here's your cup."

"Thanks so much, Mike." She filled the cup with water from the sink. "Now, let me just mix these and I'll be on my way."

Approaching footsteps startled her. She broke their embrace as a guard stopped and peered in. Time halted as he peered into the cell. He turned and vanished into the darkness.

Mike squeezed her hand. "Don't worry about him."

As she prepared to enter another time and place, she poured each herb into the water. The mixture swirled in a tiny whirlpool.

"Kylah, wait."

She looked up. "What?"

"I'm going with you. I can't bear to let you go back there alone."

Elation fluttered through her. "What made you decide this?"

He watched the cup's swirling contents. "If our destinies are to be together, I want to be by your side on this journey. I want to be there to protect you, and—" He took a few rapid breaths as if searching for the right words. "This sounds selfish, dorky, whatever you make of it, but I need you with me. I don't want us to be apart."

She stroked his cheek with her free hand. "You can come with me if you really want to. But we need another combination of herbs, the same ones in the same amounts, for you."

He looked at her over the rims of his glasses, then swept them off his face. As he focused on her, she could see him calculating what he wanted to say. "Since I make a living requiring proof and facts, and being

Irish Catholic to boot, I could never put stock in reincarnation or time travel. I can't understand how this can happen. I'll just have to put my faith in you."

She clasped his hands. "I appreciate your faith in me. But you have to accept something else on faith—what we're about to do has no scientific explanation. Even the greatest minds haven't figured out how or why. Druids take it on faith, too. Alice's spirit lives on in me. That spirit can go back and live with her body again. Just as Michael Artson's spirit now lives in you."

His eyes brightened, as if ready to sum it all up. "I contemplated doing this the whole time we discussed it, and back at your house, I agonized over it, prayed over it, but didn't want to ask—I just didn't think you'd want me tagging along. But now that the moment of truth is here, I couldn't let you go without asking you. So—here's my dose." He took the extra herbs from his pocket.

"Mike, you'd hardly be tagging along. Concentrate hard enough, keep your faith—and believe that you are Michael Artson, body and soul."

He nodded, staring at the floor.

She could tell he wasn't looking forward to the trip. He was doing it for her. Her heart swelled with love—this time without guilt.

"Let's hope your moment of truth lasts as long as the return trip." She gave him a smile that he didn't return.

"I need to do this in my car. The guards will be suspicious if they see me lying on the floor here." He glanced at the cell door. "I have a water bottle in the car I can use."

The guard walked past again, but didn't stop to

look into her cell.

She nodded. "Drink the herbs in the water and lie on the back seat. Close your eyes and concentrate very hard on Kilkenny, Ireland in the year 1324. You are Michael Artson."

"If anything at all happens, remember how much I love you." He embraced her. She basked in this moment of comfort, the magic of this new discovery of their love.

"I'll see you…back there, in our past." As he let himself out she sat alone on the cot and raised her cup in a toast. "To eternal life—together." She raised the cup to her lips.

She sputtered as the remnants caught in her throat, but her heart and breathing slowed. As she lay down, a smile played over her lips. With each inhalation and exhalation, she relaxed each muscle, one at a time, beginning at her feet.

"I wish to return to Kilkenny, Ireland in the year of our Lord thirteen-twenty-four. I wish my spirit to leave my living body and transcend the time continuum to enter the body of Alice Kyteler. Bring my spirit back to Alice's living body in the year 1324."

She then repeated it in Gaelic: "Ba mhaith liom dul ar ais go gCill Cheannaigh, Éireann i mbliain an Tiarna míle trí chead fiche cheathair. Ba mhaith liom mo anam a n-iompair ó mo choirp beo agus a teastail tríd na haoise go chorp Ailis Ní Chithlir."

She finished with the Lord's Prayer in Gaelic: "Ár n-Athair atá ar neamh, Go naofar d'ainim, Go dtagfadh do ríocht, Go ndéantar do thoil ar an talamh mar a dhéantar ar neamh. Ár n-arán laethúil tabhair dúinn inniu, agus maith dúinn ár bhfiacha mar a mhaithimidne dár bhféichiúna féin Ach ná lig sinn i gcathú, ach saor sinn ó olc, Amen."

Her breathing slowed.

Footsteps approached and faded away.

Her neck muscles released the last traces of tension. Her eyes slid shut, her body and soul at one with the universe.

She drifted away.

She woke up shivering. A cold draft blew through an open window. Opening her eyes, she looked at the empty space next to her on the bed.

She knew where she was. Fourteenth century Kilkenny, Ireland.

But Mike was not with her.

Chapter Thirteen

"Twice in one month. That has to be a record!"
Dominic reached forward and gave Brooke's thigh a
squeeze. She tittered and tugged at her skirt until it
covered her knees. "I wish we could see each other a lot
more often than this, Brookie." He affected a low
suggestive tone. "I don't mean purely for business,
either."

She displayed a professional smile and ignored his
come-on. "This can be the smash of the year if we play
our cards right." She skimmed her notes, brandishing a
smug grin. "Murder is hot. It's what the networks want.
It's what the public hungers for. And the New Age
angle is a strong hook. Not the humdrum everyday
'wife kills abusive husband in self defense.' She dosed
him with herbs. That's original, all right. That'll open
up a story about the Druid thing, and get us some new
sponsors. Companies who make holistic drugs, crystals,
runes, all that witchy stuff. They'll gobble it up like
starving vultures. Especially if there's a weight loss
remedy or a sexual enhancer involved. Advertising
revenues for my show will skyrocket." She extended
her arm.

Their knuckles met in a fist pump.

"Her arraignment is tomorrow, so the trial should
start fairly soon. Will you have somebody covering it?"
he asked.

"Maybe not every day. But definitely for the first couple of sessions, so we can get the first edition kick-started. I'd like to run it starting Monday. We get our highest ratings on Mondays. Then for the weekend edition, we'll have even more." She grabbed a folder from her desk. "Here are the questions. I'll be interviewing you for the first installment, a 'friend of the victim' feature. We'll do a run-through tomorrow."

"Before, during or after the dinner at Tavern on the Green I'm treating you to?" He threw that out there, knowing she'd never take him up on it. His fingers brushed hers as she handed him the folder.

She toyed with her diamond earring. "I can't have dinner, Dom. I've got to look over the script for tomorrow's show. This week's going to be murder—oops, bad choice of words." She covered her megawatt smile with her manicured hand.

"A raincheck, then." He flipped open the folder and glanced at the questions. "I can highlight a few things that'll make Ted look like the fallen hero, the martyr."

"Whatever you think is relevant and will arouse the most sympathy, Dom." She checked her cell phone. "You knew him better than I. And the wife. Play up her bad points even more than his good ones. We need to get all the sympathy going for him. Seventy percent of our audience is women. Women who'd want someone like Ted to take care of, to nurture. At the same time, the wife's someone the female viewers love to hate. The wicked witch, the femme fatale. Especially if she's good looking. Remember, it's all about spin."

"You got it. I can see the cover of *People* already." He stood and smoothed down his comb-over. "I'll send you this amended list of questions with my answers by tomorrow a.m."

"Awesome, Dom, thanks. Now if I can get an exclusive with her, I'll truly believe in miracles." She winked.

"I'll see what I can do. My daughter and her are like this." He held up his crossed index and middle finger. "Petra can likely talk her into it. After all, Kylah will try anything to pull the wool over our eyes and clear her name. She's not the confessing type."

"Oh, dear, no, let's hope she doesn't confess." Brooke puckered her lips.

"Nah." He waved his hand. "Her lawyer's looking to make the next Hollywood dream team, and a high profile case like this catapults him into the big time."

"Only if she's acquitted," Brooke warned.

"Not necessarily. Lee Bailey lost a few along the line. An acquaintance of mine did some digging on this counsel of hers. He got that Boston guy off—the drifter who killed prostitutes and dumped their bodies in the river. But that doctor in Quincy who killed his whole family—Richardson lost that one. The doc's serving life. Those cases put Richardson on the map. Now he's the typical hotshot lawyer. Flashy dresser, zips around in a Porsche. You know the type."

She gave him a onceover. "I sure do."

Dom guffawed. "Dearie, this is a business suit. And if I were the flashy type, I'd wear a toupee."

"And after this, you won't be?"

He fingered his I.D. bracelet. "Nah. Not my style. Grow old gracefully, I always say."

"That's your line, buddy, not mine," the queen of the nips, tucks and liposucks quipped. She didn't keep any secrets about it. She wore her scars on her show like badges of honor. It sucked her viewers in and kept her plastic surgeons laughing all the way to the bank.

****

Kylah's eyes adjusted to the fading daylight. As she stretched out on the coarse sheet, a cart rumbled and a horse neighed in the distance. A musty odor made her gag.

Mike isn't here.

Panic shot through her. Her heart raced.

Then her logical side took over. Although she wanted him here, she knew he was safer back home in the twenty-first century.

She slid off the bed. Her feet hit hard floorboards. Prickly rushes stung her feet. She looked down at the form-fitting kirtle that draped her down to her ankles. Made of off-white linen, it laced up the sides. Its wide scoop neck exposed her chest with a hint of cleavage. Her fitted sleeves reached past her wrists. She pushed them up over her elbows.

A jeweled belt circled her waist. As she ran her fingers over it, colored gemstones winked up at her—orange citrines, red rubies, blue sapphires. Well, Alice was wealthy, after all.

She slipped into a pair of pointy leather shoes. They molded to her feet, a perfect fit. Alice must've broken them in a while ago.

Curious about what she wore underneath, she pulled the kirtle up to her waist and observed her linen underpants tied around her waist with a string. A light chemise hung under the kirtle. She pulled the neckline down to see her breasts nestled into two cups of fabric attached to shoulder straps.

The chamber looked familiar, yet it seemed so foreign. She seemed to recognize the wardrobe stuffed with silk chemises, linen kirtles and velvet cloaks in her favorite shades of mauve and rose, the dresser piled with colorful gemstone jewelry, face creams lined up, just like her herb jars at home. The white ruffled curtains resembled the set hanging in her bedroom. "It's all so *me*," she marveled out loud. She'd been here before, no doubt in her mind.

Now for the moment of truth: her face. She approached the looking glass over the dresser. She studied the eyes looking back at her. Her eyes. That was her braided red hair pinned to her head, her heart-shaped face, the same smattering of freckles. Yet something looked different. A careworn edge sharpened her features, as if enduring a life fraught with hardship. What could've aged her?

Instantly she knew. She took a breath. The woman in the mirror took a breath. She smoothed her hair back, the woman smoothed her hair back. She nodded and the woman nodded, an assuring nod. They were one and the same, yet she was no longer Kylah, the twenty-first century widow. She was Alice, the woman she once was, in a distant faraway time. Yet that time was now.

It worked. Those herbs had transported her soul seven centuries into the past, into the body and life of Alice Kyteler.

She opened her mouth to speak. "I am Alice Kyteler." Her voice sounded the same, but carried a gentle Irish lilt that pleased her. She smiled and Alice smiled back.

She explored the chamber, reaching out to feel the coarse fabrics, the carved furniture. She stopped before a candle and inhaled the waxy aroma. As she focused on the Brighid's Cross on the far wall, it all came back to her. She approached a ladder back chair in the corner and gathered up her velvet fur-lined mantle, breathing its patchouli scent—her scent.

Now she knew exactly where she was.

She exited the chamber and walked through the Kyteler Inn, quiet now at midday.

The top of her head brushed the low ceiling beams as she went out the back door and into her garden. In the sun's comforting warmth, she gazed at her prized herbs, lovingly nurtured from seedlings. She knelt before the lavender, plucked a delicate blossom and inhaled its sweet fragrance. Next she breathed in the honeyed scent of her basil plant.

This was a good time to gather up the herbs for her journey back home. With her thumb nail, she snipped cuttings of rosemary, calendula, angelica and chamomile. Plan ahead, she always said. Time wasn't always on her side.

"Dame Kyteler?" She turned to face a rosy-cheeked lass, the spitting image of her friend Petra. A brown kirtle hugged her lean form. "Good morn to you."

Petronilla Meath was Alice's maid.

"Uh, good morn..." she stammered, tongue-tied. She didn't say Petronilla's name just in case. This journey was too crucial to risk any goofs.

Petronilla wiped her hands on her skirt. "I rinsed and hung the wash, now I'm off to do the milking...unless you have some other chores." A tendril of black hair escaped her cap and she pushed it back under.

"Nay, tis fine…go do whatever needs be." She dismissed Petronilla with a smile as she struggled not to look so…so stunned.

Petronilla bobbed a curtsey and scampered off.

As the sound of hooves pounded on the earth, Kylah turned to see a man on a gray horse. He slowed the mount to a halt and slid off.

"Alice, Alice, please," he begged.

His green tunic embroidered with yellow thread covered a linen shirt. Brown breeches hugged his masculine physique. Hose covered his legs from the knees down. A leather purse hung from a belt low on his hips. His attire boasted his status. He was no yeoman.

But his face and mannerisms floored her. Dark curly hair framed angular features. Thick brows intensified his green eyes, flecked with gold. Stubble shadowed his strong chin. She inhaled his essence of leather and outdoors.

Dear God, it's Mike!

"You're here!" Relief flooded her. But it vanished just as fast. He couldn't be her Mike. He'd called her Alice, not Kylah.

Now she knew—he was Alice's friend Michael Artson, the embodiment of her Mike. As the revelation nearly knocked her over, she regained her footing. He clutched her arms with strong calloused hands. "Alice, our dear friends are down with the sweat, please, you must help them!"

Oh, no.

She had no immunity from the sweating sickness. "The sweat is highly infectious, I can't be catching such a malady."

"Please, Alice, it's Brona and her daughter Margaret." His eyes brimmed with tears. "We can't let them die. You must gather some of your medicinal herbs, go there and administer them."

Who are Brona and Margaret and how are they such dear friends with Michael and Alice?

She glanced at the herbs she'd already gathered. They certainly wouldn't cure sweating sickness. "They need cardamom, coriander, St. John's Wort and a few others if those don't work. Plus divers prayers." She dreaded the task ahead. Would she ever get home?

"I'm sorry, Alice." Michael grasped her free hand, lifted it to his lips and kissed it. "But you don't know what this means to me. And Brona will be forever grateful, too. She already thinks the world of you."

She does?

Kylah nearly asked that out loud. Whoever Brona was, it was her duty to save the sick woman, and she wasn't going home until she did.

Her stomach roiled. "First I must I gather the appropriate remedies."

Michael shuffled his feet and twisted his mount's reins between his fingers, biting his lip. "My lady, you're a godsend."

"When did they come down with the sweat?" She headed back to her garden.

"Yestermorn." Michael followed her. "Many parts of the village are afflicted. After you've dispensed their medicines, 'tis best you fetch Petronilla and we all abscond to the Mourne mountains, secluded and safe. I've already had the sweat. But, Alice, I'll gladly take you wherever you wish to go."

Oh, that was so like her Mike. "We'll talk about it

after I help these ladies."

At her kitchen's butcher block, she took her clippings, placed them in leather drawstring pouches, and they headed for Michael's horse out front.

"I'll walk. Surrey doesn't like riding double." He helped her mount. She hadn't ridden a horse since college days, but couldn't tell him that. She took the reins and Surrey got off to a steady trot along the dirt road. Michael had no trouble keeping up on foot.

She inhaled the earthy air. The trees, grass, and distant hills blended in the vivid greens of an oil painting come to life. Neighing, bleating, and clucking rang out in soft harmony as she rode past a farm. She wrinkled her nose at the ripe stench of a barnyard. White sheep dotted the patchwork of pastures in the distance. Thatched-roof cottages stood alone or clustered together. Trousers and shirts in dark browns and indigos fluttered on lines in the breeze.

As they reached a village, he guided her down a narrow lane. Timber-framed dwellings hugged the road. Villagers carried baskets or bundles to and fro.

She observed the surrounding cottages. Brown timber crisscrossed the facades under thatched roofs. Doors stood low and crooked. Curtains hung in some windows, but most gaped open. She knew this was central Kilkenny without even asking. It hadn't changed much in seven hundred years. It still held all its quaint old charm, as she remembered not just from her past life, but from visits here as a student.

You've come home, her heart told her.

"Michael, I haven't been here in a while," she confessed, feeling the need to share.

"I know, you've been working way too hard, love.

After you tend to Brona and Margaret, you deserve some freedom."

"Oh, there won't be time for that." She didn't elaborate.

"Care to eat, my dear? We can nip into Tynan's for a meat pie before we get there," Michael offered.

"I've no appetite." The last thing she wanted was a pub meal, her stomach in knots. "But I thank you anyway."

"An ale then?"

They approached a timber-framed pub. Its wooden shingle hung on rusty chains, the lettering worn away. The structure leaned into the street. Its rustic charm beckoned.

"Aye, let's stop here. I didn't realize how parched I was till you mentioned it." She licked her dry lips.

He helped her dismount and tied the reins to a post. She smoothed her skirts.

They entered the dark pub. She stooped under the low doorway and the exposed ceiling beams.

Michael went up to the pitted, scarred bar and ordered two ales. The old proprietor turned a spigot on a wooden cask and the ale flowed into two dented tin tankards.

She sat on a wooden stool at a pocked table. Michael plunked down the tankards, brimming with foam.

The taste of medieval ale stirred her memory. Bitter and warm, it stung like malt Scotch. But it hit the spot.

"Ah, just what I needed." She smiled at him, marveling at how much he resembled her Mike from back home. She couldn't wait to return and tell him she'd met him in Kilkenny, in his past life, and even then the chemistry between them sizzled! "Michael, do you believe we've all lived past lives?" she blurted as he settled across from her.

He blinked in surprise, wrapped his fingers around his tankard and gazed into the suds. "I can't say I disbelieve." He looked at her and their eyes met. "Our spirits need go somewhere. I've been many places I feel I've visited before. I mean long before. But 'tis merely a feeling. I've never had proof I'd visited these places in past lives."

She smiled. "Ah, a kindred soul." But holding onto that thread of skepticism. Just like her Mike. "We believe very strongly in an afterlife, we Druids. And a beforelife, of course. Trust those strange feelings, Michael. You get them for a reason. We've all been here before." She took another cautious sip of ale.

"And how do you Druids know for certain?" he challenged.

"Places I've never been look familiar to me. Sometimes I can tell what's behind a closed door or inside a locked chest. Sometimes I meet people I feel I've known afore. And sometimes their names are the same."

"And did you know a Michael afore me?" He lifted his tankard.

"Aye, I certainly did," she said. "And I see him in you, body and soul."

"I hope he was kind to you." An amused smile played on his lips.

"More than you'll ever know," she spoke from her heart. "We should never be sad to leave our loved ones. Because we will be together again."

"Is that what you'll tell Brona and Margaret to comfort them?" The smile wavered.

Taken by surprise, she paused. "Aye, I can. But I know not if they'll believe me. I should let them know I'm not going only as an herbal healer, but as a spiritual healer as well."

"I know, dear one. And you're grand at it."

"Why, thank you." Taken off guard by the flattery, her hands fluttered about her throat. "'Tis a gift, Michael. I try to make the most of what I've been given. Do you think they'll be delirious? Will they know me?"

He shook his head. "I know not how bad they are yet. But Father Farley is calling for as many healers as he can find round here. I came out to you to save him the bother. I fear he'll be running to and fro administering last rites. That's what happened last time, remember? We were wee nippers. The sweat swept away nearly half the village." His eyes took on a faraway look, into the distant past.

She took his word for it. "Aye, it was horrid. I wish I could've done something then."

He laughed. "When we were but six? I know you're gifted, but I hardly believe you knew it then."

She gazed through the window. A cart rumbled by. "I knew I was an odd lass. I had visions, I heard voices, I made contact with the departed. I had vivid dreams, and still do. But it started very young. When I discovered Druidism I found my true calling."

"How'd you actually discover it? Growing up, we didn't dare explore any other religion or tradition or belief, only the Holy Catholic church. In my family, anyway." He took a swig of ale and wiped his lips.

"I met some Druids whilst traveling across Ireland, when I went away to study." She took another sip of her ale. "I stayed at an inn near Dublin. 'Twas full of Druids celebrating the summer solstice. They were my kindred souls, so I took a detour and joined them. I never looked back." That was the absolute truth. She had gone there in her own time as a grad student. "I worship the earth that sustains me, the trees and plants and flowers that give me life."

He nodded and smiled, so much like her Mike it scared and comforted her at the same time. "Sounds simple and basic. But for now," he tipped his tankard back and drained it. "We'd best carry on. We needed this refreshment, but we mustn't tarry overlong."

After one more timid sip, she left the nearly full tankard on the table.

Leaving the pub, she took a last look around. It hadn't survived to her century, but many others had. And they sure hadn't changed much.

****

They reached a stone cottage and Michael helped her dismount. He pushed the door open without knocking. "They cannot rise to answer it," he said.

She tied the reins to a post and followed him inside. Wooden chairs and a spinning wheel crowded the central room. Dry rushes covered the floor. Breathing in stale sweat and sickness, she pressed her hand to her nose.

A low doorway led to the kitchen, strewn with rotting vegetable peels and piles of rubbish. She gagged at the sight of a bloodied pig carcass lying in the hearth. "They need someone to help them here, Michael. I'll send Petronilla over, but they need a nurse as well."

"There are none to be found, and the well-to-do have already fled. Were it not for you, Brona and Margaret would have no hope of surviving this malady."

He led her across the kitchen to a bedchamber. A middle-aged woman and a teenaged girl lay on narrow beds. The girl slept, her chest rising and falling, a purplish burn mark on her left arm. Burns were so common in these times, from cooking over open fires.

The older woman sat up and coughed into a grimy cloth.

"Brona, how d'you fare? I've brought Alice."

Michael approached the sick woman, but Kylah held back, trying to pluck up the courage to take another step. God forbid if she brought the sweating sickness back home. How could she ever explain that to her primary care physician?

"Alice, thank the Lord you're here." Brona blessed herself. "I've been praying, is all I can do."

"You keep praying, but I'm glad to help, Brona." She physically pushed herself up to the sickbed. "I've brought coriander for your fever, rosemary for the infection. And to further speed your recovery, I also brought my special moonsbane." She held out her dark blue bottle. "This is a very rare herb, used only for the most serious of illnesses. Camma, a Druid priestess, gifted me with some seeds when I became a full Druid. I grew my own in a secret corner of my garden. I must keep it in the bottle so it won't be exposed to sunlight. I am the only Druid in Ireland who possesses it. The wrong dosage of this herb is lethal, but you need not fear my making any mistakes," she added.

"I thank you, Alice, you're my angel, and I trust

you with my life…what's left of it. I'll drink whatever you see fit to give me."

"I'm no angel, Brona, I'm mortal as you. I just happen to know which herbs to combine and which ones not to. Take these in a brew and we'll get you and Margaret on your feet. How is the colleen?" She looked over at the girl.

Whew, what a relief. She's still breathing.

"She caught it first, likely at Mass. Then folk fled like mad. My son Crispin left for business in London a mere day afore poor Maggie took to her bed." She looked over at her slumbering daughter. "I thank the Lord above for sparing Crispin." Brona's glad expression of thanks turned into a sneer. "But Father Ledrede closed up the church and fled."

"Ain't that just like the coward he is," Michael muttered. "And when he returns, likely he'll denounce those who stayed to help as witches performing magic." He headed for the doorway. "I'll fetch you some water to cool you down and for Alice to brew the herbs."

Ledrede. Kylah knew that name. Of course! The bishop who accused Alice of witchcraft. So he was the priest here, and fled his congregation at the first sign of sickness. It made her all the more determined to find out how Alice had handled her case.

"Brona, you'll rally in no time." Now over her initial hesitation, Kylah leaned over and lay a hand on Brona's burning forehead. Her drenched chemise clung to her hot skin. Sweat stained the pillowcase and the muslin rag that served as a makeshift sheet.

Michael returned with a bowl of water and a cloth. "I drew a few pails from the well. 'Tis in a pot in the kitchen."

Kylah dipped the cloth into the water and dabbed Brona's face. The woman shuddered.

She stood and turned to Michael. "I'll start brewing. Please keep an eye on the ladies."

She went back into the kitchen, averting her eyes from the filth and the fetid carcass in the hearth. Stomach churning, she managed to light a fire and boil the water in an iron cauldron. She measured her herbs—with her special moonsbane—into the pot. As she stirred with a splintered wooden spoon, she wondered when Brona or Margaret had washed last. She'd have to get Petronilla to make some soap.

She found two earthenware beakers on a shelf, and with cheesecloth as a strainer, poured her remedy into the beakers. Michael entered the kitchen and she handed him one. "Give this to Brona. Has the daughter woken yet?"

"No, best let her be," he said. "I've kept Brona cool with the water, but it needs be changed."

"All right, but first, let's get this in her." She led the way.

When she entered the bedchamber, the odors assaulted her all over again. "Brona, have you any soap?" she had to ask, putting politeness and tact aside. "Bathing will speed up your recovery and you'll feel better for it."

"Soap?" Her brow furrowed as she tried to remember. "I made some last summer, but haven't had any need for it since. Maggie may've bought some for her wedding eve bath. When she wakes I'll ask her. But it might be back at her cottage."

"Margaret is married?" Kylah blurted.

Michael cast her a puzzled glance, and she wanted

to bite her tongue off. What had she said?

"You know she wed John LePoer last June," Brona informed her with a questioning look. "You couldn't attend because you were too busy at the inn. You're fortunate in your short memory, lass. I wish mine were."

"Oh, of course, now I remember!" She held the cup to Brona's lips, confident she could slide out of this. "I'm just so preoccupied, and the inn being so busy, I completely forgot. How are the newlyweds faring?" Not too well, she expected, if Margaret was here and not with her husband.

Brona sipped and grimaced.

"Come now, Brona, drink the whole thing."

"It tastes putrid." She sputtered.

"I know, but you have to drink it all. Hold your nose if you have to." Kylah wished *she* could.

Brona took another sip, and another, resting her head against the pillow after each concentrated effort. She took the cup from Kylah and clutched it, her hands trembling. Kylah kept her grip on it just in case.

"Her husband is in London peddling his wool to the rich lords. He boasted about selling some to King Edward, but it's all twaddle and bosh." She scowled as if speaking of it left a bad taste in her mouth.

"Well, the luck o'the Irish may be with him on this venture," Kylah replied, to keep the conversation going.

"Alice, I know John LePoer in greater depth than everyone, and he's a rogue through and through." Brona sneered. "His selling wool is merely a sideline. 'Tis his vile schemes that stuff his pouches."

John LePoer? That was the same name as Alice's fourth husband, whose murder she was tried for! Could there be another with the same name? Here in this hamlet? His son, maybe? Oh, how she hoped!

Brona lifted her head to glance over at her daughter. "He cheats on my Maggie, he's taken mistresses since the day after the wedding." Brona scowled. "As a moneylender he extorts coin from poverty stricken folk till they can offer only blood, but they always go back for more. As a soothsayer, he bilks poor souls out of their meagre coin by claiming he's reading their stars. Why they don't see beyond his fakery and flubdubbery I'll never know." She coughed. "And they thank him for it."

Kylah looked away so Brona wouldn't see the surprise on her face. That's exactly what Ted did—he created detailed astrology charts for loyal clients who clung to his every word—and for good reason. His accuracy rate was astounding. But he charged only $10 a reading, and donated it all to the Wounded Warrior Project.

"An astrologer and moneylender, is he?" Kylah took the cup of water Michael gave her and put it to Brona's lips. "With his bilk—earning so much money, hasn't he provided Margaret with a comfortable life?" Kylah asked.

Brona shook her head. "Na. He spends it on his *uisce beatha.*"

Kylah was thankful she knew some Gaelic. "He spends his ill-gotten gains on whiskey? Is he a drunkard?"

"I've seen him sober—once. I loathe John LePoer, by all that is holy, I despise him. I wish it were him who got this disease, not us. He doesn't deserve to live. I wish him a slow agonizing death." Brona spat, her eyes angry slits.

Kylah's eyes grew wide at this outburst.

"Does Margaret know about John's philandering and nefarious schemes?" Kylah asked.

"Aye, but what's she to do? Divorce him? The Church will never allow it, and she wouldn't dream of it. The word is a curse to the dear lass. She lives with it, takes John into her bed when he comes back from his bilking and boozing and carousing." She forced another sip of brew and dribbled some onto her chin. Kylah wiped it away.

"Sometimes people change, Brona, maybe he'll have an attack of guilt and turn honest." Kylah tried to encourage her.

Michael threw her an amused glance, as if to say 'good job' but she rambled on.

"Maggie should leave him, that will give him a kick in the britches. Not divorce him, that's what he wants. Let him tend to his own cooking and cleaning and mending." Brona's strained laugh turned into a hacking cough.

Kylah patted her on the back and asked Michael to fetch a cup of fresh water.

"My poor Maggie knew naught about LePoer when she married the cad. I warned her, I did. I took him aside and said, 'afore you wed my daughter, you'd best learn a respectable trade, dry out and stay dry.' But he never will. 'Tis in his blood, it is. As I wish this pestilence were." She coughed. "But he'll get his, by the rood, I know, as I live and breathe. He'll get his comeuppance. Someone will do him in. The good Lord knows he's got enough enemies."

"What does Margaret see in him?" Kylah asked.

"Her feelings for him be more motherly than wifely. She cared for him when he suffered with fever, she nursed his wee lad through divers bouts of sickness. But they share a love of storytelling, dancing and song, and she overlooks his sins," she rasped.

Kylah drank this all in, knowing that she would come across John LePoer, maybe not on this visit, but on the next. "Worry not, Brona. What we reap we sow. He'll get his. Margaret will be just fine." She glanced over at the girl, beginning to stir.

Kylah went over to the other sickbed. "Hello, Margaret."

"Alice." She held out her hand and Kylah grasped it. "You are an angel. You've come to save us."

"I'm no angel, lass. Michael, fetch me more of that brew if you please." She gestured at him.

Margaret wasn't quite as sick, and Kylah hoped a fast recovery was in order, due to her youth and stage of illness. She couldn't have been a day over sixteen, and married to that cad! Kylah tried not to blanch when she remembered Alice married a John LePoer. So what would happen to Margaret? She didn't want to guess. All she knew was that the girl wasn't going to die of the sweat now.

"Michael, let's get them fed and give them some strength. Ladies, keep drinking the brew and we'll be back with a hearty repast from the market."

Margaret groaned. "Oh, the thought of food is the devil's own agony!"

"You need eat if you want to recover." She plumped up Margaret's smelly feather pillow. She might be able to re-enter a past life, but a miracle worker? Not quite.

Diana Rubino

****

On the way to market, Kylah wondered out loud, "Michael, if John LePoer is such a cheat and a cad and a drunkard, why did Margaret marry him?"

"He's nowhere the rogue Brona makes him out to be. No one, including Father Ledrede, has seen him with another woman. He's a faithful husband. Likes his *uisce beatha*, he does, staggers home on occasion, but tis always home he goes. He's a moneylender, but a fair one. He's never cheated anyone out of a groat, including me. And his fortunetelling is right on the money. She'll say aught to drag his name through the peat bogs."

"So why did she tell me these terrible lies about him?" Now she wondered how mentally stable Brona was.

"She spews all this hatred round the realm because he took her little Maggie away from her. She's attached to that lass like a yoke to an ox and hates anyone who dares threaten that bond. Including the man who rescued her from spinsterhood."

"So John isn't such a scoundrel after all." That relieved her. Maybe Alice married him for the same nurturing reasons.

"Isn't such a what?" Michael asked, his eyes questioning.

"Oh—scoundrel." She cringed. Yikes, the word hadn't yet entered the language. "Just a term I picked up from some foreign visitors to the inn. On a pilgrimage from the south of England, I believe. Must be local dialect." Whew, she got out of that one!

A young man galloped toward them, his hair streaming in the breeze. Michael halted in his tracks.

152

"This is my brother's stable lad," he said. "Hugh! What brings you here?"

The lad reined his panting horse in next to them. "My lord, the whole of Caragh Village is stricken with plague. It started near Dublin. The sickness is fast spreading west, and your brother, my lord—your brother passed last eve. I'm terribly sorry, my lord. I hate to bring such bad tidings. He lasted but two days. I immediately departed to come here."

Kylah laid a hand on Michael's shoulder. "I'm so sorry."

"Poor Eamon." Michael's voice broke. "The lad never had a chance."

"Nay, my lord." Hugh shook his head, eyes downcast. "He was one of the first to perish."

"Where are the victims being interred?" Michael asked.

"At first, they got proper Christian burials, but—" Hugh stammered and looked away. "The graveyard is overflowing. Now they bury them in a pit outside of town. Carts collect the dead, thrice a day." He regained some composure and looked back at Michael. "Eamon perished afore all this, he's buried in your family plot."

"Thank God." She blessed herself.

Each man stayed mired in his own thoughts and emotions for several minutes. Kylah closed her eyes and said a prayer for all the victims as fear's cloying grip closed in on her.

"First the sweat, now this. I need collect my thoughts. Thank you for bringing me this news, however tragic." Michael fished a coin out of his pouch and handed it to the lad.

"No hardship, my lord. I am journeying to the

midlands, where some of my kin reside. I urge you to escape here and board the first boat across the sea afore the entire land withers and dies."

Michael nodded. "Thank you, I shall heed that sage advice."

The lad tipped his hat, tugged on his reins and galloped off in a cloud of dust.

Her fingers tightened around the horse's reins. "Brona and Margaret have enough medicine to get them through a bout of the sweat, but the plague—" She tensed. "You know how that spreads. Like wildfire."

"I know." He raised his head to the heavens. "Alice, I'd best leave Ireland altogether, as Hugh is doing. I know you have no remedies for plague. Scotland should be safe. Will you go with me, bring Petronilla and your other servers?"

Kylah shook her head. "I can't, Michael, I needs run the inn. I can't leave travelers stranded. Did he say 'tis spreading to the west or from the west?"

"Spreading west. 'Tis not reached here yet, but your village may be stricken already. Plague spreads its ugly wings within hours."

She gripped the reins as if hanging on for life. "But how much can happen in the one day since we got here? It couldn't yet have claimed victims, surely."

He let out a sad chuckle. "That's what I've always loved about you, Alice. Your undying hopefulness."

"I'm not as hopeful as you think." If only he knew how the possibility of plague terrified her. She had no antibiotics, no modern drugs. She had to get home. "Naught will happen to me if you bring me back to the inn. I promise."

"And how do you know all this?" His voice took

on a sardonic tone. "Are you a seer, too, and never told me? Beholding visions of a bright and rosy future together?"

"Don't ask me how I know, but I do." She knew Alice didn't perish in this epidemic. And neither did Michael. "We'll be fine, trust me. I'm going back to my inn. You needn't tarry with me, just escort me back, then go whither you will."

He faced her with a resigned sigh. "Very well. We shall head back there, and what will be will be."

They went to market, purchased some fresh vegetables and fruit, then returned to Brona's cottage.

Kylah gave Brona and Margaret more of the brew to drink. "You will recover hastily," she assured them. "I wish I could stay, but must return to my inn. I'm sending Petronilla back here to cook and care for you. I'll give her enough money to buy some meat."

"Bless you, lass, I thank the Lord for you." Brona clasped her hands together as if in prayer. "I'll be happy to welcome Petronilla back. But I can't pay her, mind. You know she left me to work for you because I'd run out of funds to pay her."

"Of course you needn't pay her. And when you needs her back, ask me." Kylah's heart broke with pity for this poor woman, unable to keep a housemaid. She couldn't leave here without righting that.

"You do go on." A flush of color bloomed on Brona's cheeks.

That greatly relieved Kylah.

"But, Alice…" She grabbed Kylah's sleeve. "You," she whispered. "You and Michael…" she sputtered.

She leaned over Brona. "Aye, Michael's here too."

"You and him, stay together. Make sure he takes care o' you," came out so low, Kylah barely heard her.

"Me and him?"

"He does…does love you, Alice. I can see it. I always have." She coughed. "He will propose, I know sure as I lie here abed. So please do him the honor—and marry the kind soul."

She knew Michael Artson wasn't one of Alice's four husbands. Unless she married him at the very end, after vanishing from history.

Michael approached Kylah and stood at her side.

She grasped his hand. It warmed her, comforted her. She didn't repeat what Brona had said about them marrying. Maybe on the next visit here from the twenty-first century…with Mike.

****

She and Michael stopped at that same pub for supper. But the door was locked tight. She didn't see an X painted on the door, as plague victims' doors were branded when anyone inside died. No X on the back door either.

"Maybe nobody knows they're dead yet," he said.

"It spread this fast?" she asked him.

"My lady, I'm surprised our skin doesn't crawl with buboes."

She shuddered. "Don't say that. Let's just get back to the inn. I have no appetite anyway."

"Truth be told, nor do I," he said.

She mounted and they continued on.

As they traveled down the narrow road, stars twinkled overhead. The moon hid behind gauzy veils of dancing clouds, beaming enough to show the way. The horse clip-clopped through the darkness as they passed a cluster of cottages, quiet and shut tight for the night.

How many victims perished already?

They reached her inn, and he helped her dismount. With the need for human contact, she gave him a longer hug than she'd planned.

He followed her around the back, over the stepping stones, to her private entrance. It was open, the way she'd left it.

"I leave it open in case someone needs return late. Mayhap I shouldn't be so trusting," she added as foreboding crept over her. Her flesh crawled.

"Worry not about that now." He took a candle down from her kitchen rafters, lit it and handed it to her.

"Michael, I'd appreciate if you can stay the night. I mean—in one of the other rooms," she hastily added, lest he get the wrong idea. The candle cast an eerie glow. "Petronilla and the other servers have gone home."

"Did you have patrons staying when we took our leave?" he asked.

"A few. Take the large room in the front," she offered. She grasped the banister and climbed the creaky steps.

The inn sat quiet. As quiet as death.

But she put that morbid thought out of her mind as she tiptoed into her chamber, holding the candle to light her way.

She undressed in the candle's flickering flame and pulled on her night shirt.

Exhausted, she collapsed on the bed, a jumble of thoughts whirring through her mind. She wanted to help those plague victims, but couldn't dare risk dying here in the fourteenth century, never to return home. If that happened, she would change history. Alice Kyteler wouldn't live past 1324. She knew about the 'going back in time and killing your grandfather' theory, but she wasn't willing to risk changing history by coming here on an unscheduled visit and dying.

As she thrashed around, unable to get comfortable, she wondered how Mike was doing at home. She hoped he wasn't too alarmed that he hadn't come with her. She dreaded the thought of never returning to him. No, she had to send Michael Artson on his way and leave here before the unthinkable did happen—before she disrupted too many people's destinies by dying here.

At least she wasn't sweating.

Yet.

Chapter Fourteen

Kilkenny, Ireland, 1324

Kylah opened her eyes to a tarnished pewter morning. She had a good night's sleep since she and Michael returned to her inn last eve, but yesterday's ordeal drained her. Kneading her stiff neck, she slipped off the bed. She yawned, covering her mouth with her hand.

Michael entered the chamber with a cup and placed it on the table beside her bed. "Ah, I see you're awake. Here's some strong tea. I'll mix you some eggs, and you rest," he offered. "I'll stay behind instead of fleeing the plague. I'd rather be here with you and take my chances."

"Would you do that for me?" She looked into his weary eyes, sensing the deep devotion. Maybe Alice did marry Michael at some future date. Just like her and Mike back home…

"I'd rather be here with you than flee as a coward." He kissed her forehead.

"No need to rustle up a meal, my dear, I've still no appetite." She cupped his face in her palms and gave his lips a light kiss. "Go tend to your business and I'll see you in a few hours."

He nodded, his gaze lingering on her. "Ta then."

As she stepped outside, the sun brightened the sky

to the hazy azure of a newborn day. She glanced out at the deserted road and gathered her herbs. A sudden finality closed in on her.

The plague is coming to claim us.

She had to get out of here. Of course she'd return to this century on a future visit, to learn Alice's fate. But now she belonged back home.

She went into a pantry and drank the mixture in three quick gulps. "I wish to return to the minute my soul left my body to come here. I wish my soul to leave my living body and transcend the time continuum to enter the living body of Kylah McKinley."

She finished with the Lord's Prayer in Gaelic. *"Ár n-Athair atá ar neamh, Go naofar d'ainim, Go dtagfadh do ríocht, Go ndéantar do thoil ar an talamh mar a dhéantar ar neamh. Ár n-arán laethúil tabhair dúinn inniu, agus maith dúinn ár bhfiacha mar a mhaithimidne dár bhféichiúna féin Ach ná lig sinn i gcathú, ach saor sinn ó olc,* Amen."

Surrounded by silence, she closed her eyes. Her spirit drifted away.

Chapter Fifteen

Kylah woke as dawn eased through the metal-mesh window.

Am I still in the distant past or between worlds? And what happened to Mike?

She shook the fog from her mind and turned to lie on her side. The old frame creaked as she sat up. She released a whoosh of relief. A modern bed!

Forcing herself to believe Mike was home and safe, she grabbed her watch. Just after seven. She stood, stretched her aching muscles and paced her cell as though walking a treadmill. At the sight of a guard, she called out to him, "I need to make a call, please."

He let her out and led her down the hall to the phones. She entered the PIN they gave her and called Mike. His first words were, "Are you all right?"

"I'm fine, are *you* all right?"

"Yeah...it didn't work for me." His weary voice went on, "I went to the car and lay down, but I couldn't concentrate on anything, I was frantic that you wouldn't come out of it. After two hours, I gave up and went home, begging God you'd be okay."

"Mike, I have so much to tell you about my journey back in time." She struggled to keep the urgency out of her voice.

"You can tell me after you get out. I'll see you in the courtroom. I'll post bail and get you out of there by lunchtime." He paused. "I'm so damn glad you're all right. Gotta go, I'll see you soon."

Back in her cell, she lay down on the creaky bed and relived her journey to the past: bumpy dirt roads, billowing dust, the stench of sickness, waste and sewage. Breathing a heavy sigh, she almost didn't mind being locked up with indoor plumbing. Indulging herself, she closed her eyes and fantasized about Mike's lips on hers.

After an escort to the washroom, she shed her clothes and dropped them on the tile floor. The hot shower doused her in luxury, compared to that place in centuries past, where pails of cold water had to be heaved up a well. She still smelled the pungent odors, proof she'd physically been there.

Petra was waiting with a change of clothes, but she had to wear the orange jail-issued jumpsuit. At least it carried the faint fragrance of laundry detergent.

Feeling cleaner than she had since she'd made that journey, she imagined the terror Alice suffered, also accused of murder, but at the mercy of medieval zealots and kangaroo courts. Kylah shuddered. At least Massachusetts had no death penalty.

Stop!

With a smack to her head, she pushed these thoughts away. But a question haunted her:

Do I doubt Mike deep down?

The question seemed too terrifying for her befuddled brain right now.

With nothing to do but wait, she lay back down on the bed and closed her eyes, allowing herself another fantasy. In this one, they did much more than kiss.

****

Kilkenny, Ireland, 1324

Michael Artson knocked on the inn door and stepped inside. Alice ran up to him and threw her arms round his neck in greeting. He didn't return her enthusiasm.

She drew back. "What is amiss, Michael? You look troubled."

"Alice, I've come to tell you I need wed a lass from Ballyhale. She's with child." He shuffled his feet. "Mine."

She shunted her disappointment aside and dared not show it. "Well, for that I commend you," she forced a singsong tone. "I admire your honesty. You'll be a devoted da. And husband," she added.

He rubbed his temples. "We don't love each other, we just…" He looked up, searching the heavens. "I regret what might have been…" He trailed off and she didn't try to finish for him.

"There is no might have been," she answered. "Only what is."

****

Alice stood with her cuttings of lavender and wiped her free hand on her apron. Petronilla called her from the far end of her garden.

"Back here, lass."

Petronilla looked weary, for good reason. Besides running to and fro tending to Brona and Margaret, she carried out her marketing and cooking duties. "They're a trifle better, sitting up in bed longer now, and Margaret actually walked round the chamber. They're both regaining their strength, all the thanks to you."

"I'm so glad to hear that. Now you needs time to rest, dear one." Alice turned the lass round and herded

Diana Rubino

her up to the north facing chamber, the coolest. "I'll take over your duties till you regain your own strength."

"Nay, I won't let you down," Petronilla insisted, but flopped onto the bed with a throaty yawn.

"I won't hear of it. I'll go over there soon as I cut up more coriander and rosemary."

"Oh, nearly forgot to tell you, as I'm so tired." Petronilla propped herself up on an elbow. "John LePoer wishes to court you."

Alice blinked. "Court *me*? He's married to Margaret."

"Not anymore." Petronilla's lips spread in a grin. "He had his marriage to Margaret annulled."

Her jaw dropped. "Annulled? Whatever for?"

"You need ask him. Mayhap the marriage was never consummated. But he plans to call on you. Today."

"Today?" Alice went to sit next to her on the bed. "But I'm going to Brona's now."

"They're faring well enough. They don't need you right away." Her grin widened. "But John does."

"Oh, go to sleep." She swatted Petronilla on the rump and darted into her own chamber to ready herself for her caller.

As she braided her hair and wound it in a circlet round her head, she wondered: A bachelor and a widow. *How long will he take to pop the question?*
****

Two bailiffs escorted Kylah out to a patrol car. She slid into the back seat and gazed out the window as the car whizzed past historic houses, charming inns, antique shops... Her world.

As they approached the gray granite courthouse,

she fixed her eyes on the life-size bronze sculpture of Mercy Otis Warren, a Revolutionary heroine way ahead of her time. Clutching a book, she stood straight and tall. Kylah's eyes met the statue's penetrating gaze. "Give me strength, Mercy," Kylah whispered.

The front courthouse entrance was no longer used, so they drove down a side road and parked in the rear. Reporters hovered in clusters, microphones at the ready. Cameras clicked all around her as photographers followed on her heels.

"Mrs. McKinley!" A young reporter blocked her path. "How do you feel about being accused of murder?" She thrust a microphone in Kylah's face. Her police escorts pushed it away and led her inside. She had nothing to place in the bin at the metal detector, so they brought her straight into a courtroom.

Mike sat at the counsel table. She sobbed at the sight of him. She sat beside him, desperate for his touch.

But he only leaned toward her and whispered, "Out by lunchtime. Like I promised." He looked past her at the door.

As the bailiff announced, "All rise," she stood. Not having eaten much Barnstable County cuisine, she became dizzy as the room spun.

The clerk gave the judge a file.

The judge read it and addressed Mike. "How does your client plead to count one, a violation of section 382/928 of the Massachusetts Penal Code, first-degree murder?"

"My client pleads not guilty, Your Honor," Mike replied.

The judge said, "The preliminary hearing will be in

Diana Rubino

two weeks." He then explained the prosecution would have to establish that a crime had occurred and there was probable cause to believe she'd committed this crime. At the trial, the prosecution would have to show burden of proof...with her fate left to Mike's power of persuasion over the jury.

Mike stood. "May I address the issue of bail, Your Honor?"

The judge nodded. "State your position, counsel."

"The defense asks that bail be set at $500,000. My client has no past offenses, has been a model citizen of the community for the last fifteen years, has no history of violence. There is no probability that my client would be a flight risk."

She held her breath.

"Bail is set at $500,000." The judge banged his gavel. "This court is adjourned."

Mike leaned toward her. "He was more than generous. I'll go see my bail bondsman, and you'll be out of here by lunchtime—as I promised."

The bailiffs strode toward her.

"I can sleep in a real bed tonight?" she whispered to Mike before they clamped onto her arms.

"You can sleep in any bed you want tonight." Mike gave her a smile she was too nervous to return.

"And then what?" Her words rushed out.

"I know three other attorneys I want to team up with to work on your defense."

"The odds are against me, aren't they?" Her voice quivered.

"Forget odds. This isn't a poker game. You need a defense. Even if we never find the killer, I'm going to prove you innocent." He grasped her hand and she

166

clung to him.

The bailiffs stood on either side of her.

"See you in a bit and we'll go have a slap up meal." Mike's voice receded as they walked her out of the courtroom. "Everything will be all right. Have faith."

"Oh, do I ever," she whispered.

****

Back in her holding cell, she tore off the jumpsuit and slid back into her own jeans and shirt, inhaling her familiar patchouli perfume. Her energy drained, she lay down and closed her eyes, unable to get that journey to the fourteenth century out of her mind. She fell into an exhausted sleep.

The door rattled and swung open. A policeman stepped aside and Mike stood in the doorway. Still bleary-eyed, she focused on him.

"I posted your bail. Let's get out of here." He held out his hand.

She ran into his open arms. He held her tight and kissed her head, her cheeks, her neck, and finally, her lips.

"You okay?" His gaze locked with hers.

"Mike, I have so much to tell you! I went back to Alice's time. I'm sorry you didn't come with me—"

"Shh." He cut her off. "Don't say anything else until we're in the car. Come on, let's go."

A scattering of vehicles remained in the parking lot. "Man, I'm glad those media vultures are gone." He glanced around as they headed for his car. "They never let up. I'm walking to the entrance, they're shoving microphones in my face, 'How long have you known Mrs. McKinley? When does the trial begin? Do you believe she's innocent?'" he mimicked their nerve-grating cackle. "I didn't even give them the satisfaction of saying 'no comment,' which, by the way, is a comment," he added.

"They did that to me, too, on the way in," she said. "At least I had a police escort."

When they reached his car, he took her in his arms and their lips met in that toe-curling kiss she'd fantasized about.

"We'd better get going," he rumbled, "Before I take you right here."

He unlocked the car doors and they got in.

Buckling his seat belt, he said, "Like I said on the phone, I lay down in the back seat, waited and waited, but it just didn't work for me. I was too worried about you. So I went home, praying all the time that you'd be safe."

"I was fine." She gave him a reassuring nod and fastened her seat belt.

"Now tell me what happened. You're sure you weren't hallucinating? I've heard about some of these herbs, they're like those tripping mushrooms." He pushed the ignition button and backed out of the space.

She held her palm up as if taking an oath. "It's the God's honest truth. Sure as I'm sitting here, I went back to my life as Alice."

He cocked a skeptical brow. "So what happened?"

"Oh, God, it was…" She faltered, the words clogged in her throat, clamoring to escape. "What a horrible, reeking, filthy, deathly place, but at the same time it was so quiet, so serene, the sky so blue, the stars so brilliant."

He pulled out onto Route 6A. "What did you do

back there?"

First things first. "I treated two women with the sweating sickness and escaped the plague by a day or so."

"You mean bubonic plague?" His eyes darted over to her, then he focused back on the road. "How do you know you escaped?"

She laid a hand on his arm. "It hadn't reached Kilkenny yet. I'm fine. But I must get everything I can find on Alice. I have to dig deeper before I go back."

"Go back? What do you mean, go back?" He glanced at her again, his cheeks reddening. "Faith or no faith, you're messing with forces you know nothing about. Who knows how you transcend time warps to go back seven centuries? If it doesn't work, you'll be stuck there to relive your life back then—" He stopped as the car in front of him made a left turn. "I don't even know what I'm talking about." He ran a hand over his eyes.

"I know exactly what you're saying. It was the herbs, Mike. And they do work. They interact with my spirit and transport it to my previous life. Knowing I was Alice, I knew what the herbs could do. But more information will help me, because I know exactly what it's like to be Alice now, in Alice's time, how she felt about her environment, what her values were, what was in her mind, in her heart."

"And what did you find out about all that?" he asked.

"She was a loving, compassionate human being who put others' needs before her own, at the risk of her own health and life." Kylah couldn't help but smile.

"Just like you," he said.

"Well—of course. She was me. I was her. And

Mike—" A surge of happiness lightened her heart. "You were there, too, as Michael Artson. We were close friends and I believe we eventually got together in that life—because it turned into love. That's why, if the unthinkable happened, and I got stuck there and couldn't come back, it wouldn't be so bad, because you'd be there with me."

"But you wouldn't be *here* with *this* me." He jabbed a thumb at his chest.

She faltered, sighing. "Then we're back to your traveling there with me. But first you have to become a true believer. Is that possible?" Her voice rose on a note of hope.

"I need to think about it more. Where would you like to go? I mean now, in this century," he added. "We can just sit on the beach for a while. It's your call."

"The last place anyone could find us."

He nodded. "I know exactly where that is."

They sat in silence as he drove another five minutes and entered the gates of Woodside Cemetery.

****

Dominic rubbed his hands together in glee after what he just saw—Kylah and her squeeze in a passionate lip lock. And they didn't even wait till they got into the car!

He slid out from behind the wheel of his car and bounded up the courthouse steps. Spotting a bailiff exiting the courtroom, he extended his hand. "Hello, my good sir. I'm Mrs. McKinley's uncle, and couldn't get here in time. Flat tire. Did she make bail?"

"Why don't you ask her?" the bailiff retorted, pulling his arm free.

"She left. I told you, I got here late. I need to know

now, my darling niece, my late departed sister's only girl. Please, sir, don't keep an old man hanging like this. I have a heart condition." He patted his chest with his right hand, like a pledge of allegiance, to demonstrate that.

"Bail was set at half a million."

Dominic blinked as time froze. He kick-started his brain out of shock mode. "Oh! She's free on bail! God bless you, my good man." He pumped the bailiff's hand.

Shaking his head, he strode out, baffled.

He met Brooke at a café across the street. She sat waiting for him, sipping from a cardboard cup. "Free on bail, I'll be double wicked darned." He forced his eyes to stay on hers and not stray down to her teasing hint of cleavage. "Newsworthy yet?"

"Oh, you bet," she purred. "Out on bail, is she? We'll see what intruding minds want to know about that."

At her reply, a slow wink and a sultry curl of her shiny lips, a surge went straight to his loins. He grabbed her cup and took a sip from the opposite side, without the lipstick stain.

"Think of what an opportunity this is." She took her cup back. "We can watch her every move now, we couldn't do that when she was jailed. Just because she's free on bail doesn't mean she'll be acquitted. We've got the trial to go yet. And a lot more reporting to do. And a lot of ratings to rake in."

"You're right as rain, Brookie, all I could think of was 'free' and it startled me. That Richardson guy defending her isn't exactly Clarence Darrow. The evidence—and her heedless choice of counsel—are stacked against her. And from a reckless display I just saw in the parking lot, looks as if she chose her counsel with another part of her female anatomy than her brain." He smirked.

"You mean she and her lawyer are…" Brooke trailed off with a raised brow.

"Oh, yeah, I witnessed it first-hand. It's not gossip anymore. Just caught them in a liplock. Adds another dimension if you ask me." He guffawed. "So what's the next step?"

"We get a crew out to her house and start asking questions. Then we start interviewing neighbors. We'll track down the murdered husband's biker friends who showed up at the wake, that blue-haired matron you were cozying up to…" She trailed off and gave him a sideways glance.

"Oh, Enid Streetman? She's a nice lady, don't bother her."

"Who is she?" she probed, her gaze staring daggers.

"Ted's ex-mother-in-law. She's raising her grandchildren since her daughter committed suicide. She's been through enough." Fondness for Enid softened his heart.

"All right, I won't." She gave in as her eyes narrowed to mascara-coated slits. But she still looked the way he felt—hungry for a meaty story the scandal-starved public could sink its fangs into.

"But I won't waste a minute." She reached into her purse and plucked out her cell phone, slid it out of its leather case and tapped on a contact name.

****

Mike stopped his car in Woodside Cemetery and

cut the engine. She slid out and raised her face skyward as the breeze whispered through the leaves. Hand in hand, they strolled the landscaped grounds among rows of tombstones, weather beaten with the ravages of time.

She led him to a familiar stone lying flat on the ground. "On every visit here, I kneel before this tiny grave. Infant Healy, daughter of Ebenezer and Hanna, 1797. May 8. Five months. These are my ancestors, Mike. Ebenezer and Hanna Healy were my great-grandparents seven generations ago. Healy means 'artistic, scientific.' The Gaelic equivalent is 'ó hÉalaighthe'. My mother taught me that name before I learned my own."

He knelt beside her as she drew her hand over the rough, worn surface, her fingers dipping into the etchings of letters and numbers that marked her ancestors' short time on Earth.

"Are they all resting here?" he asked.

"No, some are here, some in Boston, some went back to Ireland and died there. I hoped to find a connection to Alice Kyteler, but we're not related. We have an undeniable connection, but it's not blood." She stood and brushed small clods of dirt from her knees.

He rose beside her and she clasped his hand. It felt so alive after the hard stone.

They left the children's plot and she led him deeper into the graveyard. She stopped at a stone with a curved top, leaning over as if too old and tired to stand upright. They knelt together. Covered in yellow moss, the gravestone stood in a circle of brown earth.

"In memory of Mr. Ebenezer Gage. He died November 1, 1830, aged 78 years and three days. Remember me as you pass by, as you are now so once was I, as I am now so you must be, prepare for Death and follow me," she read out loud.

"Old Ebenezer didn't have much hope of an afterlife," Mike commented.

"Maybe not then, but now…" She sighed. "I'm sure he's in a better place. I always read it for that very reason, because I know how wrong he was."

"Whatever you say." Mike thrust his hands into his pockets as they walked. He gave her an encouraging smile.

She headed for another familiar soul, the young Mercy Hallet. "She only made it to thirty." Another leaning headstone, its curved top pitted and decayed, it read: "In memory of Mercy Hallet, wife of Randal Hallet. She died September 8, 1831 in the thirtieth year of her age. Thirty was middle-aged in those days," she said. "I always wonder what could have ended Mercy's short life—childbirth? Smallpox?" She took a deep breath of the cleansing air. "I'm not looking forward to all the dirty looks and snickers at the trial—and I'm not talking ghosts here. I mean from the live ones."

"Ignore the live ones," Mike said as they moved on, circling gravestones with grinning skulls etched into them. "You're innocent until proven guilty. What's more, a judge has freed you on bail, showing the public that you're not a flight risk, or any kind of danger. You're innocent, so you're entitled to live an innocent life."

She shook her head. "But I'm sure that's not how they'll see it."

"Who's this ubiquitous *they* and what right do *they* have to judge you?" His rising voice cut into the peaceful quiet.

"They are the public, my customers, anybody who knows about this and rushes to judgment."

They stood at another tiny stone, the lettering barely readable.

"Joshua G. Thacher, son of Edward and Lydia T. 1829—May 19. One month. Look at this. A grief stricken mother stood on this spot and buried her infant, probably not even recovered from his birth. So sad." She moved on and he followed her.

"I've never known you to care what fools think," he said.

"I don't, but I've never been accused of murder before."

"I've seen how prejudgment can condemn the innocent. Rational thinking people know you're innocent until proven guilty." Mike put his arm around her. "The others can go to hell."

She recoiled. "I never heard you talk like that."

"I know, but that's how I feel. I get involved in my cases to the point of obsession, and since this is you, I can't find words to tell you how I feel about this. My own fate is on the line. I couldn't be more emotionally tangled up if it were me on trial. I just want you to know that, in case you didn't already."

She turned to face him. "I know, and I appreciate it. But I've worked hard to gain a good reputation around here, a respected store owner, helper of people who need their homes freed of unwelcome spirits, all that. Now Ted is gone..." She closed her eyes and pictured Ted alive, his gray ponytail and stubble-covered chin, slumped in his wheelchair, dreaming of what might have been. "I don't want to put on a brave face or strut around like a diva. Or go around convincing people I'm innocent. I don't give a damn about all that. All I want to do is find out who killed him. That means trips back to Alice's time—the year of her trial, and reliving what she went through." She gazed up at the clouds sailing by on the breeze that rustled the leaves around them.

"You'd better not," he warned. "You need to show up at your own trial every day."

"Mike, the two days that passed in the fourteenth century were just hours here, in the middle of the night. I can leave and come back and no one will know my spirit transcended this dimension to enter another. No one ever will know except you and I." She knelt and ran her fingertips over three tiny gravestones huddled together in a row, "Baby Murray" etched into all three.

"I wish you wouldn't do any more time travel." His voice wavered as he knelt beside her. "It's too dangerous. I wanted to go back with you because I can't live without you, and I can't live without you here either."

His entreaty tore at her heart. "But I have to go back. Just one more time." She stood, brushing her hands on her jeans. "Going back and living her life again will tell me what happened then, and will tell me what is happening now."

"Kylah, we're not married yet, and when we are, I can't order you around, so I'm asking you, please don't go back there again." His eyes pleaded. "Okay, I'll admit it. I'm begging you." His tone softened.

"I need to." She gathered him in her arms. "You can still come with me."

He looked away, shoulders slumped in defeat. "You're as stubborn as a...cat."

"Not stubborn. Determined. Let's just take one thing at a time."

They continued winding among the tombstones.

"I'm moving into the upstairs of the store. It's got ghosts, but at least they're friendly." She smiled, thinking of her mischievous little friends.

He shot her a look over the rims of his specs. "How do you know that?"

"I told you it's haunted. Sometimes I hear marbles rolling around, sometimes I hear giggling. They're playful children. They just like to hang out and play."

"Won't that upstairs be too small after living in your big house?" he asked.

"I can adapt. I don't think of that big house as home anymore. There's nothing for me there now. Not even the garden. I'll grow another one—in our house, when we're married."

"It can't happen too soon for me." He gave her a one-arm hug. "So, with those little ghosties playing hide-and-go-seek over your store, you won't be alone after you close up shop. And it'll be convenient to the store, too. You won't even have to drive to work. In that regard, I'm glad you're out of the house." He stopped and faced her. "I'll help you move. Then I have to get back to work on your case, I can't waste a minute."

"Can you waste a minute to hug me?"

He opened his arms and they shared an embrace, the only two living souls among all the departed.

"Of course, my love. I'm all yours now," he whispered into her ear. "And just like in the fairy tales, hokey as it sounds, we will live happily ever after."

She wanted to laugh, but it seemed disrespectful

showing any form of amusement here. "From anybody else it would be hokey, but from you, it's very romantic."

"I wasn't trying to be either." He winked and squeezed her hand.

She led him to a stone bench inscribed with the name "DiMartile." A stone angel about a foot high sat at the edge of the bench, her arms crossed in her lap.

Kylah sat and patted the bench next to her for him to sit. She placed her other hand atop the angel's head. "For the first time in my life, I feel helpless. I lost control of my destiny. Just like these poor babies who never had a chance at life, snatched away by some horrible disease, their grieving parents standing here to see them lowered into the ground. That little Healy girl didn't even live long enough to have a name. She'll be 'infant Healy' for all of eternity, with those three Murray babies."

"I'm steering the ship for you right now," Mike said. "Go about your usual business."

She stood, clasped his hand, and they strolled farther. She halted before a tremendous tree with multiple intertwined trunks. "Look at this. Isn't she magnificent? I adore this tree. I've spent many a day and evening sitting under her. I feel a strong connection to her... I talk to her sometimes, and I know she's listening. After all, trees are alive." Taking a breath, she hesitated, wondering whether to tell him something else. She decided to share. "I call her Kallie. It's Gaelic for 'from the forest'. I gave her a name beginning with K like my own name."

He squinted up into the sunlight-sprinkled branches. "Yowee. Kallie must be an old timer. It—er, *she* must've seen the Revolutionary War. I've never seen a tree with all these twisted trunks like that. Is she an oak?"

Kylah smiled at how fast Mike adapted to calling Kallie 'she.' "Yes, she's a swamp chestnut oak. The mighty oak is the most sacred of trees to Druids." She lovingly ran her hand down Kallie's rough brittle bark. "Folks of ages past worshipped oaks. Actually, the word 'Druid' is derived from the Greek for 'oak.' " She circled the wide trunk. "Oh, if Kallie could talk, what stories she could tell."

"How can trees teach us about time? Except to show us how long they can outlive us." His tone grew serious, thoughtful.

She answered, "Druids believe when you've come upon a grove of oak, ash and hawthorn, you've encountered a place where faeries congregate." She captured a leaf and circled her fingertips over its back and front.

"Faeries in an old cemetery? I guess they're everywhere." He surprised her by reaching for her free hand. He pulled her to him and gave her a warm kiss.

She caught her breath as a spark of desire jolted her. "That was magical. I've never been kissed in a graveyard before."

"I'm sure your departed friends—and Kallie—will understand." He led her back in the direction of the car. "The faeries made me do it."

****

Mike pulled up to Kylah's garage door and cut the engine.

She stared at the house she shared with Ted. "I feel detached, as if I've never seen it before. I have no more feelings for this house." She cringed, as if the house harbored hostility toward her. "It's just a piece of real estate."

"Then you're sure to get yourself comfortable in the space over your store." His tone carried warmth and assurance.

"Oh, yeah." She pictured the former colonial tavern and smiled. "In a way it's home already, I spend so much time in the store. I can never come back and live here. It'll never be the same." She closed her eyes, shutting out the sight.

"I understand. I feel the same way about my house."

She looked over at him. "You're selling your house, too, aren't you?"

"Already listed it." He draped his hand over the steering wheel. "I told the realtor I'm a motivated seller and to put that in the listing. I just want to unload it."

She blinked in surprise. "You put it on the market even before you knew I'd marry you?"

"I knew you'd marry me."

His smile sent liquid fire through her.

She tilted her head. "How?"

His gaze intensified. "Deep down I knew we'd end—I mean, wind up together, somehow, someday."

That struck a chord echoing from the distant past. "That's just what Brona said about us back in the fourteenth century."

"Who's Brona?" he asked.

"The sick woman I tended to." She repeated Brona's prediction: "He does love you, Alice. I can see it. I always have. He will propose. So please do him the honor—and marry the kind soul."

"She said all that?" Mike's eyes became unfocused, as if he were drifting into deep thought.

She reached over and grasped his hand. "What is it, Mike? You look like you just saw a ghost."

"No, not a ghost." He shook his head. "Stranger than that."

She waited, but he sat in silence, looking lost in his thoughts. "Well, come on, what is it? You can tell me."

He scratched his arm and adjusted his glasses. "Not long ago, Ted told me something strange."

Her breath caught in her throat. "What?"

He captured her gaze. "He knew you and I would wind up together someday. I jumped in with, 'Well, Ted, our lives took different paths and it just didn't happen, and now that we're married to other people…' but he cut me off, told me to shut up and listen. Then he told me someday you and I would fall in love and get married. He seemed to be foretelling his own death, and knew what would happen afterwards."

She studied the wood grain of the dashboard. "That really is strange, because Ted never said anything like that to me. Where was I?"

"I don't know, in the kitchen, I guess. It wasn't a long conversation. We were talking about his stepkids, and somehow it just evolved. You know the way conversations go." He shrugged. "It just drifted. I don't know how he came out with it. Then he changed the subject just as fast, and we started talking about the Red Sox or something."

She released a deep breath. "I wonder how long he felt that way."

"He wasn't blind, Kylah." Mike clasped her hand.

"Yes, but to come out with something like that, it's

scary. Especially since it happened exactly that way in my past life…and yours," she added.

He glanced away. "That's another story."

"We can talk more later. Let me get some clothes and things and get out of here." She reached for the door handle.

"You got it." He hopped out of the car.

She started up the stairs and turned around to see him standing in the entry hall looking out the window. "It's okay, you can come up."

"You sure? You don't feel uncomfortable with me in your bedroom?"

"Not at all." She gestured for him to follow.

In her bedroom, she got out her luggage, a makeup case and a garment bag from her walk-in closet. Then she went over to her nightstand, slid the drawer open and took out some papers. "Ted liked to send me notes in code, 'message within a message' notes." She unfolded the first one he'd ever given her. Her eyes misted over. "This is how he proposed to me." She showed him the note. "See what it says here? 'I want you and me to be together and happy for the rest of our lives, you and me, Ted.' But certain letters are slanted just a bit more than the others. Those letters spell out a note within the note." She pointed out the *m* in 'me,' the *a* in 'happy.' the *r* in 'for,' the *r* in 'rest,' the *y* in 'you' and the word '*me*.' "It spells 'marry me.' " She closed her eyes, remembering that night.

"Hey, that's really neat." Mike leaned over to read it.

"Here's another one." I am *t*aking you on the va*c*ation of your dreams, to a place like now*h*ere else on Earth that you can *i*magine in our wildes*t* fantas*i*es!

"The slanted letters spell 'Tahiti.' He took me there on our second honeymoon."

Mike nodded. "Yeah, I remember when you went. You were so excited about that trip."

She folded the notes and slid them into her overnight bag. As she packed some more valuables, he glanced out the window. "There's a Lexus nosing down the street, slowing to a stop in front of the house. Here we go with the rubbernecks," he muttered, turned away and paced the room. "I swung by Market Basket the other day, and at the checkout I saw two of the tabloid rags with blaring headlines about your upcoming trial, 'Accused Husband-Killer Released on Half a Mil Bail' and some other garbage about 'Druid Ghost Hunter'. I bought them all, took them outside and dumped them in the trash bin."

"Thanks, Mike, I appreciate that. But I'm sure it hardly made a dent. I'm surprised Brooke Hill didn't jump us at the courthouse." Kylah capped her lilac cologne bottle and placed it in her cosmetic case.

"Brooke Hill from that tabloid TV show? She was there?" He shook his head, his tone swathed in disbelief.

She chose a gold lipstick tube from her makeup caddy and added it to the bag. "I'm surprised the *Globe* or at least the local paper didn't get to me first." She hung a garment bag over her closet door and unzipped it.

"What I'd like to know is how Brooke Hill found out about the case so fast." He went back to the window and looked out. "Good. All clear."

"They have their informers, don't they?" She took two pairs of gladiator sandals from a rack.

"Yeah, but she didn't waste a second. Looks like they need to create another sensationalized story, since spousal murders are cash cows for ratings these days."

"That's what keeps their ratings up." She folded a pink bra and panties and placed them in her overnight bag. "Preying on other people's tragedies."

"You sound awfully understanding."

He looked away when she folded another bra. She hadn't realized it was making him uncomfortable. She shut her underwear drawer. "That's because I get accused of the exact same thing, with my paranormal investigations," she said. "Duping people who think they see ghosts. Only I help people, they don't. And I don't take money. But from the perspective of the ignorant, it's the same thing, isn't it? Right, counselor?" She gave him a sardonic grin.

"Objection!" He made a fist and pounded her bureau. "I'm a defense attorney!"

She chuckled. "We'll have to learn how far to push the envelope with our joking around."

He stepped up to her from behind and wrapped his arms around her waist, nuzzling her neck. A warm thrill spiraled through her.

"I can take all the lawyer jokes you can throw at me. They bounce right off. I've heard them all. And most of all, I'm glad you can see humor in any of this," he spoke between light kisses on her neck.

A hum of pleasure sounded in her throat. "You have to, or you'll lose your sanity. Ted had a wicked sense of humor, he told some pretty sick jokes in his time, and I know he wouldn't want me to just wither away with a permanent scowl on."

"Good for you. I'm proud of you." He took a deep

breath. "Oh, that perfume of yours…" He drew away and stood at arm's length. "If Alice wore that, no wonder she snagged four husbands."

She went into her closet and came out with an armful of clothes. "Oh, she wore perfume, all right. I know a lot of her intimate details. But I need to do more research on her."

He looked at the stack of books on her nightstand. "I'm still not clear on how that helps you with this case. What if you can't find anything out, or if you find out she really did kill her husband?"

She stopped packing and looked at him. "I know she didn't. I know very little about the events in her later life, but I know what was in her heart, just like I know what's in my heart. Just as I'd never kill anyone, especially not my own husband, I know she didn't kill hers. We share the same spirit, Mike. You must understand that, especially now, after what you told me Ted said."

He gave her a lopsided grin. "I guess I'm just one of those mundane guys who's permanently grounded. Maybe Ted did have a premonition or just something about us made him see that."

"But it almost proves you were Michael Artson in our past lives. For God's sake, you've even got the same first name." She raised her hands and let them fall to her sides.

His lips curved in a fuddled half-grin. "Well, I have a confession to make."

"What?" She folded a pair of slacks.

"My full given name is Michelangelo." His eyes darted around and down to the floor. "But I hated it so much growing up, and was the object of so much ribbing, especially from the girls, I changed it to Michael in about sixth grade, when I couldn't take it anymore." He twiddled with her hairbrush and put it back on the vanity. "I wouldn't even let my parents call me Michelangelo anymore, so they started calling me Mike. My mom still honors my wishes."

She stared at him, open-mouthed. "Michelangelo?"

"Yes, but if you don't mind, if we're going to spend the rest of eternity together, I'd prefer you call me Mike. Or darling." He turned to look out the window again.

She answered in a near-whisper, "Michelangelo is a beautiful name." She approached him. "After a near-immortal legend. But if you prefer Mike—or lickety-yummy soufflé, I'll simply provide the whipped cream."

He turned to face her. They exchanged a knowing smile, but didn't move closer. The tension sizzled.

"You and Michael Artson look so much alike." She feasted on his features. "You have the same mannerisms even. Just the way I saw myself in the mirror when I was back there. I was dressed like Alice, but I was definitely carrying my body around."

"So it's not just the spirits, but the bodies, too?" A spark of interest lit up his eyes.

"Not always." She shook her head. "We can come back as the opposite sex, or a person who looks entirely different. But in the majority of past and present lives, we have the same features, the same genetic makeup."

"So if Michael in the fourteenth century had some illness...I'll get it too?" His hesitant words carried a hint of fear.

"Not necessarily. Most of the time we share a lot of

the same physical characteristics with those we were in past lives. That doesn't mean there's some guy walking around Boston who's a dead ringer for Henry the Eighth. He could be reincarnated as an Indian guy or a Chinese woman. But he'll definitely share the same spirit."

"So there's another Bluff King Hal out there?" He cocked his brow as the left side of his mouth lifted in a half-smile.

"Maybe not right this minute. Maybe he lived in the eighteen hundreds, or he'll come back in five hundred years. But he came back, and he will again." She nodded, her voice steady and confident.

"And that goes for Hitler and Mussolini?" he continued his line of questioning.

"I believe so. Eventually, but their spirits have a lot to learn first."

"Scary," he concluded, his gaze landing on her wooden sculptures of hooded wizards and mushrooms carved from dead trees.

"It doesn't have to be scary. Just think. You and I have been together before, and always will be." She folded a white blouse and placed it in her overnight bag.

He paced back and forth. "When I think about how powerful the universe is, creating life, death and what follows, it sounds too logical—even scientific—to dismiss it as mumbo jumbo."

"Spoken like a true lawyer." She looked up from her packing and smiled at him. "The evidence is there."

"So it's possible Alice could've killed any of those husbands in order to run off with Michael Artson," he said.

She looked him straight in the eye. "No, it's not possible. Do you think I'd ever kill anyone?" Her voice rose, sharp and indignant.

"Of course not," he retorted a bit too forcefully.

"Then you can't believe she would." Her gaze still pinning him, she added, "She is me, Mike. And I'm her."

He sat on the edge of the bed, hands folded between his knees. "You came back safely the first time. But who knows what might happen if you chance it again? You can die of the plague or some highwayman can kill you."

She shook her head. "Alice survived her trial. It's *after* the trial I don't know about."

"It's too dangerous," he insisted.

"You say that because you don't truly believe." She put a pair of shoes into a zippered bag, finished hanging her dresses in the garment bag and zipped it. "But I'll make a believer out of you yet. Now let's get out of here."

Downstairs, she took one last look around her earth-toned living room. "I had some happy times here. But now it's time to move on." She walked out the door and closed it behind her, locking away all the memories of the past ten years. "I'll have to come back for the clocks. No—wait." She opened the door and dashed back in, grabbed her tiniest clock, set into the heart of a Claddagh, and enclosed it in her fist. "I got this in Ireland. It's my favorite. I'll get the others another time."

They headed to his car.

"After I'm acquitted, we'll go house shopping," she said with a resolute nod.

He put her bags in his trunk. "As long as I can keep my lumpy recliner that doesn't recline anymore."

"Why doesn't it?" she asked over the roof of his car as he opened the driver's side.

"It broke. Don't ask how." They got in.

"Then we'll have to buy another one and break it— or at least break it in."

"You got it." He winked.

They shared a smile. This temporary semblance of normalcy made her spirit soar.

As they drove down the street and turned the corner, she made him stop beside a red car.

"What is it?" he asked.

"That's...back up a minute." She leaned forward, squinting.

He shifted into reverse and she peered at the car's back license plate.

"I'll be damned, that's Charlotte's car!"

"Charlotte? Ted's stepdaughter?" He shifted into park. "What's her car doing here?"

"I'll bet my bottom dollar it has something to do with Brooke Hill." Her teeth clenched. "Brooke must've met her here and is grilling her somewhere. Probably at the mall bribing her with a new wardrobe."

"That Lexus I saw stop in front of the house must've been Brooke's. You want to wait?" he asked. "Charlotte has to come back for her car sometime."

She shook her head. "No, what's done is done."

"That vulture," he muttered, shifting the car into drive and heading up the street. "She's pumping Charlotte with all kinds of questions now."

"It doesn't matter, Mike. We're going to come out of this, aren't we?" she urged.

"Of course. But in the meantime, the media can make your life a living hell."

She let out a sardonic laugh. "Even more than it is now?"

"Much more," he warned. "I'll say it again. You need bodyguards. The media can be more dangerous than whoever you thought was trying to run you off the road."

"I know, but let's take one step at a time. Let's get my stuff into the apartment over the store first." She changed his radio station from Fox News to The Joint, which played reggae.

"What the hell's all this?" Mike braked when he reached her store. Cars filled the small lot in front and were parked along both sides of the road. An army of bodies armed with microphones and cameras blocked the store entrance.

Someone sighted Mike's car, signaled the others, and in less than two seconds, the vultures swarmed the car from all directions, thumping on the widows. The car swayed. The press of bodies blocked out all sunlight. Kylah breathed deep and fought off the beginning of a panic attack.

Chapter Sixteen

Dominic treated Enid to lunch at The Colony Diner, hardly a tourist trap and well within his price range. "Mark my word, Enid, when business picks up it'll be dinner at L'Espalier and Red Sox tickets behind home plate." He cringed at that empty promise, knowing business wouldn't pick up, and if he wanted to treat her to either of those delights, he'd have to donate blood—gallons.

"Oh, you don't have to, Dom, I'm a cheap date." Enid's diamond ring flashed as she sprinkled salt into her pea soup. She looked over at him and leaned in a bit. "I haven't been in the loop about Kylah's ongoings. Did they set a trial date yet?"

He squirted ketchup on his fries. "I'm not sure, but Petra told me she's out on bail. Miscarriage of justice if you ask me. I wouldn't be surprised if she jumps bail and flees the country."

Enid emptied the packet of oyster crackers into her soup. "You really think she killed Ted?"

"After careful deliberation I've arrived at that conclusion. No one else had a motive to kill Ted. Her lawyer has his work cut out for him, I'll tell you that much. But he sure don't mind." Dominic glanced over at the next table to make sure no one was listening. "Now I have proof they're slippin' between the sheets. I saw them in a lip lock. In full view of the courthouse!"

Enid *hrmmph'd*. "I still can't fathom why Ted tolerated the shameless carryings-on of those two." She scowled in disgust. "How's your daughter handling it all?" She picked up her soup spoon and dipped it in the bowl.

He tightened his lips. "I'm worried sick for her. She's running that store all crazy hours. But she still insists she enjoys it. I'm trying to talk her into leaving that rat race to get away from this mess."

"Kylah must be paying her a good salary," Enid said.

He shook his head. "Nah, she wants to run the store because Kylah is such a good friend to her and she thinks she'll be part owner someday. If you ask me, Kylah ought to give up ownership of the store now— before she's found guilty. She's incapable of running a business in the situation she's in. And once the trial's over, who'll wanna buy a store from a murderess? Who'd even want to shop there?" He stabbed his fries with his fork.

"You'd be surprised, Dom. I drove past the place a few times. The parking lot was packed, cars parked all along the road. There was a line to get in." She sipped her soup from the spoon and wiped her lips, leaving an orange lipstick smear on the napkin. "And I don't want to scare you, but your daughter's far from safe there. There are such things as serial killers, you know." Her voice went low, her tone menacing. "Not every killer kills…just once."

That pushed his panic button. He yanked his cell phone from his pocket. "That does it. Excuse my rudeness, but I want her out of there, not in the line of fire. I need to talk to her now," he said as the phone rang at the other end. "Petra, this is Dad."

****

Kylah entered her store through the back door and waited until Petra finished ringing up a customer. She handed the woman a bag—one of the big ones. Even on a slow day, Petra outsold anybody else she'd ever hired.

As the customer turned to leave, Kylah sneaked up from behind and poked Petra between the shoulders.

She turned and her eyes grew wide. "Hey, you look wicked awesome!"

"Thanks. I had to sneak in the back door." With all the customers browsing, there was no line. "Nice to have a lull, isn't it?"

"Whew!" Petra swiped at her brow. "This is the first breather I've taken all day. That woman who just left dropped three hundred dollars and change on incense, Wicca books, and Tantric motion lotion. I guess you know there's a cop stationed at the front door."

Kylah nodded, looking at the entrance. "Yeah, I wouldn't mind one at the back either."

Petra chugged water from a plastic bottle. "Apparently the story made the New York papers, because half the people I talk to are from there. They drive here from all over the place, hoping to catch a glimpse of—" She clamped her mouth shut.

Kylah nodded. "Yeah, I know. I'm a celebrity. I'm surprised nobody's asked for my autograph yet."

Petra gave Kylah another hug. "Oh, I'm relieved beyond words you're well enough to come back."

"I'm surviving. I'm moving in upstairs. Mike just dropped me off." Kylah rang up two more sales and served a woman wearing a New York Yankees T-shirt.

Diana Rubino

"Is Mrs. McKinley here today?" Yankee Lady dropped an array of rings, bracelets, and flavored condoms on the counter.

"That is I." Kylah held her head high, ready to deal with her public.

"You—" Her jaw dropped. "I thought you got arrested for murder!"

"I was accused of the crime, which I did not commit. I am out on bail and trying to resume my life. Anything else you'd like to know?" she asked.

"N—no, just—are you going to keep your store open?"

"Can you think of a reason I shouldn't?" she shot back.

"Um, uh," the woman stammered as Kylah ran the credit card through and gave her the slip to sign.

"And I hope you'll return, because I truly appreciate your business." She wrapped the items in lilac tissue paper and placed them in a gold bag displaying the store's name.

"Uh, wait—just a minute. I want to get a few more things." She left her newly purchased goods on the counter and dashed away to snap up some more loot.

"Well, that's one way to drum up business," Petra said.

Kylah smirked. "Mike is right. I'm a one-woman freak show. So I might as well make the most of it, right? Lemonade out of lemons?"

"Kylah, you're a very brave lady," Petra said as Kylah rang up another hefty sale. "If it was me, I'd cringe in a dark corner of the cellar afraid to come out."

"I have nothing to cringe from, Petra. I'm innocent, Ted knows I'm innocent, Mike knows I'm innocent,

194

and God knows I'm innocent. That's all that matters. And karma will take care of what is meant to be." She straightened a row of bracelets hanging from a velvet bar on the counter, then rang up Yankee Lady's other items.

"I know it will. Go make tea or something." Petra stood back as the next two gawking customers recognized Kylah, nudged each other and dropped their purchases onto the counter.

"Thanks." She closed her office door and leaned on it. "Whewww."

Shutting the bustle out, she sat at her computer, logged onto the Internet and did a Google search on Alice Kyteler. A new item came up on the Richard III Society website. Her eyes widened. "Oh, sweet!" She clicked on the heading and flipped on her printer, reading the screen as the printer spit out the pages.

According to the article, Alice's last husband John LePoer had fallen ill with a mysterious disease. He wasted away to skin and bones, his nails dropped off and his hair fell out. His sons found a sack of 'horrible and detestable things' in her kitchen. When John died, his sons dragged Alice before the bishop. They accused her of bringing slow-wittedness onto them and killing their father by sorcery. John—and her previous three husbands—bequeathed all their wealth to her, to the sons' impoverishment. As the bishop interrogated Alice, her 'incubus lover' named 'Son of Art' who 'had carnal knowledge of her,' stood at her side.

"Incubus lover? Hmmm." Kylah grinned as she continued reading. He was a barrister, a lawyer in American terms. He defended Alice at her trial for poisoning John to death. "Son of Art?" Kylah read the sentence again. "Artson. Michael Artson was her incubus lover." She laughed and continued reading. "This incubus made its appearance under various forms, sometimes as a cat or a hairy black dog, and three Ethiopian men."

Kylah's Mike did have a cat and a hairy black dog. His wife was likely to get custody of them. But three Ethiopian men? She doubted Mike knew any.

Too jittery to sit and read the rest of the article, she skipped to the end. And not a moment too soon—when she read the last paragraph, her jaw nearly hit the floor. Alice swore that she'd been set up by her husband John's murderer—and she knew exactly who that person was. She set out to prove the killer's guilt and her own innocence.

"Holy moly, Alice knew the killer?" When she saw the next line, *to be continued next month,* she pounded the desk with her fist. "No, don't do this to me! I need to know now!"

She looked up the article's author, Pamela Butler. Determined to contact Ms. Butler, she found the e-mail address of the Richard III Society's American branch president and hunted down the addresses of New England chapter members. With trembling hands, she composed a message online, including her phone number, and copied it to all of them.

She worked off her nervous energy by going upstairs to sweep and scour the space into livable condition. She never dreamed she'd live in it someday. But it just showed how life threw curves when least expected.

She began by vacuuming the dust, dead bugs and cobwebs from the floors, corners and window sills. She stopped every fifteen minutes to run back downstairs and check her e-mail. Nothing from any Ricardians yet.

On her fourth trip back upstairs, she filled a pail with ammonia and water. Her cell phone rang as she stood on a ladder scrubbing a window.

She pulled off her dripping rubber gloves, sat on the floorboards and swiped the screen. "Mike, hi, what's up?"

"Hey, honey, a few things. I called on some expert witnesses to testify at the trial. A photo lab tech, who can analyze that photo of the car in front of your house to determine if it was altered and when it was taken, and a handwriting expert who can tell if Ted was under duress when he wrote that final entry in the notebook. That'll help in our defense to show that somebody set out to kill Ted and made it look like he was referring to you in the note."

"I know that photo's a fake—I simply was not there at that time," she insisted, gripping the phone so hard her knuckles ached.

"There's a lot of ways to analyze photos to prove they're doctored," Mike said. "We're not dealing with Einstein here."

"We sure aren't." She got up and paced the creaky floor.

"I have a few other tricks up my sleeve," Mike said. "Lawyers use theatrics to get a point across to a jury. I'm going to eat some of that moonsbane to show it's harmless, then eat an unnamed herb. 'It's so harmless, you can throw it in the air,' I'll tell them. I'll take catspur, fling it in the air, breathe it in—it's just one tactic I plan to use. My other tactics are more fact-based. Including the fact that you weren't anywhere near Ted when he died."

"I'm keeping the faith, Mike," she assured him.

"I have no doubt you are. I'll pick you up about six. We'll have a nice quiet dinner at Scargo's and go for a walk along the beach—or through a cemetery, anyplace you want."

"I can't wait!" Once again, she bounded down the stairs to her computer. "Oh, sweet! I got a message back."

"Message?"

"Yeah, there's something I need to show you, an article I found online. I'm waiting to hear back from some historians, and it's got me so worked up, I've been going around the upstairs like a tornado scouring the place between checking my e-mail every few minutes. I'm a nervous wreck waiting for it."

"Good, catch you later." He disconnected.

She hunched over and read:

Dear Kylah,

I haven't yet found the info I'm going to write about next month. I'm still digging to find out who framed Alice.

Kylah forced her frown into a smile as she read on:

I have 3 British Library historians & an Oxford medieval scholar helping me. A producer friend wants to make a BBC special out of the story. So I'm hustling. When I find out anything, you'll be the first to know.

Best regards,

Pam Butler

Clasping her hands together to stop shaking, she dragged herself back up the staircase and went on with her window-scrubbing. The mindless physical labor gave her a chance to think about Alice's predicament and how she found John's killer.

As she poured the dirty pail water down the drain, she plotted her next move. "I have one shot at this," she muttered.

With a resolute nod, she crossed the hall, intent on keeping busy. As she polished bathroom fixtures, her stomach rumbled. A glance at her watch told her why. "Yikes! Ten to six?"

She bolted down the stairs and gave herself a rapid makeover in record time. The side doorbell rang as she gave her lashes a final flick of mascara.

Mike stood at the door holding a cardboard box. A bottle of wine stuck out of the top. "Just a few basics you might need, and not-so-basics you might not need, I wasn't sure what you had here."

"Oh, that's so thoughtful of you, Mike, thanks." She helped him set it down on the floor and grabbed her jacket from the hall closet. "Look what I found." She led him to her office and showed him the pages she'd printed.

As he read, she said, "Alice knew exactly who John's killer was. She's just about to show the court who this person is and how he or she killed John. Then the article ends. Pamela Butler promised to get back to me when she finds out more." Unable to keep quiet as he read, she rambled on, "I have e-mails in to some other people, too, for backup. But I'm not holding my breath waiting for them to get back to me."

He looked up over his specs from the printout. "All right, what's the subtext of that?" His eyes pierced her.

She could've bitten her tongue. "N-nothing. I mean, people don't reply in an instant. I can't sit here and expect them to zap me answers when it's convenient for me. That's all." She stopped there, not wanting to protest too much. But, hell, did he know her!

His gaze softened and he went back to reading. "Yeah, well, I've learned how to read between your lines."

She circled the office, emptying her incense burner, straightening pens.

He put the pages down. "So this historian claims Alice knew who murdered John, but she hasn't found out *how* or *if* Alice proved her own innocence."

She stopped fidgeting and turned to face him. "I know Alice was resourceful and determined to find John's killer and clear her own name. I'll learn that soon enough. I just need to know who the killer is in *this* life—the bastard who killed Ted."

He approached her. "I have every faith in you, honey, but just in case the truth continues to elude, I need to do my job. I'm not going to slack off and let you do everything."

"I have every confidence in your abilities. But I need to be the first to find out the truth." Her voice trilled with excitement.

"If it's a race you want, watch me win." He crossed his arms over his chest, as if he were giving his opening statement.

"I'll tell you what." She planted a light kiss on his lips. "The winner decides where we live after we get married. And gets to pick out the house."

He whistled. "Wow. You're way ahead of me. I just started shopping for rings."

Her eyes widened and an overall glow warmed her. "Rings? I didn't even think of that."

"Well, we can't get engaged and married without

rings, now, can we? We can do without a house for a while, but what's an engagement and wedding without rings? I don't want to formally propose without presenting you with a rock." He took her left hand in his and kissed it.

She tingled all over. "Formally? You mean on bended knee in a tux on a moonlit night in a Parisian garden with the scent of gardenias and Chopin playing in the background?" She moved a step closer. "Complete with poetic monologue in a voice cracking with emotion?"

"I'll go for the trip to Paris, the garden and the Chopin. But let's ditch the tux." He grinned. "I was hoping to get away with sweats and my Sox cap."

She stepped into his embrace. "So you're hinting you'd rather propose on the Jumbotron at Fenway Park during the seventh inning stretch."

"If that's what you want." His lips sought hers.

She responded to his warmth. Closing her eyes, she pressed her body to his. As he eased away, her lips tingled from that teasing, too-short kiss. Her fingers laced round his neck and she drew him to her. Wanting to reclaim his lips, she whispered, "Mike, what would happen if we made love right now?"

"We'd enjoy it, I expect." His voice wavered. "But we'd regret it later. It will be worth the wait, I promise. Here and now isn't the best time to take it to the next level. We both know that. Besides—" He gently ran his thumb over her bottom lip. "You don't have a bed in here."

She smiled and nodded her acquiescence. "I have that sexy room in the back filled with all those toys and DVD's and slippery stuff. And I'm having a bed delivered tomorrow."

"And we'll break it in—or maybe just break it. But we shouldn't—not with the trial pending. The media vultures have enough on you already. Let's not add 'suspected husband-slayer and her attorney are lovers' to give them more ammunition."

She backed away, her desire withering as her stomach rumbled. "We really should wait. So let's go to dinner."

Once again her appetite won over her hormones. That was happening more and more these days.

Chapter Seventeen

After a steak dinner and a bottle of Chateau La Fleur-Petrus, Mike pulled up to her store. The red alarm lights glowed from inside. "Are you sure you'll be okay alone here? Without even a bed?"

"I have a down mattress cover I'll spread out on the floor. I'll light a cheery fire and will be very comfortable over the store. It's only for one night," she assured him as he cut the engine.

"And you'd rather not go back home, just till you get a bed here?" He turned to face her.

"That house Ted and I shared is not home anymore. This is my home now." She gazed at her colonial building and its grounds with a new appreciation. It survived the ravages of three centuries and still it stood, an American icon. "Friendly spirits live here, and I feel a warmth and belonging here that I'll never feel again in the other house. With Ted gone, everything's gone with it. I don't care if I ever set foot inside it again." Her voice quivered as she fought tears. For some reason she didn't understand, she didn't want Mike to see her cry.

"Yeah, I know the feeling. But I'm staying in my house till it sells. The kids didn't move their stuff out yet." His sympathetic tone touched her. "But I can't wait to unload it. I'm selling it at a loss and don't even care." He leaned his head against the headrest and closed his eyes.

"We'll make a beautiful home together," she promised. "And I was just kidding about the winner deciding where we live. I'll go wherever you want."

He slid her a sideways glance. "I have only one requirement. That it's in this century."

"It's a deal." She leaned over and brushed his lips with hers.

He saw her to the door. She hesitated, not wanting the evening to end. They stood facing each other, putting off the good-nights.

He gathered her in his arms. "Everything will work out, I swear," he said.

"I know." She nodded. "But how, I don't know yet."

As he kissed her, she fought the impulse to take him upstairs and seduce him.

But he ended it before she did. "See you tomorrow." He gave her cheek a gentle touch and left her.

She went upstairs and as a double shot of anticipation and fear jolted her heart, she carried out the plan she couldn't tell him about.

She mixed her herbs to the exact formula, poured them into a cup of water, took a deep breath, and drank. Sitting cross-legged on her comforter, she said, "I'm returning to 1324 to enter Alice's body and live through those events, to find her husband's killer. I can't wait around for scholars to write back. I must take fate into my own hands."

But she added a small detail—this was to be on June 30, 1324, three days before she was arrested for the murder of her husband John. She needed those three days to get oriented.

She lay on her back, closed her eyes, and pictured the Kyteler Inn as it looked, felt and smelled on June 30, 1324—the bureau with the oval looking-glass, the ladder-backed chair under her diamond paned window. The warm breeze brought the odor of waste as the knocker clanged against her front door.

****

Kilkenny, Ireland, June 30, 1324

"Alice! Alice, open up." The steady pounding alarmed her. She stopped stirring her porridge and headed for her front entrance.

The banging grew louder as she unlatched the door and swung it open. Her brother-in-law Arnold Wolfe shuffled from one foot to the other, wringing his hands as if warding off the cold on this sultry summer morn. He was also seneschal of Kilkenny, so she sensed this wasn't a social call. "Arn! Why do you shiver so? Come in." She stood back and let him enter.

"Alice, I regret needing to bring you such unsettling tidings, but alas, I am the one to—"

"Quit waffling and tell me, Arn." She clutched his sleeve and pulled him inside.

"Bishop Ledrede demanded that you appear before him for questioning in the murder of John—by sorcery."

"I refuse to go." She placed clenched fists on her hips. "His charges are beyond the church's jurisdiction. Sorcery is a secular crime. If it is a crime at all. Either way, you can tell him where to put his demands. Or, rather, shove them."

Arnold cast her a wry grin. "I be one step ahead o'you, my colleen. Roger Outlawe declined to issue the writs for your arrest. I then told Ledrede to stop his proceedings against you. Now you want to hear the capper?" His hand-wringing became hand-rubbing, as if he'd pilfered Kilkenny's treasury. He licked his lips as if tasting his words, finding them tasty indeed.

"Firstly, thank dear Roger for me," she said. "I relish cappers as much as anyone. So cap away." Her fists unclenched. "But I know Ledrede. The miserable old wretch is doing this because he hates me. I'm loved, happy and rich—everything he ain't."

"Stephen carried out his first arrest since becoming my officer." Arnold's grin widened as he spoke. "Quite happily, I might add."

"Good for Stephie." He was one of her former in-laws. "Whom did he arrest?"

"Why, as I live and breathe—he arrested dear old Bishop Ledrede!" Arnold guffawed, slapped his knee and stomped his feet in a sprightly jig.

At first she tried not to let mirth get the best of her but keeping a straight face was harder than when thinking of a joke in church. She forced her lips into a dignified line.

Arnold carried on, "As the bishop cools his heels in Kilkenny Castle's prison, pacing with outrage and righteous indignation, the faithful of the church began bringing him food and ale, yet more ale than food, I expect. So he dispatched his messages of outrage through his faithful flock. He placed the entire diocese under interdict. But I, being his official gaoler, foiled him before he could finish imbibing his ale. I summoned the chief constable, who issued strict orders. No one can access the prison except one brother for companion, one servant to make the bed, and one lad to prepare his meals."

"Bully for you, Arn. No female company. He's sure reapin' what he's sown." A wave of satisfaction lightened her mood. "Justice is served."

Arnold nodded. "I sent a crier round every market village in Ireland to proclaim in public, 'if you wish to lay complaints against Bishop Ledrede, his clerics or household, come to me and I shall provide every redress with grace and favor.' He'll need explain to the Archbishop of Dublin why he put the diocese under interdict. Then we'll see who comes up smellin' like roses. Heed me, Alice, this could get ugly."

She stood her ground, her back ramrod straight. "I still refuse to appear before the ecclesiastical court for a secular offense. And you can tell him that. Now may I return to my porridge afore it grows cold and pasty?"

"Do that, o lovely one." He tipped his hat and backed out.

Chuckling and shaking her head in amusement, she went back to her kitchen and served herself a heaping helping of porridge.

As she sat down to eat, Petronilla came in carrying a basket of cabbages. She set it down as Alice gestured to her porridge. "Care to partake?"

"Nay, thank you." Petronilla stood closer. "I bring sad tidings. That lass from Ballyhale that Michael Artson wed…she passed a fortnight ago from fever. I just heard about it when I was at market."

A pang of sympathy shot through Alice. "Oh, I'm so sorry…the poor lass. And she was with child."

"Was she?" Petronilla's eyes widened.

"Tis why he married her. I'll send him my condolences. Oh, damn these horrid fevers." She made a fist and struck the table.

"I often wonder why some are spared and some are not." Petronilla tucked wisps of hair under her cap.

"As long as we're on this side of the grave, we're not privy to that reason," she replied, heaving a sigh. "Oh, the poor lass and her babe. And I thought I had problems."

****

July 2, 1324

"Alice? Alice..." A gentle nudge woke her. She opened her eyes to Arnold beside her bed, brows knitted, hands trembling.

"Arn? What is amiss?" She focused fuzzy eyes on him and yawned.

"I'm so sorry to wake you this early, but I needed to tell you, Bishop Ledrede has been freed from prison."

"Whom did he bribe?" She smoothed strands of hair off her forehead.

"No one. When I was busy holding my inquests against the bishop, the king sent two justices here. In their presence, I summoned all the nobles and people in the county to make inquiry into the bishop and his ministers. These depositions contained wild accusations against the bishop. But the jurors were loathe to accuse him because they could not do so truthfully, nor did they depose anything against him."

She sat up, her elbows supporting her. She clutched her nightshirt over her décolleté. "But we all know what a prat he is. Surely they could rustle up something truthful."

He replied, "Someone cited an old false accusation against the bishop that he seized the property of an intestate person for himself. They showed me the document, hoping it might lend support for the bishop's unjust incarceration. So I sent messengers to the bishop in prison, seeking his sureties that he'd answer the charges in the secular court."

"As if the bishop would tell the truth," she scoffed.

"Ah…" Arnold held up his pointer finger. "The bishop replied he's subject to God alone, not bound to stand trial before any mortal." He took a few rapid breaths. "The reason he was imprisoned had naught to do with secular law. In addition, the men who imprisoned him were excommunicate. Therefore, the bishop was not bound to answer charges. So I sent for the sheriff of Kilkenny. The Lord Chief Justice also came here from Dublin. They brought a warrant to the castle constable, sealed with my seal. It stated that the bishop is to be released."

"Where does that leave us?" She swung her legs over the side of the bed and her feet hit the floor.

"I must relay you this message about Bishop Ledrede and your…your heresy charges."

"Oh, nay." She stood, stretched and pulled on a robe.

He stepped back to give her room. "Ledrede and some of his flock stormed into the Kilkenny judicial hall where I was presiding. They demanded to be heard, but I tossed him out on his arse. Then just this morn, Ledrede was allowed to speak in the dock, you know— where accused criminals stand—and demanded that you be turned over to him for punishment. I waved him off. 'Go do your preaching in the church, old bean,' I dismissed him. But having to make his grand exit, Ledrede read out the names of the accused and the

Diana Rubino

charges against them."

"Them? What other poor souls did he drag into this?" She dipped her face cloth in her water bowl on the stand.

"I'm sorry to say, but Petronilla, your housemaid." He shuffled his feet. "He arrested her on heresy charges."

She turned to face him, her face cloth dripping water onto the floorboards. "For the Lord's sake, why her?"

"She's a servant of yours, why else? Ledrede will stop at naught. If you want my legal opinion, I strongly urge you to indict him for defamation."

"I was thinking along those lines." She braided her hair, her gaze fixed on a flower petal lying on the floor. "But what I had in mind for him was more illegal."

"The Dublin clergy won't be sympathetic to him, I assure you," Arnold said. "There's no love lost twixt them. They lately accused him of being a truant monk from England. Being a foreigner, he'll never be in their good graces."

"I did not kill John and I'm no witch." She tucked her braid under her cloth cap. "But poor Petronilla—what can we do about her?"

"Leave that to me. At present I need file defamation charges against him. But I warn you—you will be arrested. I expect a constable will be by shortly." He headed for the doorway. "Wherever they bring you, to Kilkenny Castle's gaol or anywhere else, I shall proclaim your innocence."

"Thank you so kindly, Arn." She clasped his hand.

"I must go now, but be assured I am on your side." He quit the chamber.

She dressed without the help of her maids and headed to her desk to dash off a fast note to Michael. She needed to save her life—and poor Petronilla's.

I'm about to be arrested for John's murder and need your help...

****

She knew Michael's knock, four rapid raps, a pause and three more. It symbolized the fourth of March, the day they first met. What a sentimentalist!

With a quick glance in the looking glass and tug on her skirts, she scampered down the hall to let him in.

"Top o'the mornin' to you," he greeted her with two bottles he held out to her. "Mead for my honey from the Dunguaire winery in County Clare. And I shall defend you to the death—mine, that is—from this false accusation."

"Thank you kindly." Her mouth watered at the thought of the sweet honey wine trickling down her throat. "Michael, I heard about your losses. I am so sorry. Please accept my deepest condolences."

A pained look filled his eyes. "Thank you, Alice. She ailed for quite a while. It was more of a blessing she no longer suffers. I am keeping my mind fully occupied. Hence, I shall prepare your defense and want you to know that justice will prevail."

She stepped back to let him in. "It will be nigh on impossible to prove my innocence unless we find John's killer. His sons accused me of killing him by sorcery—but even were I capable of sorcery, no form of hocus-pocus causes the wasting sickness that befell John."

"I'm starting by questioning the sons." Michael followed her into the kitchen. "Of course they're suspects."

"But I'm the prime suspect because John's sons found a sackful of 'horrible and detestable things,' which they gave to two priests. Then he died and that's when his sons dragged me before the bishop and accused me of sorcery."

She went to her herb cupboard and unlocked it.

"But where did they find this horrible detestable sackful? Your cupboard there?" He pointed at the wooden cabinet.

"Nay. I keep it locked and hide the key. It wasn't herbs they found in the sack. It was full of dead insects I use as fertilizer. The insects provide minerals and nutrients plants need to thrive. But they must've believed I'd collected them for some ritual and they went into a panic."

"And devout as they were, they ran to the priests." Michael sat, chin resting on palm.

"Aye. One thing John and I did not see eye-to-eye on was my Druidism. So we agreed to disagree on that." She opened her cupboard door. "I needs put away the sage and coriander I cut this morn." Looking inside, she noticed a space twixt two bottles where her moonsbane should be. She looked closer. "Where's my bottle of moonsbane?"

"Pardon?" Michael came up behind her.

Counting the jars, she noticed her moonsbane was missing. "The moonsbane's gone."

"Are you sure?" He bent his knees to peer into the cupboard. "Did you mayhap use them and not remember?"

She turned to face him. "Moonsbane is for the most sacred of ceremonies and healing deadly disease. 'Tis far too powerful for casual use. I've not even seen the toadstools growing in the last twenty years. I always kept the bottle hidden in the back. I'm the official guardian of this scarce supply for all of Ireland. Any Druid wanting it must come to me and show just cause to have it. And now it's gone!" Her mouth dried up as her heart raced.

"When was the last time you used it?" he asked.

She focused on the floor, trying to remember. "I can't recall. God's truth, I've hardly ever used it." She paced in circles, tapping her fingers to her head, shut her eyes and concentrated.

"Right!" She halted. He bumped into her back. "The outbreak of the sweat earlier this year, before John began courting me. We went to Brona and Margaret. I'd told Brona a pinch of moonsbane would serve as her cure. I told her how rare and special it was. I told her the wrong dosage was lethal. I even showed her the dark blue bottle I stored it in. It needs storing in a dark vessel to keep light out. I had to bring it to her house still inside the bottle so it wouldn't be exposed to sunlight."

They turned to face each other at the same precise second.

"Brona!" they proclaimed in unison.

"She got to my herbs somehow." Her fists pumped the air. "No one hated me—and John—more than his former mother-in-law."

"I recall that as if it were yesterday." Michael nodded. "We came back here to fetch the herbs, you gave Brona and Margaret the mixtures, and that's when Brona spewed forth that venom about what a wild rover John was."

"Of course that venom was unfounded," she said. "John was a devoted husband to me during our short marriage…the best of all four I married. And never would I steal a man from anyone! I refused to even let him court me 'til after his annulment from Margaret. I wouldn't let him bed me 'til the wedding night."

Michael shuffled his feet, head down, clearly embarrassed.

"Sorry, Michael, you needn't know that."

He led her to a chair, but she couldn't sit. She paced to and fro, floorboards creaking. He fell into step beside her. "Now how can I *prove* Brona pilfered my cupboard and fed John enough moonsbane to wipe out all of Kilkenny?"

"Let's start at the beginning." Michael stood still. "When could Brona have snuck in and pinched your moonsbane?"

"Any time I wasn't here," she replied. "Guests come and go all the time, but that cupboard door always stays locked. No one even goes near the cupboard. The lock hasn't been disturbed. The culprit obviously sprang it."

"Could Brona be that clever, to spring a lock?" Michael asked her.

She halted and looked him in the eye. "Nay, not Brona. But I know who could. Her son Crispin. Believing I stole John away from her daughter and was after his money, Brona hated me for marrying him, and got Crispin to do her dirty deed."

"Is he the sort who would commit such a hateful act?" Michael asked.

Her lips spread in a sneer. "To be sure as I'm standing here. Crispin's been in gaol more than not for most of his years. Burglary, petty theft, breaking and entering, he has more offenses than his head has lice. He can pick a lock faster than he can pick a pocket."

She went to her desk and studied her guest book. "Crispin's never been a guest," she said as Michael stood beside her. "He wouldn't have dared stay here; besides, even if he had, his carrot orange hair is hard to miss."

"He'd worn a disguise, then." Michael peered over her shoulder at the book.

"I insist every guest sign my book, but I know better than to believe they all sign their real names." She eliminated the folk she already knew, her repeat guests who came for single-night trysts and signed out the next morn, their ladies in tow. "Some travelers stay here whilst passing through." She checked those names. "Since John died, there've been four. The first three I remember." She looked up and focused on a knot in the wood on the far wall. "They were together and shared the chamber across from mine. The last traveler arrived after the moon sank." She ran her finger down the page. "His name is here in the book—Kevin Kelly from Donegal. I gave him the chamber at the end of the hall." She shut her eyes tight and tried to picture him. "Dark hair, a long beard, dirty nails, old and tatty shirt and trousers. Crispin has orange hair and no beard. If this were he, you are right, Michael, he'd been disguised."

"When could he have forced this deadly brew upon John?" he asked.

"The morn after Kelly checked in, I rose early to do chores and left John abed. I spent a long time in the garden, cutting herbs, watering flowers, planting seeds. I returned to see John drinking tea in our chamber.

Diana Rubino

Then he said he was going out. When I went to the guest's room and knocked, the door stood ajar. Kelly was gone." She closed the guest book. "Let us take a look upstairs."

They climbed the staircase and she led him to the chamber she'd shared with John.

She halted in the doorway, inhaling John's residual scents of sweat and outdoors. An unbearable wave of grief and loss shook her. "Michael, I can't bear to go in since that day." She hung back at the threshold.

"I understand." He entered the chamber and looked round.

Standing in the doorway, she noticed the teacup he'd used on the bedside table. "When had John got up and made himself tea?" she wondered out loud. "He hadn't said aught about making tea that morn. Someone must have brought it to him. He woke and saw it on the table. Thinking I'd brought it, he drank it." The truth jolted her like a bolt of lightning. She grabbed the door frame to steady herself. "Michael! That cup...look inside it."

He picked it up and peered in. "Some tea leaves are at the bottom."

"Those aren't tea leaves." Shaking, she clutched the door frame with both hands. "Tis the deadly moonsbane that Crispin got from my cupboard. He broke in and found that same blue bottle. Tis the only blue bottle I keep. Brona told him about it. So he was able to distinguish it from the others." She paced in circles, fists clenched in rage.

Michael came out of the chamber. "You've just but won the case. We can testify how the disguised Crispin knew you had the only moonsbane in Ireland." He

216

clutched her arms and brought her to him in a tight embrace. "Alice, you've saved your own life."

At a pounding on the door they broke apart. "I know this is the summons for my arrest. The time has come, Michael."

"I am behind you, dear one, through this entire ordeal. And you shall walk free whilst that murderer rots. You have my vow." He crossed his heart, took her hand and led her down the stairs.

She opened the door to two men in matching blue doublets, swords at their belts. "Dame Alice Kyteler?"

She nodded. "That is I."

"We are sheriff's men of Kilkenny. Several articles were read in the presence of the lord justiciar and the king's council acknowledging your heresy and were publicly attested to. On the unanimous agreement of the clergy, you've been pronounced a heretic. We are ordered to confiscate your goods and you to appear in secular court to be punished for your demerits."

"My goods?" She looked from one to the other and back again, unable to read their blank stares. "What goods?"

"Any goods pertaining to your dealings in witchcraft, Dame Alice. You must come with us now."

With a final glance at Michael, she went, knowing what she had to do whilst they ransacked her house.

"I shall get Arnold or one of his officers to question Brona and her son," Michael promised her. "You shall see me again soon."

After a desperate embrace, they parted.

****

With a guard clasping each arm, she descended a flight of worn stone steps and down a dark corridor.

With a skeleton key, they unlocked a door, a small barred window cut into it.

"When may I see my counsel again?" She turned to face them as they nudged her inside and prepared to bolt the door.

"Afore the morn, I expect," said the guard holding the door.

"Will I be served a meal?" she asked.

He guffawed. "You're a witch. Conjure up a bowl o'toadstools."

"I am not a witch, you silly sod!" she hissed into his face.

They answered that with a slam of the door. The finality of the locking latch plunged her into despair. Fighting the urge to collapse and weep, she turned and looked round the stuffy cell. A narrow bed with a ratty mattress stood against the wall next to a battered table holding a wash bowl. A chamber pot stained yellow with urine sat at the foot of the bed.

Shivering although she wasn't cold, she hugged her arms to her sides. The stale, musty air choked her. She coughed and spat on the dirt floor.

Knowing she wouldn't be here long gave her a spark of hope. With naught to do, she lay on the bed and pictured a grassy meadow, fragrant herbs, warm sun on her back. She drifted off.

She woke to the jiggling of the key in the latch. A guard escorted Michael in. She fell into his arms and clung to him, cherishing his presence.

"I will make sure you're set free, or they can hang me. Brona is not going to send you to your grave," he vowed, his tone resolute. "And because a husband always takes care of his wife..." He knelt before her and clasped her hands. "Alice, will you marry me?"

She gasped. "Oh, Michael..." She caught her breath, flooded with joy. "Of course I'll marry you!"

He glanced around. "I know this place is the furthest thing from romantic, but I couldn't wait. I'll propose again in a more appropriate setting."

"Any time is fine with me." She captured his lips with hers.

"'Tis the strangest thing." He looked into her eyes. "Remember a while back, you told me Druids believe in a beforelife and an afterlife?"

She nodded.

"I wasn't so sure about it back then. But it's been happening to me again and again. I go somewhere and I know I've been there before. And now, once again..." He took her hands in his. "I know I've been here before. With you."

Chapter Eighteen

Now that Dominic considered himself and Enid an 'item,' he planned to take her to a slew of places they'd enjoy together...Plymouth, Salem, Boston, with the Barnstable ghost tour first on the list. Good for a few laughs, it was also convenient, and best of all, free. The guide, Josh, was a buddy of Petra's, so he offered them the tour gratis. It evolved into a family outing when he invited Petra, and Enid managed to bribe Charles and Charlotte with new headphones if they tagged along.

On a moonless night, the little 'family' joined a group in a stroll through Cape Cod's Barnstable Village. Dominic still had all this figured for mumbo-jumbo, but he got a kick out of seeing Enid and Petra so enthralled.

After introducing himself as their guide, Josh brought the group on a stroll, stopping at landmark buildings along the road and delighting them with one spooky story after another. Their tour began and ended at the seventeenth-century Old Gaol.

Josh herded the group into the rear of the clapboard building and shut the door. "These were the holding cells back in the day. Those holes in the walls are where the jailers passed food to the prisoners."

As they all stood engulfed in total darkness, he spun more ghostly tales.

"So that concludes our tour." He opened the door

and turned on a light. "But before we head out, does anyone have a story they'd like to share?"

"I do," one woman spoke up. "I just got back from England. I was in Canterbury Cathedral, standing on the spot where Thomas Becket was murdered in the eleventh century."

The group listened, rapt with attention.

"Out of the corner of my eye I saw a figure dressed in brown. When I moved over to let him pass, no one was there. When I got home, I Googled 'Canterbury Cathedral ghosts' and learned that a monk in a brown caul haunts that very spot."

A chorus of *ooo*'s resonated through the jailhouse.

Another man boasted about his eighteenth-century home's resident ghost. "I named him Ollie after the sea captain who'd built it. Ollie likes to hide things and make me find them. He's just having fun." He went on, "I saw a figure in old-fashioned clothes standing at my bed a few times. One time he pulled my covers down."

Then, to Dominic's surprise, Enid nudged her way forward, turned and faced the group. "I have more than ghost stories to tell. I've had this verified by three mediums over the years. I am the reincarnation of a woman who hunted down witches in medieval Europe. On each of my many past life regressions, I've gone back to that same life, where I have a young daughter who looks like my dear departed Jill…" She paused to catch her breath. "But I couldn't find out my name. The mediums couldn't come up with a name, either."

"Maybe you're not meant to know yet," Josh offered. "When and if it's time to find out, you will. And not necessarily while you're here on Earth."

"I'm having another regression tomorrow," she

announced. "I'm praying I'll find out more about this lady. But I've just about given up hope. After twenty-five years of regressions, I get the same details, nothing new. While in that past life, I devoted my time to annihilating witches...and caring for my daughter."

"How do you feel about witches now?" Josh asked her.

"I'm completely understanding and open to them. Some of my best friends are Wiccans. I hunted witches in my past life because I believed they put spells on me to make me ill and infirm. But now, in hindsight, we all know that's nonsense. My grandson and granddaughter have a few stories to tell, too. They lived previous lives as a prostitute and a pirate."

With that, Charlotte and Charles elbowed their way through the group and left the building.

"They're kind of shy about it." Enid excused herself and bolted out the door after them.

"I believe I was reincarnated, too," offered a girl wearing a Claddagh design on her shirt. "I lived in Ireland in the seventeen-hundreds. My name was Dair, Old Irish for 'oak.' I was a Druid."

Petra gasped. "Wicked cool! Are you one now?"

"No, but I've always been interested in Druidism," she said.

"We'll have to talk later!" Petra gushed.

"Anybody else?" Josh scanned the group.

Dominic checked his watch.

A middle-aged man stepped up, unbuttoned his collar and shined his flashlight on himself. A thick red mark circled his neck. "I was hanged in a previous life as a highwayman in the sixteen-hundreds," he divulged. "Sometimes birthmarks we have in this life correspond to an old wound from a previous life."

Dominic shuddered, completely creeped out. He nudged Petra. "I've had enough storytelling for one night," he stage-whispered to her. "Somehow it's not the same without a campfire and s'mores. Come on, let's get out of here. I promised Enid I'd take her dancing at the Irish Village."

****

Kilkenny, Ireland, July 2, 1324

Sweat trickled down Alice's back as two guards escorted her into the crowded courtroom. She breathed through her mouth to ward off the repulsive odor of unwashed bodies, but it penetrated her fabric, her skin and her taste buds. She fought the urge to vomit.

Vicious stares followed her as she strode up the narrow aisle. Chancellor Edward de Burgh, perched on a dais like a king, motioned for her to sit on a bench facing him. A smirk crossed Bishop Ledrede's wrinkled face. She looked through him as if he didn't exist.

Michael strode in, a sheath of papers clutched in his hands. She released a sigh of relief at the sight of her savior. He sat beside her and their eyes met. He nodded at her silent plea, but said nary a word. The steely determination and confidence radiating from him said it all.

With a metallic clang of his gavel on a slab, de Burgh called the court to order. "Dame Alice Kyteler, on the unanimous agreement of the secular and religious courts, on account of various acts of sorcery and manifold heresy, and having made sacrificial offerings to demons, you are judged an heretic by brother Richard, Bishop of Ossory, with Lord John Darcy, the Justiciar of Ireland, Roger Outlawe, the Prior of Kilmainham, Chancellor and Treasurer as witnesses. The sheriff of Kilkenny sent his men to ye Kyteler Inn to confiscate your goods. Sheriff, take the oath and state your case."

The sheriff, dragging his lame left foot, wooden cane thumping on the floor with each step, shuffled up to the witness box. The bailiff gave him the oath on a tattered Bible.

Bishop Ledrede stood, his scarlet robe knocking the bench askew. "Sheriff, tell the court in the name of God what you found in Dame Kyteler's inn that serves as proof that she is an heretic and murderer of her spouse John LePoer."

"We found a teacup on the bedside table of John LePoer containing the remnants of four herbs, foxglove, mandrake, hemlock and moonsbane. As determined by our alchemist, moonsbane is deadly in certain combinations. According to Druid bard Lord John Darcy, Dame Kyteler is the only Druid in all of Ireland who possesses spores of the deadly moonsbane. No one else could have administered moonsbane to John LePoer."

Michael stood. "Objection. But someone else *did* administer it. Brona Merivale also knew Dame Kyteler possessed the moonsbane. On the third of June, Brona ordered her son Crispin to don a disguise as a guest at the Kyteler Inn. He signed in as Kevin Kelly. He picked the lock of Dame Kyteler's herb chest, pilfered the moonsbane, and served it to John LePoer in brewed tea. It directly caused his demise. Brona's motive has always been strong, as she believes John deserted her daughter Margaret for Dame Kyteler, although that is not true. John annulled their marriage for…" He cleared his throat. "For personal reasons. Brona and Crispin are outside the courtroom awaiting my cross-examination."

"And how did Brona Merivale happen to know Dame Kyteler is the only Druid in Ireland who possesses the deadly moonsbane?" Ledrede's condescending tone dared Michael to render a believable reply.

"When Brona and Margaret suffered from the sweat, Dame Kyteler brought it to her and showed her the distinctive blue bottle. Moonsbane is also used to cure terminal diseases, in the proper dosage. And most importantly…Dame Kyteler *told* Brona she is the only Druid in Ireland who possesses moonsbane. That is reason enough," he added for effect.

Ledrede huffed, puffed, and rested his case.

Michael brought in Crispin and Brona.

"I never stayed at the Kyteler Inn in disguise or otherwise, under my own name or that of Kevin Kelly," Crispin countered. "I deny that accusation!"

Brona testified under oath, "I never made threats to neither Dame Kyteler nor John LePoer for causing my Maggie such anguish and grief."

Michael also brought in a moneylender who attested, "Crispin used the name Kevin Kelly when trying to secure a loan from me, wearing the same wig and whiskers."

Alice fixed a smug smirk at de Burgh. Her heart slowed down. Brona and Crispin stood nary a chance now.

"I call Petronilla Meath to the stand," Michael announced.

Alice's maidservant approached the stand, swore to tell the truth, and sat.

"Were you Brona Merivale's housemaid for a time?" he asked the pale housemaid.

"Aye, from last April to November," she replied, her voice shaky.

"Did Brona ever mention John LePoer and Dame Kyteler?" he asked.

She nodded. "Aye. Brona told me divers times that she vowed revenge on John and Dame Alice for the death of her daughter Margaret," Petronilla testified. "She said 'My poor Maggie's death will be avenged, if I have any power to do so,' many times whilst in my presence."

A collective gasp filled the musty air.

Petronilla, unblinking, held her head high and faced de Burgh. "And under the influence of the said Dame Alice," she now stared Alice straight in the eye, "I have rejected faith in Christ and the church, and three times on Dame Alice's behalf, I sacrificed to demons." Her voice steady, she spoke as if reciting from a script. "On one of these occasions, by the crossroads outside the city, I made an offering of three cocks to a certain demon from the depths of the underworld. I poured out the cock's blood, cut the animals into pieces and mixed the innards with spiders, with a herb called milfoil as well as other herbs. I boiled this mixture in a pot with the brains and clothes of a boy who had died without baptism and with the head of a robber who had been decapitated. This was all done at Dame Alice's instigation."

Alice sprang to her feet. "Nay, Petronilla, you know that's not true!" She shook her fist. "Who put you up to this? As if I didn't know!" She glared daggers at the bishop. All heads turned to stare as her rant hung in the stale air.

"Silence!" de Burgh ordered. "One more word and you'll not have a chance to say your prayers!"

Petronilla went on, "I also made many concoctions, lotions and powders to cause injuries to the bodies of the faithful and arouse love and hate as well as make the faces of certain women appear before certain people with horns like goats when incantations were added." Her eyes narrowed to slits as she went on, "Dame Alice and I had put our own husbands under the sentence of excommunication, by lighting waxen candles and spitting various ways as the ritual required. And although in our unholy art I was the mistress of the ritual, I was nothing in comparison with my mistress, from whom I'd learnt all these things and many others. In fact, there is no one in Ireland more skilled than Dame Alice, nor do I think there is anyone in the world her equal in the art of witchcraft."

Petronilla's testimony almost knocked Alice off her feet. Forced to stand in silence, she recoiled at these outlandish accusations. She tugged on Michael's sleeve. "That never happened! The church must have tortured Petronilla into this confession, as they always do on these diabolical witch hunts, with Ledrede as the prime instigator. They forced her to say all that!" she hissed.

He held his finger to his lips. "Shhh. This has no bearing on your case. She just signed her own death warrant."

With no more witnesses, Michael rested his case.

De Burgh stared Alice down, his eyes narrowed to hateful slits. "Dame Alice Kyteler, you are hereby judged, proved and condemned as a heretic and consigned to the flames and burned at the stake tomorrow at high noon."

Shock struck Alice numb. She swallowed a lump and shuddered.

The guard dragged Alice back to her cell, shoved her inside and slammed the door shut. She stumbled and tripped over the chamber pot. It turned over, urine soaking the dirt floor. The sour odor hit her in the face. As she turned away, gagging, a dark figure hovered on the other side of the barred window like a ghost. She took a step closer. Sharp features came into focus— black brows furrowed over slitty eyes, a long nose pointing like an accusing finger, thin lips spread into a sinister snarl, deep lines etched into a bony face.

"Brona! What are you doing here?"

A cackle escaped the woman's throat. Alice's flesh crawled. "I hate you and your dead husband for all eternity." Her gravelly voice echoed and died in the chamber's depths. "I promise you'll never see old age in this life or any other. You will never rest in peace."

Alice's breath halted as those hateful words struck her like a blow to the head. "Then it was you...you murdered John." She approached the hateful creature and grabbed the bars, fists clenched. "Why? Why did you do this to us?" She spat, teeth clenched in rage. She wanted to reach through the bars and strangle the life from this old crone. "You cruel wretch!"

"It was your fate. And it is far more cruel than I." She backed away, turned and vanished into the dark maw of the prison.

Alice dragged herself to the straw bed, dropped to her knees and curled up, hugging her knees.

Fate. How can it be so cruel, so heartless?

The biggest question of her life entered her mind

again.

How much free will do we mortals really have? Does fate drag us through our lives, rewarding and condemning us here on Earth and our souls through eternity?

She had only one way to find out.

Emerging from her depths of despair, she breathed deep as a steely determination quickened her heartbeat. Unfolding her body from her fetal position, she stood tall, thrust out her chin and chest, pushed back her shoulders, opened her stance to the universe. Shaking a fist at fate, she vowed, "I shall fight you with my last breath. You hear that, fate? I shall kick your bloody arse!"

****

The next morn at sunrise, the guard nudged Alice from a restless sleep. "You're to appear in Dublin before the Lord Dean of St. Patrick's church."

"There are worse places to appear than Dublin," she muttered as a steward brought in a wooden trencher and an earthenware jug.

He placed it on the floor before her and slipped out.

Thirsty, she took a sip of the liquid—warm bitter ale. She spat it out, wondering if it was poisoned with her own herbs. The trencher held a slice of brown bread. She scowled.

Didn't even butter it, cheap sods.

****

In the wagon on the three-day journey to Dublin, she repeated her vow, now a mantra: "I shall fight you, fate, and I shall win!"

Two priests met her wagon at the church and helped her down. She settled her gaze on God's house towering over her, its magnificent spires stabbing the sky.

The ruddy-faced Lord Dean sat behind a desk that looked more like a pulpit.

"I respectfully request that a day be set for my response," she spoke up.

He took a breath, looked up at her and his ice-blue eyes met hers. "Your request is denied, Dame Kyteler."

"For now, mayhap," came her answer.

Back in her cell, she knelt and repeated her mantra. "Watch me, fate, you heartless bastard, I won't let you defeat me." She chanted herself into a deep sleep.

Her cell door groaned open. Jolted awake, she squinted in daybreak's gauzy light. A guard led Michael in.

"Tell me the good word, Michael. I know you've come to set me free. It couldn't happen any other way. I fought fate and won."

He approached her and gathered her in his arms. "Crispin confessed to donning the disguise as Kevin Kelly and giving John the deadly brew of moonsbane. He even produced the blue bottle he'd pinched from your cupboard. He wanted to confess and serve his time so God would forgive him. But he didn't mention that his mother manipulated him into the murder on her behalf, so she went free." He paused to take a breath and sobbed, holding her fast to him. "And now, my love…you're free."

"I knew it." Emotionally drained, she pitched forward.

He brought her to the bed and sat her down. "Here. Sit for a moment."

Too exhausted to sob with relief, she babbled,

"Where will we spend our new life together? England, I want to go to England. I feel I've been there before and belong there. I need return and finish my life there."

"Your wish is my command." He bowed before her. "But first we're going to your favorite place, the dolmens in the Boyne Valley. The most fitting place I can propose marriage to you...properly."

Chapter Nineteen

Dominic pulled into Enid's driveway, his stomach growling. This invite to a home cooked dinner saved his hide—and his shrinking wallet.

He grabbed the twelve dollar bottle of table wine he'd bought at Shanley's Discount Liquors, strode up her walk and rang the bell.

She answered, swathed in chiffon, her signature diamonds glittering. "Dom, so glad to see you. Do come in."

"Enid, I can't tell you how much I appreciate your inviting me over. I crave your companionship." *And this free meal,* he added silently. He handed her the wine bottle. "I hope this will go with dinner."

"Why, thank you, how nice." She glanced at the label with thinly disguised disdain.

As they sat and chatted over her baked lasagna and meatballs, he emptied the last of the wine into her glass. "Your grandkids seem kinda shy," he remarked as she passed him the bread across the table set for two. The grandkids were out or hiding.

"They do their own thing, they don't want to hang around with Nana anymore." Her bangle bracelets clinked as she lifted her glass and sipped.

He smiled in appreciation at her upswept hairdo and buffed nails. What a class act, this lady. And an admittedly cheap date to boot!

"Speaking of the kids, they looked real uncomfortable in the old gaol when you started talking about their past lives." He helped himself to another square of lasagna. "They bolted like they'd seen a ghost—heh, heh, bad word choice. Are they squeamish or nonbelievers or what?"

Enid cleared her throat, as if deciding what to reveal and how. "Oh, they're believers, all right. They bolted because they refuse to share this with anybody. They both have psychic gifts. Because they're so gifted, they don't even need to be regressed to reveal the memories of those past lives. But they told me when they lived in the distant past, they did bad things." She folded her hands under her chin. "There's nothing to be proud of in being a pirate and a prostitute. These memories tormented them so badly, I took them to a child psychologist. He rattled off the standard theories—it's their overactive imaginations, they'll grow out of it." Enid let out a whoosh of disgust. "I should've taken them to a shaman or a medium instead of a doctor brainwashed in the ways of Western medicine. But the children never spoke of it again." She slid a bite of lasagna onto her fork. "Neither of them have mentioned their past lives in, oh, I'd say at least seven years now. Just around the time Jill died, they withdrew and hardly shared anything with me. Except tidbits about Ted and Kylah." She halted her fork halfway to her mouth. "You know, the loud fights over his drinking, and her, uh...*friendship* with Michael Richardson, her, uh...*lawyer.*"

He nodded. "Have you always been a believer in the supernatural?" Dominic sipped the fizzy wine, cringing in shame. Oh, if only he could afford a nice red Zinfandel instead of this rotgut.

"I'm a big believer in the spirit world and past lives." She paused. "For many reasons."

He sensed she didn't want to elaborate on that. But if they didn't find some common ground, he was afraid she'd call this budding courtship quits. "So, tell me...that story of the past life you told at the gaol, being a witch hunter...that was amazing. And I never thought I'd admit this, but all this stuff is beginning to fascinate me. Petra's been pushing me to get into the Druid thing, and..." He knew this was the wine talking, but this would bring them closer, "and I'm getting sucked into it, but in a good way." A grin came easily to him. "This feels so natural to talk about it. Before, I'd have laughed out loud. But now, the more I learn, the wider my sights. By that I mean I'm more open-minded. For some inane reason, it's all beginning to make sense to me. It's filling a void in my life."

"Well, I'm glad to hear that, Dom." She raised her glass in a toast and clinked it with his. "There's a lot more to this world than what we can see or hear."

Now she seemed to be opening up—the right time to dig deep. "Did you go on that regression you told the group at the gaol you were going to?"

She nodded and held the glass to her lips.

He figured that was a prop to hide behind.

"Yes, I did." She still waffled, like she couldn't decide how much, or what, to divulge. "And it wasn't pretty."

"So did it turn out you were a witch and somebody hunted you down?" He was so full, he needed to loosen his belt, but kept eating. Where would another slap-up meal like this come from? He banked on her being flattered at his asking to take some leftovers home.

"No, but I was worse than any prostitute or pirate," she admitted, still hiding behind her glass.

"What happened?" He put his fork down for the first time since he'd sat at the table.

Her lips tightened and she shook her head. "I can't tell you, Dom. It's shameful."

He tried not to sulk, but heck, he was disappointed. He wanted to hear all the gory details. "C'mon, you can tell old Dom. We've become…well, close by now. At least I hope so."

She twirled her glass by the stem. "Maybe I'll tell you later. It's not exactly table talk."

"Petra thinks she lived a past life, too, in the Middle Ages," he divulged, his tongue nice and loose. "She didn't say anything at the gaol and I'm not surprised. She doesn't want to face it, either." He eyed her questioning expression and went on, "She was executed in that life. Horribly."

"Oh, Lord above, what for? Does she know?" Enid clasped her chest in a gesture of horror.

"For being a witch. She was burned at the stake. And has a mark on her arm that she was born with. Right about here." He held up his arm to show her the area. "She insists it's a carryover from her atrocious end."

She gasped. "It's barbaric what those brutes did to those poor souls. Does she have difficulty with it, or has she managed to put it behind her?"

"I think the Druids have helped her." Dominic debated whether to grab another piece of bread. He didn't want to make a pig out of himself. "She seems a different person since she joined them, I must admit."

"Since you've shown some interest, I strongly suggest you become more involved, too," Enid urged in a sharp tone. "If my Jill had that in her life, she would have been so much happier. She may not even have killed herself, wouldn't have let Ted and Kylah get to her the way they did. But it's all speculation now. At least you have Petra and this is a way to be closer to her, and to your spirituality."

He reached across the table to grasp her hand. "Enid, I thank God for bringing you into my life. You've helped me like you'll never know. And you know what would help me even more?"

"What?" Her eyes widened.

He glanced at the pan between them, one square of lasagna remaining. "Whip me up one of these every week and I'm forever in your debt."

****

Emerging from a deep sleep, Kylah sat up. Familiar surroundings welcomed her—her lilac comforter, her white ruffled curtains. She breathed the sweet fragrance of vanilla. "Oh, thank God I'm home..." The trauma she'd just suffered in that past life came rushing back. But the mystery was solved. John LePoer's ex mother-in-law Brona was the mastermind behind John's murder and she'd framed Alice. The parallel to this life hit her so hard she reeled as if whacked on the head. Who is Ted's ex mother-in-law?

"Oh, my God. Enid!" Realization struck her numb. Gasping for air, she grabbed her phone. "Mike, I know Enid killed Ted. She planned it all out. She got into the house, killed Ted and framed me," she rattled off in a single breath. "She killed him with the same herbs Brona used on Alice's husband John in 1324. The exact same events happened, seven centuries apart." She gulped air.

"Okay, okay, stay put, I'll be right over."

Shaking, she took a few breaths and headed for her closet to get dressed. "What the..." Her Levi's were missing. She pulled slacks, skirts and blouses off hangers, tossed sweaters aside. No sign of those jeans. Did she lose them in the move from the other house? No, that couldn't be...

She looked to see if anything else was missing. Sure enough, her blue striped shirt was gone. And her blue hat with the orange band. Come to think of it, she didn't remember even packing those things. They disappeared before she moved out of the house. "Enid, you monster," she growled through clenched teeth.

****

"My jeans and shirt are missing. I know she was there. She wore my clothes to look like me in case someone saw her," she told Mike as they sat at her new dinette set in her living space over the store.

"We need more evidence for probable cause against Enid before an arrest can be made," he told her. "I'll tell the police about your missing clothes and your suspicion that Enid has them, and I'll have a detective question Enid and her grandkids. They can get a search warrant to see if your clothes are in her house." He got up to leave. "I'm not wasting another second, I'll get back to you." He kissed her and hustled out.

With her trial in less than twenty-four hours, she bowed her head, pictured her sacred oak in the cemetery, and prayed.

****

Kylah's cell phone rang ten minutes into her lunch

break. A local number. Not the *Boston Globe* or a TV station. "Kylah McKinley speaking."

"Mrs. McKinley, this is Detective Lieutenant Frank Munn. I've been questioning Mrs. Streetman here in my office, but she insists that you be here before she says another word. Are you able to come down here now?"

"Enid needs me there? What for?" She shook her head, baffled.

"She won't say until you get here, ma'am."

"Uh…" she sputtered. "Okay, I'll be right down."

On the drive to the police station, she didn't even play the radio. *What could Enid possibly need me there for?* she repeated over and over in her mind. The detective hadn't subpoenaed her. She could've refused to go.

But she was too damn curious.

****

The lady officer behind the window pointed to her right. "Detective Munn's office is the first on the right."

Kylah knocked on the door.

"Come in."

She entered and the detective greeted her from behind his desk. "Thank you for coming in, Mrs. McKinley. Have a seat. You know Mrs. Streetman."

A pearl-necklaced Enid nodded, straight faced.

I can't stand the sight of you, sat at the tip of Kylah's tongue as she sat next to Enid and gripped the chair arms.

"Mrs. McKinley, we called Mrs. Streetman in for questioning, which I taped. She insisted that she needs you to hear this, and something else she has to say." Munn hit the play button on his recorder.

She leaned forward to listen.

"Mrs. Streetman, thank you for agreeing to talk to me," Munn said.

"I am happy to cooperate, Detective." Enid's voice came through clear as if it were live. "I want justice done like everyone else."

"You don't need a lawyer, we just need some information. Now...can you please go through every step of the day your late former son-in-law Ted McKinley died, from the time you got up?"

Kylah pulled the chair closer to make sure she caught every word.

"I hadn't seen Kylah for months...or Ted, for that matter. I wanted nothing to do with either of them. I loathed them, but I despised her more. I know Kylah was responsible for my poor Jill's untimely demise..."

"Mrs. Streetman," he cut in, "not to interrupt, but we must stick to the subject at hand. Please give me an account of what you did that day."

"I was out of town."

As if that solved the case. Kylah shook her head in disgust but didn't dare say a word.

"Out of town where?" Munn prodded. "I need specifics. And can you provide documentation as to where you were? Receipts for gas, restaurants? Was anyone with you?"

"Why, of course, Charlotte was with me. We went to..." She paused.

Kylah's ears perked.

"Uh...I have no receipts. I throw them all out. I was...four days..." She faltered. "No, that was the week after..." She rambled on, barely coherent.

Kylah's chest tightened, every muscle tense as a coiled spring.

"Calm down, Mrs. Streetman," Munn's recorded voice went on. "You can't think straight when you're all flustered like this." His tone gentled. "I know it was a while ago, but can you tell me if in fact you were on a trip that day?"

"Of course I was." Her voice took on an accusatory tone. "How dare you question my veracity. I was nowhere near that woman—or her husband." She audibly huffed and went on, "Kylah killed Ted, and I can tell you why she killed him. For his money."

Kylah's jaw dropped.

"She never made a decent living in that perverted store of hers. Or hunting ghosts or fortune telling with those silly cards," the tape went on.

"Mrs. Streetman...you need to get back on track," Munn's insistent voice gained volume.

"I wanted nothing to do with either of them. We have absolutely nothing in common."

As her babbling continued on tape, Kylah watched Enid's eyes wander from one point to another...the window, the file cabinet, the computer, darting around like pinballs. Her hands fluttered.

Her recorded voice continued, "Detective—" She cleared her throat. "I need Mrs. McKinley here before I say another word."

Munn hit the stop button. "All right, she's here now, Mrs. Streetman. What do you need to say to her?"

Kylah looked over at Enid. Their eyes met.

The lines around Enid's mouth deepened. She gulped, pulled on her fingers, scratched her head. "Kylah, I had to stop accusing you the instant I looked at..." She pointed straight ahead. "At what's behind the detective."

Kylah craned her neck to see.

What's back there?

Enid seemed to hold her breath. Her body froze. She stared as if mesmerized. A sob escaped her throat.

Kylah followed Enid's pointing finger. Next to Munn's photos on the wall hung a plaque made to look like aged parchment.

"What are you talking about, Enid?" Kylah's blood boiled. Her fingers clenched the chair arms. She wanted to reach over and strangle this woman.

Munn turned to look. "My Saint Patrick plaque?"

"My name is Patrick," Enid read out loud from the plaque. "I am a sinner, a simple country person, and the least of all believers. I am looked down upon by many." Her voice broke.

Kylah studied Enid's dazed expression. Munn said, "That's Saint Patrick's Confession. I got that in Ireland years ago."

"I know all about him." Enid folded her hands. "Irish pirates captured him when he was sixteen, brought him to Ireland and enslaved him for six years. In *The Confession* he wrote that his time in captivity made him evolve spiritually. God forgave his sins and he converted to Christianity."

"That's right." Munn nodded. "So why call Mrs. McKinley in here?"

"I am Irish and always was." Enid's voice lowered.

Kylah strained to hear her.

Munn hit the 'record' button on the machine.

"I have a strong connection to Patrick," Enid went on. "I always knew I lived a previous life in the Middle Ages, but on a recent regression, I found out exactly who I was. I was Brona Merivale, in fourteenth century

Kilkenny. After my son-in-law John deserted my daughter Margaret, he married Alice Kyteler. When my Margaret died I always blamed those two for her death." She focused pleading eyes on Kylah. "I did it." She laced her fingers. Blue veins stood out on her age-spotted hands.

"Did what?" Munn asked.

"I planned the murder of John in that life." Her voice quivered. "I got my son to give him a deadly brew of herbs. I was never brought to justice, I never served my time as I should have. Guilt gnawed away at me." She gazed at the plaque, as if speaking to it. "In that past life, I knew how Patrick's time in captivity brought him to God. In 1375, I made a pilgrimage to his tomb at Downpatrick. There I had a vision." Enid's eyes stayed focused on the written Confession. "Patrick appeared before me. He urged me to confess, repent, serve my time and God would forgive me. But I never got the chance. I was killed on the way home, run over by what I don't know. It happened so fast, I didn't know what hit me."

Munn let out a whoosh of breath.

Kylah sat stone still, more in shock than when she got Munn's phone call.

Munn sat up straight. "I'm sorry about your messy fourteenth century demise, Mrs. Streetman, but that's slightly out of my jurisdiction." He glanced at his watch.

Enid held her head high as if testifying before Congress and turned to face Kylah. "When I was Brona in that life, my son-in-law John lusted after Alice Kyteler. He annulled his marriage to my daughter and married Alice. And guess who Alice Kyteler is in this life? Kylah McKinley." She turned to Munn. "And she can prove that beyond any doubt. I lived it as much as she did."

Munn looked ready to call the men in the white coats. But it all came together now. Enid just proved she really was Brona.

"Enough about the reincarnations, Mrs. Streetman," Munn cut in. "Now let's get back to the present and Ted McKinley."

"I was just about to. Detective. I can't live with this on my conscience, vexing and haunting my soul, for the rest of this life." She took another breath. "And future lives, as it did in my past life as Brona. So I must confess." She spilled her guts. "I also killed Ted McKinley in this life."

Munn frowned.

"I knew it!" Kylah stared, shaking. She forced every ounce of willpower not to scream her throat raw at this woman.

"Go on, Mrs. Streetman," Munn urged.

"I followed Kylah for two weeks, getting her schedule down pat, so that I knew when she'd be out of the house. She left for her store at 9 a.m., very punctual, wanting to be there one hour before opening. She parked her car in the converted carriage house behind her store. She went home at lunch time, noon sharp, and stayed half an hour." Enid clutched her pearls. "Then the kids told me that she did inventory twice a year on a Sunday, in June and December, and stayed in the store till late at night. She closes the store early on inventory days so she can go in the back and work in peace. The kids know this because that's when they and Ted went on their bi-annual trek to Provincetown, rain, shine, snow or sleet. It was a ritual with them. But on this day, Ted cancelled on them. He didn't give a reason."

"Go on," Munn urged, glancing at Kylah.

"A week before the murder, I bought a train ticket to Columbus, Ohio under a false name, went to a dealership there and purchased a white Mustang convertible, identical to hers, with cash. I drove it back and hid it in my garage. I put Massachusetts plates on it, the special plates that say 'Cape Cod and Islands' with the picture of the lighthouse on them."

Munn opened a bottle of antacid tablets and popped one into his mouth. "And then what happened, Mrs. Streetman?"

"I bought an outfit to wear to her house, a colorful Bohemian-looking skirt, blouse and big hat that was her style. On the day she did her inventory and Ted cancelled on the kids, I drove to Ted and Kylah's in the Mustang I'd bought, so any neighbors would see the car and testify that she'd been there at the time of Ted's death.

"I rang the doorbell and heard Ted wheeling himself to the door. He opened it and gasped in shock to see me standing there. He said something like, 'Enid! What are you doing here?' I kept my eyes downcast, trying to look uncomfortable, like it was a major struggle to force myself to go there. I told him I couldn't live with myself anymore and broke into wracking sobs. I needed to sound like they shook me to my soul. I recited my bogus confession, 'Ted, I've been meaning to come to you for several years now, and never had the guts to bring myself here. I know you're not too fond of me. I now realize you left Jill for good reasons and enough time has passed for me to look at this whole thing objectively. I just wanted to come by to say—I'm sorry. I'm sorry for all the misery I've caused you and Kylah, and I hate myself for it.' I made my voice quiver, and forced a new flood of tears to come. I'm good at that, you know."

Munn sucked on his tablet and popped another one.

Kylah's breath caught in her throat. Her heart all but stopped.

"Ted said something like 'Well, Enid, we make mistakes, do and say things we regret, but that's where forgiveness comes in.' I told Ted I came over because Christ led me, but now I begged Ted to forgive me. He said 'Okey dokey' with a casual shrug. He wasn't very religious, you know."

Munn nodded. "I didn't know him, but go on."

"I took a step toward him, bent down and wrapped my arms around him. I think he realized this was the first time we'd ever had any physical contact. Never had we even shook hands. Then I offered to make us a pot of tea. He told me Kylah's teas were in the cabinet above the stove. The kids had told me the exact location of Kylah's secret herb cupboard. They knew because they'd seen her mix some of her concoctions. So I headed straight for it. It was locked. I broke into it with a knife and opened the door. I felt I'd just stepped into a pharmacy: rows and rows of jars lined up with military precision, each labeled in block lettering, in alphabetical order. I got out the piece of paper with the Druid formula on it. I knew about the moonsbane being in a blue bottle from my past life as Brona. So my perfect murder was halfway done."

Munn swallowed. Kylah trembled with rage. "You evil monster," she muttered.

Enid took a breath, her eyes still fixed to Patrick's Confession. "I went into the kitchen and fetched a teacup, then went back to the cupboard to fulfill my mission, to mix these herbs and cause Ted a slow, agonizing death. Hemlock, mandrake, foxglove, and of course the moonsbane, they were all there, waiting for me to combine them into the deadly formula. I deliberately put the bottles back in the wrong places, to make it look like someone was in a hurry to concoct this potion, and that someone, when the police investigated Ted's death, would be Kylah." She glanced Kylah's way.

Kylah couldn't stand the sight of this woman. She looked at Munn, his gaze fixed on Enid.

Enid went on, "Detective...and Kylah, there's a deeper reason I behaved the way I did. I hate myself. I always had self-loathing from the day I emerged from the womb. Why? Because my mother died giving birth to me and my father always threw that in my face, I killed her. So I needed to do something heinous and get punished, which is what I always believe I deserved. In both lives."

He cut in, "Mrs. Streetman, I'm not a psychiatrist. You can get counseling later."

"I believed Ted left Jill for Kylah, and wanted to punish him and Kylah both. I also wanted revenge at my father for hating me," she rambled.

"I'm sure your father is cowering in his grave, Mrs. Streetman." He glanced at his watch again. "Now get back to the facts. This battery only lasts two hours."

She cracked her knuckles. "Then I mixed the lethal herbs, brewed it in water, and gave it to Ted. After Ted drank his deadly dose, I told him the truth—that I was killing him for all the misery he and Kylah caused Jill, for driving my girl to suicide. I explained how it happened the same way in our past lives as Brona, her daughter Margaret, Alice Kyteler and John LePoer. Brona killed John with the same herbs and set Alice up to take the blame, as I'd just done. By then Ted had minutes to live." Enid cleared her throat. She avoided eye contact with either of them. "He pointed to a spiral notebook and pen on his bookshelf and asked me for them, to make one last entry. I said if he mentioned my name in there, I'd burn it. He wrote his entry, then I took it from him and read it. It didn't incriminate me. In fact, it looked as if Kylah had killed him and he forgave her. And he had some ramblings about Poe on the page. All in red ink. I put the notebook and pen down on the table. I saw a handgun on the table, took it and held him at gunpoint so he wouldn't try anything. He was in a wheelchair, but he was strong, you know. When I saw him groan in agony and clutch his stomach, I knew it was the end. He fell onto the floor." She dabbed at her eyes with a tissue. "After I made sure he was no longer breathing, I went into Kylah's room, got a pair of jeans, a shirt and a hat to make sure I looked more like her than when I'd come in. I let myself out and took off my gloves. I got into the Mustang and drove away, believing I'd committed the perfect murder. Just as I did in Ireland seven centuries ago." She took a deep breath and said no more.

Munn rested his chin in his palm. "Mrs. Streetman, can you give me any details that show definitively that you committed this murder?"

"Of course." She didn't miss a beat. "Ted was lying on his right side clutching his middle when I left him. The wheelchair was also on its side, he knocked it over."

"That's exactly the way I found him, lying on his right side clutching his middle, and the wheelchair knocked over!" Kylah shouted, unable to hold back any longer. "No one else could have known that, Detective."

"Please keep your voice down, Mrs. McKinley," Munn said.

Kylah seethed. Her fists clenched. "I knew it," she said. "When I saw my clothes were missing, I knew it was you who killed Ted, like you killed John in that life as Brona. But why this sudden guilt trip, Enid?"

"It's hardly sudden, dear." Her voice quivered. "As I said before, Saint Patrick urged me to confess when I made a pilgrimage to his tomb in 1325. But I never got the chance. I was killed on the way home. I thought if I don't confess to this murder now, I'm doomed to repeat my sins and my soul will never see peace."

As Munn sat there, shaking his head, Kylah read his mind: this is a doozy for Cape Cod.

"And to remove any shred of suspicion against you and prove my guilt beyond any doubt, I had to state that I knew Ted was lying on his right side clutching his middle when he died. With the wheelchair knocked over and his notebook open on the table. Oh, one other thing…I put his gun on the bookshelf, not back on the table where I found it." Enid stood and held out her hands, wrists up. "You're going to cuff me now, Detective?"

"No. I'm not arresting you at this point. But I'm going to detain you here until I get some of these things verified. Then I have to contact the District Attorney."

He then asked, "But about this fourteenth century life of yours in Ireland, why are you so sure it ties in with Kylah and Ted McKinley?" He looked at Kylah and back at Enid.

"Because I've traveled back to that lifetime. And now, in this life, I'm getting my karma back. As is Kylah." She nodded in Kylah's direction. "If we don't learn from our history, we're doomed to repeat it." She said all this without blinking an eye. "Karma will take care of what is meant to be."

"Mrs. Streetman, you can talk more, but I need to read you your rights," Munn said. "It's our policies and procedures."

She nodded.

"You have the right to remain silent, anything you say can and will be used against you in a court of law, you have a right to have an attorney with you when you're being questioned. If you cannot afford one, one will be appointed by the court to represent you. You can decide at any time to exercise these rights and have a lawyer with you. You can stop answering questions at any time. Do you understand these rights as I've just read them to you?"

"Of course." As if she'd been through this routine before. "I waive my rights. I'm ready to pay my penance."

He hit the stop button on the recorder and held up his hand. "Mrs. Streetman, can we pause here, please? I'll take you into the waiting room to sit for a while. Mrs. McKinley, I'll be right back."

Kylah sat there, stunned. So Enid had accused her, then Saint Patrick got her to confess. She bowed her head. "Thank you, Saint Patrick."

Munn came back in and closed the door. "We have to go through the motions with her now, Mrs. McKinley. You can go."

****

She walked out of there in a daze. Picking up her pace, she fished in her purse for her phone and almost tumbled down the steps as she called Mike.

"Call me back, you're not gonna believe this."

She got into her car, but didn't drive back to the store. She needed a few moments alone, in silence.

She headed to Woodside Cemetery to sit with her angel.

****

"So she confessed, how 'bout that." Mike opened a bottle of champagne and filled their flutes as they snuggled before her hearth's dancing flames.

"The detective didn't believe a word of it until she said Ted was lying on his right side, clutching his middle, the wheelchair knocked over and the notebook open on the table. That clinched it. That's when he read her her rights." Kylah took a sip of the sweet bubbly. "I'm still worried, though. What if her lawyer gets her off? An insanity plea wouldn't be much of a stretch." She took another sip, then a gulp, welcoming the buzz soothing her fears.

"She's the one who's big on karma. That's why she confessed in the first place." He stroked her hair. "She'll probably waive her rights to a lawyer and a trial. Don't let your doubts get the best of you. And don't ever go on any more of those trips to the past. I can't handle it."

She smiled and took a deep cleansing breath. "There's no need to. It's not like I wanted to go back. I had to."

"Good. Let's enjoy the present and look to the future. I've had enough of the past." He took her glass, put his down, and opened his arms. They embraced as their lips met in a lingering kiss.

Her phone rang.

"Let it ring," she sighed and recaptured his lips.

Later, she checked her missed call. It was Charlotte, Enid's granddaughter, Ted's stepdaughter. "Now what would she want?" Kylah muttered, making a mental note to call her back.

****

The bells on her store's door jangled as Mike entered with a jaunty step. Since Kylah was no longer a one-woman freak show, a cop no longer guarded the entrance. She dashed around the counter to greet him.

His smile told her she had nothing to fear this time. "The prosecutor moved for a continuance, delaying your trial pending closing of the investigation with Enid as the new suspect." He clasped her arms and went on, "Her public defender tried to have her confession thrown out, but she insisted that it stand. She was arrested and arraigned. Her lawyer entered a plea bargain and she was sentenced to twenty years." His hands slid down to clasp hers.

Kylah took a deep breath and whispered, "I'm free," as Mike's arms enveloped her. Warm cleansing tears fell from both of them.

"Now we can begin our life together, our next life," he promised her.

****

Kylah got her mail, went inside and opened the package from the County Courthouse. She knew what it was—her jeans, shirt, shoes, hat, sunglasses—and Ted's spiral notebook the cops found on the table next to Ted, that same page facing out, his entry in red ink.

She put her glasses on and read, "You did what you had to do. And I forgive you. I'm going to a better place and can go with a clean conscience. I had nothing to live for here anyway. Whoever I was in any past lives, I hope to return to Earth as a writer as gifted and with a sense of humor and the macabre as the man who, with pen and paper, created worlds beyond anything we mortals can imagine on Earth or beyond, who I idolize more than any other: Eddie Poe. Gotta go. Ted."

This was the entry Officer Hughes read to her when she didn't have her reading glasses. Glasses on, she was able to see it was much more than what Enid called "some ramblings about Poe." It was one of his note-within-a-note messages to her. He'd written certain letters more slanted than others. They spelled out three words.

Enid poisoned me.

She pressed the notebook to her heart as Ted's aroma of pine aftershave, manly sweat and marijuana surrounded her. "I know she did, Teddy. She's paying for it. And I know you and Eddie Poe are kicking up your heels together. I bet he wishes he could have made this all up."

****

Fenway Park, Boston, Massachusetts

The night couldn't be more perfect for baseball. The gentle breeze carried the aromas of peanuts and roasting hot dogs. The sun sank behind the bleachers and the floodlights illuminated the field. Kylah got up from her seat in Field Box 28 along the first base line.

The Red Sox were ahead six to one and it was only the bottom of the fourth inning.

"I'll be right back." She pulled down the brim of her Sox cap. "I'm going for ice cream. You want a cone?"

"Kylah, wait." Mike grabbed her hand.

"Why? One more strike and he's out. I want to beat the line."

"I'll go with you. I just enjoy seeing the Yanks strike out." He pulled her back down to her seat.

She chuckled. "All right."

Strike three. The inning ended. Music blared from the speakers as the Sox trotted off the field.

She stood again, but he grasped her hand.

"What is it?" She pulled away. "The line'll be—"

"Ice cream can wait. Trust me." He pointed to the Fenway Park scoreboard above the bleachers. "Look over at the board."

A dazzling display of lights flashed on the scoreboard, spelling out KYLAH, WILL YOU MARRY ME? She stared, dumbstruck.

Mike dropped to one knee right there in the box and pulled a diamond solitaire from his pocket. He took her hand and slipped the ring onto her left ring finger.

Her tears turned the sparkling diamond into a blur. "Oh, Mike…of course I'll marry you."

The crowd roared, cheered and whistled. He got to his feet, and before 37,000 fans and thousands more watching on television, they shared a warm embrace, savoring the moment.

"They don't wait for the seventh inning stretch, and I couldn't either," he whispered in her ear.

****

Still on a high from that unforgettable moment, she held her hand out to Petra. "Here it is close up. Too bad they didn't zoom in on it with the TV camera," she said over a laugh.

"Oh, it's gorgeous. Wow, what a dazzler." Petra turned Kylah's hand from side to side. "Look at the way it catches the light." She squeezed Kylah's fingers and gave her a smile. "I was bawling like a baby when I watched that last night. It was so romantic. I'll bet it's gone viral on YouTube already. Hey, I'm glad this all worked out for you. You deserve it."

"Thanks." She exhaled as peace washed over her. "I, uh…I was wondering, has your dad been in touch with Enid, visited her in prison?" Her gaze roved around her store, landing on the new display of silver bangles, exactly what Enid would've worn, stacked up to her elbow.

Petra's brows shot up. She paused, as if the question shot her between the eyes. "Well, yeah, he's crazy about her. Still." She fidgeted with her pendant. "He visits her all the time. He's hoping they'll reduce her sentence so they can…you know, he wanted to marry her."

Kylah straightened a stack of "Along 6A" tourist newspapers on the counter, her store featured on the front page. "I've been thinking about Enid. I dreamed about her a few times…I have to say, I respect her for confessing and owning up to her fate. It takes a lot to admit you deserve what's coming to you."

Petra nodded, lips pressed together. "Yeah, but as much as I'm amazed she confessed and insisted it stand, I'm so glad she did. It saved you from a trial…but I know you would've been acquitted," she hastened to add.

"You have to believe in karma, Petra. She shouldn't have killed Ted, but..." She splayed her fingers. "We come from the same place."

"You mean Ireland in the thirteen hundreds?" Petra asked.

"I mean our beliefs. Our demeanors. Warped as it seems to the rest of the world," she replied.

"Would you have killed someone if you were in her situation?" Petra moved closer and lowered her voice, although the few customers in the store stood out of earshot.

"No, I couldn't commit murder." She traced the edge of the newspaper, watching her diamond catch the light and sparkle. "I'm grounded enough in this world to respect lives and the law. Enid took it a step further...and believed she'd get away with it." Kylah took a breath. "But she couldn't. And that's why I can't hate her. She admitted she was wrong, the law prevailed, and there she is."

"You have a very forgiving heart, girl," Petra commented. "There are killers out there I'll never forgive who've killed people I've never met, but if somebody killed my own husband..." She shuddered.

"I wanted to strangle her at first," Kylah said, "but at the end of the day, I'm free, Ted is at peace, she's in prison, and..." She shrugged. "I feel sorry for her. I even want to go visit her."

Petra rested her elbows on the counter. "Then go. She can't harm you from there."

Kylah looked up and smiled at a customer heading for the counter, arms laden with books. "No, she sure can't. Now I can walk down the street without worrying about getting mowed down."

They shared a laugh as Kylah got ready to ring up another sale.

****

Mike put down his salad fork and it clanged against the plate. "You want me to go visit her with you? Why? I have nothing to say to her. I can't believe you want to see her ever again."

Kylah refilled his wine glass. The savory aroma of filet mignon floated from her kitchen. Her mouth watered. "I should've waited till after dinner to talk about this, but it's been on my mind. Charlotte called the other day. I returned her call and we talked a while. She was crying, so upset at her grandmother spending the rest of her days in prison, she was the nicest to me she's ever been. She told me about visiting hours, and I told her I'll go visit her grandmother tomorrow."

"I hope you find something to talk about." He sipped his wine.

"She's a pitiful soul paying her penance, and she'll probably die there." Kylah picked up their salad bowls. "She's at the Correctional Institution in Framingham. When I Googled it, I found out it opened in 1877 and it's the most overcrowded in the state."

"Well, she does seem like the gregarious type."

"Dinner's ready." She pushed her chair back and stood. "But I hope you'll at least think about going there with me."

He followed her into the kitchen and she put the salad bowls in the sink.

"I think it'll be helpful for you to visit her," Kylah said. "Closure, the whole coming-full-circle thing."

"That's your trip, babe." He checked to make sure

the steaks were ready. "Let's eat first. I make more rational decisions on a full stomach."

****

She approached the Massachusetts Correctional Institution and eased up on the gas pedal. "Well, it's not a medieval dungeon." A chill prickled her skin as she remembered that horrible torture chamber from the distant past.

She parked, cut the engine and turned to her right. "Thanks for coming with me, Mike."

"I feel bad..." He paused and grinned. "I didn't bring her any chocolate chip cookies."

Kylah rolled her eyes and slid out of her car. They walked across the parking lot toward the prison entrance.

She held onto her keys. "They'll want me to surrender these at the metal detec—"

Before she finished her sentence, an engine roared and a car headed straight for them. "Mike!" she shrieked. He hurled her out of the way. She stumbled and fell on her hands and knees. The car struck Mike with a sickening thud, tore through the lot, and hit a tree head-on. An ear-piercing bang shook the ground. Metal crunched. Glass shattered. Steam poured from the hood, crushed like a tin can.

She crawled over to him, one arm flung over his head, his features twisted into a tortured grimace. "Mike!" She scrambled to her feet to get help.

As she ran to the entrance, uniformed guards burst through the door and headed for Mike.

She knelt at his side as the guards surrounded him. One of them pressed his fingers to Mike's wrist. "Pulse is steady. But he might have internal injuries."

"Ambulance is on its way," another guard said. "We called when we heard the crash."

She grasped Mike's hand, his eyes shut, his jaw slack, the contorted grimace of pain now relaxed into repose. "Mike, an ambulance is coming, I'm right here with you…"

The horror of Ted's accident came rushing back and drowned her in fear. "Breathe, Mike, breathe," she urged. "God, I beg of you, let him live. He did nothing to deserve this." She bowed her head and whispered the Lord's Prayer in Gaelic… "Ár n-Athair atá ar neamh, Go naofar d'ainim, Go dtagfadh do ríocht…"

Sirens wailed, an ambulance screeched up to them. She scrambled into the back and knelt at Mike's side. In a haunting repeat of that night outside the bar, she chased the ER surgeons down the hall to an operating room.

"You can't go in there, ma'am." A nurse barred her entrance.

The scene played over, in exact sequence. She sat in a plastic chair and prayed. "No, he cannot die!" She made a fist and pounded the wall beside her. "This isn't supposed to happen!"

Prayer got her through the agonizing wait. A doctor walked up to her. Her heart surged.

"He's had some internal bleeding and will be in ICU for a while, but his injuries aren't life threatening."

"He'll be okay?" She stood on wobbly legs and clutched the doctor's sleeves.

"Yes, he's been stabilized. But he's sedated. He can't talk to you."

Awash in relief, she gasped for breath. "Thank you, doctor, thank you so much…" She sobbed as a surge of hope lifted her spirit.

****

She slept like the dead that night, out of sheer exhaustion.

"He'll be all right, he'll be all right..." she chanted over and over, between prayers and on her drive to the hospital the next morning.

The nurse looked up from her chart, her face devoid of emotion. "He slipped into a coma, Mrs. McKinley."

Those words hit her like a punch to the stomach. She doubled over. All hope drained, leaving sheer terror. "Can I see him?" she rasped, her throat raw.

The nurse led her into the ward. Monitors beeped, tubes stuck into him. He lay still as death, his face drained of all color. His mother stood next to the bed. They embraced and watched over him, clasping hands.

"That was so beautiful, the proposal on television." Her future mother-in-law gazed at Kylah's engagement ring, tears spilling down her cheeks.

"I can't live without him, Rose," Kylah whispered.

"The police called and told me who did this," his mother said.

"I know, too, but we shouldn't talk about it. The nurse told me to be careful what we say, he can hear us," she cautioned.

Hours and days went by in a blur. Friends came over, sat with her, prayed with her, cried with her, cooked meals she couldn't eat. Struck numb, she drove to the hospital twice a day to keep vigil over his bed.

When she managed to corner his doctor, "We can't predict..." seemed to be the catch phrase.

"If I hear 'we can't predict' one more time, I will

scream," she vowed out loud, teeth clenched.

****

Day four...or five...she laid her hand over his heart. "Take my strength, let my energy heal you, I'll be your lifeline."

The monitors' beeps and blips counted a steady beat as tubes fed him air, nourishment, life.

"We're getting married the day you get out of here. I'd marry you right now, but you'd never remember it." She watched as his lips crept into a tiny curve of a smile. "Oh my God!" She dashed out to find a nurse...anyone. "He heard me, he smiled!"

How many hours passed, she didn't know. But visiting hours were over. She sat out in the hall, fell asleep in the chair.

"Mrs. McKinley?" She opened her eyes to Mike's doctor standing over her. "He's out of the coma. He's in room 314."

"Oh, thank you, doctor, thank you, God." Kylah threw her head back, laughed and cried.

She sat by his bed watching him eat ice cream, thanking God and his doctor over and over for giving him back to her.

"I remember flinging you out of the way, but that's it. Next thing I remember was waking up with a nurse shoving a pill into my mouth." He scraped the spoon along the bottom of the bowl.

"A few more things happened in between, but you don't have to know that now. I'm so thankful you're all right, you have no idea." She tried to steady her trembling hands. The combination of fear and relief drained her.

He winked and nodded. "Oh, I have an idea."

She opened the *Boston Globe* she'd brought and folded the page back. "But there's something I do want you to know. Right here. It says who tried to kill us and crashed into a tree. The head-on collision paralyzed her from the waist down. She's spending the rest of her life in a wheelchair." She took a breath. "Enid's granddaughter. Ted's stepdaughter. Charlotte."

He shook his head and whistled. "I've heard of poetic justice, but is there a such thing as poetic karma?"

She smiled and tossed the paper aside. "There is now."

****

Gray's Beach, Cape Cod

Kylah and Mike cuddled on their blanket, arms entwined, the sea crashing in the distance. Mike's lips captured hers in a long, dizzying kiss.

She caught her breath and inhaled the warm salty air. "Mike, can I ask you a personal question?"

"Ask away." He planted tiny kisses on her neck.

"Have you ever made love on a beach?"

He shook his head. "Never had the privilege."

A wicked thrill spiraled through her. "Well, there's a first time for everything." She began nibbling on his ear and playfully bit his lip.

Their thighs pressed together, their mouths met and their tongues mingled. Blood rushed through her veins. She expelled short, hot breaths from her parted lips as he pulled away. She moaned in frustration, her body aching for more of his warmth, more of his caresses. His fingertips glided over her curves as she opened his shirt buttons and wriggled closer against his mat of chest hair, thrusting her fingers through the spindly roughness, such a contrast to the smoothness of his face.

"Lie back. I want to do everything," he murmured, his voice rumbling from the depths of his throat.

She stretched out as his lips played upon her cheeks, her eyelids, her chin. Hot shivers rocketed through her. He searched out the hollow of her neck, teased and tasted her perfume with every beat of her pulse. He slipped her shirt and shorts off her. She arched herself against him.

When he made love to her, she soared into another existence, her body one thirsty sponge of receptiveness, responding, begging. Their shared climax erupted in an explosion of pent-up tension.

Their breathing calmed as she rested in the crook of his arm, gazing into the heavens. The velvet sky sparkled with glittering stars. The full moon cast a shimmering streak of silver on the bay before them.

"Look, Kylah." He pointed upwards.

A shooting star streaked across the heavens, a diamond tumbling over velvet.

"Make a wish," he urged.

"I'd rather not, Mike. I have everything I could ever want. But you go ahead. Just watch what you wish for. We're both living proof that you always get it."

Author's Notes

This story is based on what actually happened to Alice Kyteler of Kilkenny, Ireland, in the fourteenth century. All the people involved in Alice's arrest and trial are historical figures. The trial happened as written. Alice then vanished from history. According to legend, she fled to England.

Bishop Ledrede tortured Alice's maidservant Petronilla Meath into a confession as a heretic witch. The court condemned her for sorcery and offering sacrifice to demons. On November 3, 1324, four months after Alice's trial, Petronilla was burned at the stake, the first woman in Ireland to be executed this way.

The steward's name was Arnold LePoer in 1324 Kilkenny. I changed his last name to Wolfe as not to confuse, because Alice's last husband's name was LePoer.

I'd never heard of Alice until I read an article by Pamela Butler titled "Witchcraft & Heresy" in the Spring 2004 issue of *Ricardian Register*, the Richard III Society's quarterly publication. I asked Pamela what inspired her to write this article and publish it in the *Register*.

She replied: "You asked why I wrote about Alice Kyteler, who preceded Richard by a century-and-a-half. I only wrote it because others on the listserv encouraged me to write about witchcraft, a subject about which I knew very little. I ordered three books from Amazon.com on the subjects of witchcraft, heresy, Satanism, etc. for research reasons. That was my basis, plus I searched the Internet. The *Malleus Malleficarum* was published in 1487, just two years after Richard's death, so it's almost contemporary. I chanced across Alice in this reading and thought that it was an interesting case. Witch burning was fairly rare in Ireland, and wasn't as bad in England at that time as it had been on the Continent. I wish that the M.M. had never been published; still, the fact that it was published and accepted may reveal the mindset of those times."

The Richard III Society has greatly enriched my life. Please visit the website at http://www.r3.org

If you visit Cape Cod, the Barnstable Village ghost tour is a very enjoyable evening stroll. For details, please visit:
http://caiprs.com/Barnstable%20Ghost%20Hunters%20 Tour.htm

Sources

Butler, Pamela, *Witchcraft & Heresy*, the Ricardian Register, Spring 2004

Davidson, L.S. and Ward, J.O., *The Sorcery Trial of Alice Kyteler*, Medieval & Renaissance Texts & Studies, Binghamton, NY, 1993

Sutton, Maya Magee, and Mann, Nicholas R., *Druid Magic:The Practice of Celtic Wisdom,* Llewellyn Publications, Woodbury, MN, 2000

Llywelyn, Morgan, *Druids,* Del Rey, New York, 1992

Green, Miranda J., *Druids*, Thames and Hudson, London, 1997

www.salempress.com

www.hoganstand.com/general/identity/extras/supernat/stories/banshee.htm

www.geocities.com/nulliusinverba/Kyt.htm

http://www.capecodgravestones.com/yportwood.html

A word about the author...

Diana has written several historicals and paranormals set in England and the U.S., and three time-travel romances.

Diana is a member of Romance Writers of America, the Richard III Society, and the Aaron Burr Association. She and her husband own CostPro, Inc., an engineering business based in Boston. In her spare time, Diana bicycles, golfs, plays her piano, and devours books of any genre.

www.dianarubino.com
www.DianaRubinoAuthor.blogspot.com
https://www.facebook.com/DianaRubinoAuthor
on Twitter @DianaLRubino.

~*~

**Other Diana Rubino titles
available from The Wild Rose Press, Inc.**
A BLOODY GOOD CRUISE—Vampire Romance
FOR LOVE AND LOYALTY—Time Travel Romance
with Richard III
*FAKIN' IT (*Romantic Times Top Pick)
and
The New York Saga Series:
FROM HERE TO FOURTEENTH STREET (1894)
BOOTLEG BROADWAY (1933)
THE END OF CAMELOT (1963)

Thank you for purchasing
this publication of The Wild Rose Press, Inc.

If you enjoyed the story, we would appreciate your
letting others know by leaving a review.

For other wonderful stories,
please visit our on-line bookstore at
www.thewildrosepress.com.

For questions or more information
contact us at
info@thewildrosepress.com.

The Wild Rose Press, Inc.
www.thewildrosepress.com

Stay current with The Wild Rose Press, Inc.

Like us on Facebook

https://www.facebook.com/TheWildRosePress

And Follow us on Twitter
https://twitter.com/WildRosePress

www.ingramcontent.com/pod-product-compliance
Lightning Source LLC
Chambersburg PA
CBHW060531260626
47161CB00003B/845